The Worst Deceit

Annie Harper Trilogy, Book Two
- The Golden Fleck Series

Hil G Gibb

Haruki Publishing

For Ben and Helen Glover

aka, Dad and Mum

Copyright ©2024 by Hil G Gibb

All rights reserved.

No part of this publication may be reproduced in any form or by any means – graphic, electronic, or mechanical, including photocopying, recording, taping or information storage and retrieval systems – without the prior permission, in writing, of the author.

The right of Hil G Gibb (Hilary Gibb) to be identified as the author of this work has been asserted by her in accordance with the UK copyright, designs and patents act 1988.

No portion of this book may be reproduced in any form without written permission from the publisher or author, except as permitted by U.S. copyright law.

Contents

Chapter One	1
Chapter Two	18
Chapter Three	34
Chapter Four	45
Chapter Five	63
Chapter Six	80
Chapter Seven	89
Chapter Eight	93
Chapter Nine	102
Chapter Ten	109
Chapter Eleven	120
Chapter Twelve	131
Chapter Thirteen	142
Chapter Fourteen	155
Chapter Fifteen	163
Chapter Sixteen	172

Chapter Seventeen	181
Chapter Eighteen	190
Chapter Nineteen	197
Chapter Twenty	204
Chapter Twenty-One	215
Chapter Twenty-Two	226
Chapter Twenty-Three	233
Chapter Twenty-Four	240
Chapter Twenty-Five	245
Chapter Twenty-Six	253
Chapter Twenty-Seven	264
Chapter Twenty-Eight	270
Chapter Twenty-Nine	275
Chapter Thirty	286
Chapter Thirty-One	298
Chapter Thirty-Two	309
A Word from Hil	314

Chapter One

Lucan howled loud and long, like a savagely, and mortally wounded animal.

Annie had successfully led Finwe, Elva, and Lucan through her personal portal, and they had all had the air punched out of their lungs as they landed hard onto the damp ground in the Necropolis, Glasgow.

Varis, the fifth member of their party, wasn't with them. He had not made it through.

"He is lost!" Lucan cried out again and again while punching the unyielding ground with his large, and tightly clenched fists. Not knowing quite how to approach Lucan, for that had been Varis's gift, the others tentatively moved towards him, and crouched down beside him. Tacitly, they let him know that they were there for him — to do quite what, they didn't know. Lucan's dreadful distress was both painfully palpable and heart-wrenching.

"It should be *me* that is lost," he wailed, his faced etched deeply in anguish. "I ordered him to be the lead elf behind

Annie, but he tricked me. He was hellë-bent on taking the most treacherous position at the back of our dicrad daisy chain!"

Again, Lucan repeatedly pounded his large fists upon the earth — so much so, that Annie, while trying not to make light of this most serious situation, couldn't help but think that he might disturb the dead person whose plot he was beating to a pulp.

It was nighttime with a bright, full moon that revealed its many craters to the naked eye. Annie was acutely aware that the overly zealous security guards could be out patrolling the grounds at any moment. She also knew they would be especially curious about, and attracted to, someone weeping and wailing between the gravestones, and pounding the earth in the dead of night — *no pun intended*, she thought. She was more than a little ashamed that she could find humour at such a time, but then, humour and sarcasm, had been her emotional armour for as long as she could remember.

"I'm really sorry, but we are going to have to get Lucan to be quiet," she urged the twins. "Otherwise, we are going to attract some very unwanted attention and our quest could be over before it's even begun."

Nodding to indicate that she understood, Elva lent forward and gingerly placed a comforting hand upon Lucan's broad shoulder. He instantly shunned her, twitching his shoulder aggressively and weeping louder still. Finwe shrugged his shoulders at Annie and Elva, accepting that it was now *his* turn to try consoling Lucan and, even more importantly at that moment, to shut the commander up. In line with his usual style, Finwe took a far more direct approach. Without any hesitation, he knelt behind Lucan. In one swift, strong movement, he wrapped his long arms around Lucan's shoulders and dragged him back, and tightly into his chest.

That's more like a rugby tackle than an embrace, thought Annie, but she had to admit that it was having the desired effect. After a few seconds of alarmed, violent, and angry protest, Lucan had slumped into Finwe. Within the next moment, Finwe had managed to muffle Lucan's sobs into somewhere between his chest and his armpit. The pair huddled in this awkward and clearly uncomfortable embrace for more than a minute. Without the need for any discussion, Elva and Annie stood facing outwards to keep watch for any unwanted attention.

"He is lost," Lucan repeated, more and more quietly, until his voice was just a whisper. "He is... lost. He. Is. Lost. Lost."

It wasn't until Lucan had been got under some sort of control that Annie, Elva, and Finwe were also deeply struck by the loss of their wise, kind, and brave friend. Without a word, Elva and Annie joined Finwe, and Lucan to form a tightly knit huddle of aching grief on the damp grass, beneath the full moon.

For the moment at least, their quest to retrieve the sacred Labradorite Amulet and save the elven realms, could wait.

<><><><><><><><>

Meanwhile, Varis was trapped somewhere within the portal itself. He was suspended between the Sun Elven Realm and the Human Realm. While travelling through Annie's portal, he had seen his mother, who had died while giving birth to him. Varis had never felt her embrace. He had never heard her voice or seen the lights that twinkled in her eyes as she laughed. That said, he had immediately recognised her from the likeness of her that his father had carried with him at all times. The precious likeness had been in Varis's keeping, together with his father's likeness, for the last two hundred moons.

This unique experience inside Annie's portal corridor, had drawn him powerfully towards his mother. While being drawn, he had also felt the pull of Lucan's hand as their link in the daisy chain through the portal was put under immense strain.

He had seen the desperate yearning in his mother's large, golden-brown eyes and felt it mirrored, tenfold, in his own heart.

Surely, just to touch her with the tip of the fingers on one hand cannot do any harm, he had thought. *She is my mother after all. My mother.*

The primal urge for Varis to go to his mother had been just too tantalising to ignore. He had stretched his free hand towards her and Lucan's grip on Varis had been stretched to a point where only the last joints on their fingers were firmly interlocked.

As soon as his mother's fingertips touched him and clasped his hand, Varis had been instantly steeped in an all-encompassing, unconditional mother's love. He could feel his mother's love fill him up entirely, and he had openly wept with an equal measure of joy and sorrow. Then Varis's other hand had slipped out of Lucan's grip completely in order to fully embrace his mother.

At the very same moment that Varis and his mother embraced, his four companions had been unceremoniously ripped forward and away. To them, it felt as if they were on the back of a majestic, greater gold-tipped soron that was midway through an inverted loop in the convection currents, high above the Woodland Realm.

The link between Lucan and Varis had been broken, and now it was just Varis, and his mother. Within seconds, his companions became the tiniest of pinpricks in the far distance. But, the warmth and love of his mother's embrace meant that he barely noticed they had gone. All he could think about was all his mother's love that now enveloped and swaddled him, and all his love that he could finally express to her.

He was safe. He was loved. He was home.

<><><><><><><><>

As the four friends finally released their tight and consoling embrace of each other, they sat in silent contemplation, each with their head hung low, and their eyes downcast.

"He was so much more than my second-in-command," Lucan said quietly, his voice shaking and choking a little from all his spent emotion. "He was more than my friend. He was... he was my... my soulmate."

Elva's, Finwe's, and Annie's heads popped up like meerkats, in surprise. They all knew that Lucan and Varis were an incredibly close unit. There had never been any doubt about that. They had trained as soldiers together and fought together for most of their lives. It just hadn't occurred to any of them that Lucan and Varis were anything more than that.

"That must surely make his loss all the more terribly painful, Lucan," said Annie with a clear note of deep compassion. She just hoped that Lucan would not be offended by her stating the bleeding obvious. With his eyes still cast down, Lucan nodded. He then raised his head slowly to look directly at Elva and Finwe.

"And you?" he asked, with a glint of defiance in his amber eyes. "What do *you* think and feel about it?"

Elva and Finwe exchanged looks in a tacit conversation. Annie was confused.

Clearly this news is a very big deal, she thought. *But what kind of big deal is it?*

Lucan's head sorrowfully drooped again.

"There is no need for you to say a single word," he said with obvious bitterness and gloom. "I already know what you will think. I suppose you are going to report me upon our return to the Sun Elven Realm. I understand that you will not have any choice."

"Report you?" Annie blurted, disbelievingly. "Report you for what? For you and Varis being soulmates? For being in love? You've got to be kidding me!" She was getting her dander well and truly up, now. "When I think about it, it's so obvious that you two have — I mean *had* — a deep and meaningful relationship that went far beyond soldiering together. It's not like it's a crime, is it."

"But that is just the point, Annie," Lucan replied, his red, tear-filled eyes looking directly into her earnest bright blue ones. "It is just that. It *is* a crime."

"What?" Annie exclaimed. As her exasperation increased, thick, dark clouds started to roll across the full moon.

"And it is not simply because I love a male Sun Elf," Lucan continued, his head now buried in his hands. "It is made worse by the fact that Varis is — I should say...was — a *half* Sun Elf. While his father was a Sun Elf, and a captain of the guard no less, his mother was a Woodland Elf, and a lowly birth one at that. King Peren regards such matches as impure, and their offspring as 'less than', as 'half elves'."

"Well that's just bloody typical of Peren," Annie raged, spitting the king's name from her lips, as if it tasted of the sourest milk. "He doesn't mind the likes of Varis serving him and risking their lives though, does he? Oh no, he doesn't mind *that* at all."

Elva and Finwe nodded in silent agreement with Annie's assertion. As Woodland Elves themselves, they found King Peren's view of what he called Half Elves absolutely disgraceful.

"Varis was a supreme soldier," said Lucan, his voice petering out through emotional exhaustion. "He worked twice as hard as other elves, to simply get half as far. He more than earned his position. Varis was the best of us all. He was the best of me."

There was a tense and extended silence between the four of them. It was broken by Finwe as he placed a firm grip on Lucan's shoulder that Lucan sagged beneath and made no attempt to repel.

"Varis was, indeed, the very best of us," he affirmed. "And it matters not one iota, that he is... I mean was... a so-called 'half elf'. For what it is worth, in my view, it also matters not that you and he are... were... in love. When you find your soulmate, you should never feel ashamed.

You should be able to embrace it and each other when, and wherever, you please. You should be able to shout it from the very rooftops." Finwe's look of pure defiance changed to one that was far more difficult to read. Was it wistful or wishful thinking? "I know I would shout it from every rooftop, if I could."

There wasn't time to explore this mysterious and palpable change in Finwe, for Elva was also up on her feet and firmly gripping Lucan's other shoulder.

"I agree wholeheartedly with Finwe," she asserted. "Why should a genuinely loving relationship be deemed unlawful just because of the prejudice and bitterness of one old, and twisted, monarch? No," she continued while holding up a hand to stop Lucan's weak attempt at defending his king. "It is about time there was a more reasoned and compassionate leader in the Sun Elven Realm, and I for one cannot wait for Adran to come to the Sun Elven throne."

In an extremely uncharacteristic display of gratitude and affection, Lucan put his arms around Elva and Finwe, and squeezed them to him. He then extended his left arm to also bring Annie into his grateful embrace.

He hugged them all tightly to him and wept once more.

Finwe, Elva, and Annie reciprocated the squeeze and wept with him.

<><><><><><><><>

With her head deeply buried in among her friends, Annie felt the initial stirrings of an idea. That idea had the making of a possible means of saving Varis. Scared that she might kill the idea before it would have the chance to take proper root, she remained very still, and quiet. She noticed her golden fleck stirring gently in her eye. It was an indication that inspiration was on the very cusp of bursting forth.

Suddenly, and without any warning, Annie sat bolt upright on her heels. The idea had now taken root, grown, and fully flowered in her mind.

"That's it," she exclaimed. The others' sallow faces looked at her in an equal measure of surprise and confusion.

"What is it?" Elva asked, sensing Annie's air of all-consuming inspiration and excitement. Annie looked intensely at her three comrades and smiled at each of them in turn.

"I think... no, I don't think... I *know* how to save Varis."

"Do not joke with me," sniffed Lucan. "It would be too cruel to bear if you promise this and then do not achieve it."

Annie confidently took his large hands in both of her much smaller ones, and looked deep into his red-rimmed eyes.

"I would *never, ever* joke about something as important as this," she assured him. "I truly believe that I have a really robust solution for giving Varis his best chance of being rescued — of bringing him back to us." Her look now changed from one that was telling, to one that was asking for Lucan's blessing. She held his face in her hands now, and Lucan made no effort to resist.

"Will you at least let me try?" she asked, gently.

Finwe and Elva held their breath while waiting for Lucan to reply. It was all down to Lucan now. Whatever Lucan decided, would be the final word. After several moments that felt like an absolute age, Lucan closed his eyes and started to, almost imperceptibly, nod his head. He was too scared to even dare hope that Varis could be brought back to them — be brought back to him. Annie didn't require any clearer signal for agreement, and she jumped to her feet.

There wasn't a single moment to waste.

"What are you planning to do, Annie?" Finwe asked.

"You'll see," she said, smiling at the sensation of her magic powerfully building up within her and her golden fleck enthusiastically performing encouraging figures of eight. She moved to stand next to her gravestone portal. She breathed deeply, filling up her lungs in an effort to steady her jangling nerves.

She didn't want to touch the stone too soon.

She mindfully drew on her strong emotions associated with the loss and shock of losing Varis. She wanted her magic to amplify, and to only touch the stone portal once her magic had peaked — when she simply couldn't hold it any longer. She was starting to understand and master the fact that, the more concentrated her magic, the more effective it would be.

The speed of her fleck's figures of eight had increased to the point where it became a golden, flickering blur. The bubbling and spitting cauldron of her magic inside her was starting to boil over. Another moment, and she would lose control altogether. If that happened, there would be no telling what carnage would ensue.

It was now or never.

And so it's now, she thought.

Annie's fingertips lightly grazed the gravestone and the entrance to her personal portal sprang open.

The very instant that Annie touched the stone, she was pulled forward, hard. But, rather than being pulled all the way in and through, she was held back. Something or someone was holding her other hand and lower arm. Annie had to force her head to turn, and she looked over her shoulder.

It was Finwe.

He'd had the presence of mind to realise what she was about to do and, at the moment she opened her portal, he had grabbed her arm and leaned back with all his might. Seeing Finwe's actions, Elva and Lucan had both jumped into action, and wrapped their arms around his waist. They would be Finwe's ballast, and Finwe would be Annie's anchor.

Bringing her head forward again, Annie leaned farther forward and slowly entered her portal. The behaviour of atoms here warped absolutely everything — stretching and condensing, fragmenting and reconfiguring — all at once. Finwe, Lucan, and Elva appeared like they were hundreds of feet away and yet, at the same time, Annie could feel Finwe's strong, long-fingered hand tightly clasping her smaller one.

Come on! That's quite enough basking in the glorious weirdness of my physics-defying portal, she thought. With one last look back she gave Finwe the slightest of smiles. She then turned her attention away, to focus back onto her immediate mission.

Now, let's find and rescue Varis.

<><><><><><><>

Varis was so blissfully happy, basking in a seemingly unending pool of nurturing contentment. He had talked and laughed with his mother for what felt like many, many moons. His mother was filling and swelling his heart, his mind, and his very soul. All else and anything else had almost evaporated: the dying realms, his friends, Lucan, everything. It was as if he were right back in the womb, where every baby was completely at one with its mother. Where the mother is the baby's whole universe, its whole everything. Varis wanted to believe that there could be no end to this all-encompassing joy.

But there was a tiny kernel of something that refused to be quashed. It was right there, at the very back of his mind, and tucked away in a corner of his heart.

What is it? he thought, frustrated that it persistently niggled and interfered with his contentment. *No, wait,* he continued. *It is not a what. It is a who. Who is it?* Varis couldn't quite grasp it, like trying to hold specks of dust as they danced in bright sunbeams. And yet, he felt an urgency to grasp it all the same. It felt important. Supremely important.

Looking lovingly back at his mother, he noticed an almost imperceptible glitch. Part of her cheek pixelated for a brief moment and hastily reconfigured. Wait — there it was again. This time, the glitching happened to the entire left side of her face and her voice muted momentarily as well. Something wasn't right. In fact it was very wrong. The energy that was creating his mother in the portal corridor was starting to fail, and was failing fast.

As the energy failed, the tiny kernel of something, or rather, someone, grew. Suddenly, the tiny kernel exploded and entirely filled Varis's mind and heart.

"Lucan!" he exclaimed. He turned back to his mother. "Where is Lucan?"

But his mother, increasingly glitching and intermittently muting, simply stroked Varis's face and attempted to draw him back into her warm embrace. Now awakened to what was really happening, Varis resisted.

"No, Mamma," he said, holding her delicate hands in his large ones. "You are not real. You cannot be real. Please believe me when I say that I deeply, deeply wish you were, and yet, you are not."

But Lucan is very real, he thought. I need him. He needs me. I need to get back to him. I need to get back to him, right now.

Varis firmly pulled away from his mother and turned towards where Lucan's hand had slipped from his. He attempted to carry on through the portal corridor, but he couldn't make any headway. A terrifying thought struck him. Soon, as the portal's energy powered down completely, his mother would be gone and he would be lost, alone and trapped in this limbo, perhaps forever.

All the while, Varis's head was clearing and his thought of — and feelings for — Lucan, his friends, and the dying realms came flooding back with all the strength of a tsunami. He continued to struggle with all his might in his endeavour to move forward, but it was all to no avail. In deep and heartbreaking frustration, Varis let out a booming roar of distress, and despair.

Annie heard what sounded to her like the roar of a lion in the night.

<><><><><><><><>

"Varis? Varis, is that you?" Annie called.

"Annie?" shouted Varis with equal measures of relief and disbelief. He was frantically searching for the source of the voice. "Annie, I cannot see you."

A moment later, Annie's small, square hand came into view, as if forcing its way through heavy blackout curtains. It was still some distance away and Varis's efforts to take hold were being thwarted. Once more, Varis let out his lion's roar of frustration.

"I cannot reach you Annie. I cannot move. I believe that I am done for."

Varis let his arms fall limply to his sides in melancholy resignation.

"It is no use, Annie," he said, quietly. "The portal is failing and I am to be trapped within it. You must carry on with the quest for the Labradorite Amulet. You must save the realms. Tell Lucan... tell Lucan —"

But Annie was having none of it.

"Stop that talk now," she barked assertively. "You can tell him yourself. Now, try again. Try harder. Reach farther. Reach farther, now. We can do this. I know we can." She too, could see Varis's mother becoming increasingly pixelated with the waning energy of the portal corridor. Instinctively, she knew that if she couldn't get Varis out now, there would be nothing left of him by the time they made their return journey back to the Sun Elven Realm.

"It is too late, Annie. I am lost," he said, squaring his shoulders and resigning himself to his tragic fate.

Just then, Varis felt himself move forward slightly.

How can this be? he thought. *I am making no attempt to move and yet I am moving.* It was then that he felt what was left of his mother's arms wrap around his waist and squeeze gently. Although it had become thin, reedy, and intermittent, he could hear her voice.

"You are... needed, my... son. You must... leave here. Just... know... that... I love... you."

And with that, his mother sacrificed the very last of the portal's energy that had created her, in order to propel Varis, her beloved son, forward towards Annie's hand. As his body gently floated forward, Varis looked over his shoulder to see his mother for one last moment. For a split second, he saw her smiling, loving face before it atomised completely.

Annie's fingertips made contact with Varis's and, quickly, they each grabbed tightly to hold on to each other. As this was Annie's third time through her portal, she wasn't surprised when both she and Varis were abruptly and unceremoniously, thrust into what felt like the world's largest rollercoaster, that was midway through an inverted loop high above the theme park. Somehow, all the while, Finwe had maintained a tight hold of Annie's hand. With all the various shenanigans that she'd experienced since her birthday, in Glasgow, Annie had completely given up trying to understand how space, time, and any other kinds of physics worked within the portal. Her only concern in this moment was saving Varis.

For what felt like hundreds of moons, the pair experienced steep rising, plummeting falling, and stomach-churning somersaulting. They were completely out of control and unable to scream, for it felt like any air they'd had, had been brutally punched out of their chests.

Finally, Annie and Varis could see the tiny figures of Finwe, Elva, and Lucan in the portal's aperture. Within a blink of an eye, they were bearing down on them, with no signs of slowing. They were then rapidly spat out of the portal. Lucan, Elva, and Finwe fell backwards into a heap, and the violently ejected Annie, and Varis crash-landed on top of them.

Grunting and groaning, they all rolled off each other, and lay flat on their backs in a haphazard, and heavily panting circle. No one moved or said anything for several moments. They were all too preoccupied with regaining their breath and steadying their pounding hearts. All, that is, except Lucan, who sprang up and launched himself at Varis.

"Why in Volta's name did you damn well disobey my orders, you pustid pellöpe?" he growled fiercely, while tightly gripping Varis's collar and shoving his fists up, and under Varis's jaw.

"You know why," Varis simply, while dangling like a limp puppet and finding it difficult to speak with Lucan's fists partially blocking his airway. Looking around at the others and placing both palms firmly on Lucan's chest, he added, "And I think they do too."

The two elven soldiers just looked at each other for a long moment, each traversing a vast range of conflicting emotions. Finally, they entered into a strong and gruff embrace that soon melted into one of utter bliss and joy.

Both openly wept with relief and gratitude.

Annie, Elva, and Finwe all shrugged at each other and, without a word, moved as one to envelop the Sun Elven pair in their heartfelt embrace.

Chapter Two

As the reunited group of friends disentangled themselves, Annie noticed that the night was warm.

That's weird, she thought, *in just the few moons that I've spent in the elven realms, October has turn into... what? May? June? It looks like the Wise One's hypothesis was spot on. Time really does move differently between the Human Realm and the elven realms.*

For the first time since landing in the Human Realm, the elves had a chance to take in some of their surroundings.

"What *is* this place?" Elva asked in an awed whisper.

"This place?" Annie replied casually. "This is the famous Necropolis in Glasgow. I think over fifty thousand people are buried here."

"Fifty thousand!" Finwe exclaimed in the loudest of stage whispers, as if not wanting to disturb those who had 'passed over'.

"Are there thousands of leaders of a few realms, or a few leaders of thousands of realms?" asked Varis, who had just surfaced from his reunion with Lucan, and had instantly resumed his characteristic curiosity, and thirst for knowledge. Annie was clearly perplexed.

"What? No," she said, with a shake of her head. "These people aren't leaders of realms. They are just... just... people."

Looks of surprise and disbelief passed between her elven friends.

"Why? What's so very strange about that?"

"Well," Elva replied, sharing knowing looks with the others. "In our elven realms, we only have very few markers such as these. Only the leaders of the realms are afforded such permanent monuments of remembrance."

"And so, what happens to the rest of you?" asked Annie.

"So," Varis interjected, "Sun Elves are taken to the mountaintop and set alight when the suns are setting. The Shoreland Elves are set adrift on the oceans where they slowly sink and become nourishment for the carnivorous creatures of the seas."

"Woodland Elves are lightly covered with nature's bounty of flowers, so that they might quickly become completely one with the forest again," explained Finwe. He hesitated for a moment, and then added, "Like we did with young Lilyfire."

On hearing Lilyfire's name, a large, choking lump of sorrow caught in Annie's throat and the group bowed their heads. They each took a moment of silence to think about their little comrade whom they had so tragically lost in the Woodland Realm.

Dragging herself out of her sorrow and back into the present moment, Annie asked,

"And the Shadow Elves? What about them?"

"No one knows for certain, but it is thought that the Shadow Elves are simply left to rot wherever they die," said Varis. "There is no ceremony, no remembrance, no thanks, nothing."

"Oh, that's cold, even for them," said Annie.

"What do you expect?" said Lucan, with undisguised disgust written across his face. "They are Shadow Elves."

Thinking about Shadow Elves brought her beloved Carric flooding into her mind. While they were on a mission to retrieve the sacred Labradorite Amulet, poor Carric was being held and tortured by Shadow Elves in the dark tower, King Tathyn's lair.

The thought of brave Carric suffering, and Tathlyns' dreadful, secret deal that she had reluctantly agreed to, made Annie feel sick to the bottom of her stomach. Tathlyn had his minions kidnap Carric from their chartered Shoreland Elf ship, as she and her comrades had journeyed back to the Sun Realm. Tathlyn had forcefully encroached on Annie's mind and shown her what he would do to Carric if she did not bring the Labradorite Amulet directly to him. The only way to definitely secure the release of her love, was to betray her friends and all those in the elven realms.

She hated herself for agreeing to it, but what else could she do? She loved him.

"What do you think Annie?"

Annie was only vaguely aware that she was being asked a question, and had to force herself back into the here, and now.

"I'm sorry," she said, apologetically. "What did you say, Lucan?"

"I said," repeated Lucan, now sounding much more like his naturally starchy self, "although it is dark, are you able to start your search for the Labradorite Amulet with your human eyes? As you know, time has never been so very much of the essence."

Annie quickly pulled herself together and affirmed that she felt confident that she could use her magic to light the way. Although, her friends' elven eyes were better able to see in the dark than hers, without the need for magic, they didn't know where they should look.

With considerable effort, Annie put her thoughts and feelings about Carric out of the forefront of her mind, and, metaphorically, parked them somewhere round the back, out of sight. She trained her focus on producing an adaptation of the palm bombs she had developed a knack for while on the Shoreland Elven ship, fighting, and failing, to save Carric from the intense swarm of Shadow Elves.

With a familiar, bubbling surge from her stomach, and a flick of her golden fleck, a palm bomb almost effortlessly formed in the centre of her small, square-fingered hand. That was the easy part. Preventing the palm bomb from efficiently blasting several gravestones to rubble, and attracting unwanted attention, would be more demanding.

Annie closed her eyes and, with effort, slowed her breathing. She figured that calming her inner workings down would, essentially, dial down her palm bomb into a sort of palm light.

Breathe in for four, three, two, one, she told herself, *and out for eight, seven, six, five, four, three, two, one.* After two rounds of this slow and controlled breathing, the palm bomb ceased wrestling to be unleashed. Following a further round of slow and steady breathing, it sat comfortably, and inert in her hand.

She slowly opened her eyes, as if trying not to startle it into weapon status once more.

There in her hand sat a beautiful, iridescent sphere of light. It had a satisfying, solid weight to it, and it gave off an air of contentment. Annie afforded herself a little smile. She was pleased with her creation.

The amulet can't be very far from here, she thought. *It was no more than thirty seconds between the jobs-worth guard spotting me, me running, and then accidentally colliding with my portal.*

She had been just about to touch the amulet when she was rudely interrupted and scared away by the graveyard's security guard. She turned away from the gravestone that was her portal, to face the direction whence she believed she had come running that night.

And so to work, she thought as she squeezed her shoulders up, back and down, and confidently stepped forward with her palm light. The light was really effective at revealing her immediate surroundings in the dark. Lucan, Varis, Elva, and Finwe followed in single file for fear of distracting Annie from tracking down her quarry.

Without warning something lightly brushed past Annie's cheek, causing her to startle. Instantly, her palm light ramped up to palm bomb status and she found that she could barely hold onto it. Whipping round, she brightly illuminated Lucan's face. Their considerable difference in height meant that Lucan's face was lit from below, causing it to take on a hideous, ghoul-like quality. This did nothing to effect the downscaling of Annie's palm bomb.

"What the *hell* was that?" she hissed, aware that she was sounding more than a little hysterical. Finwe overtook the others to stand beside her.

"It is all right, Annie," he whispered. "Look." He brought his left arm into the palm bomb's pool of light. They all gasped in awe and delight, for there, happily perched upon Finwe's arm was a stunning barn owl.

Annie realised that she was holding her breath in fright and made a concerted effort to return to her slow, steady, and calm breathing. Thankfully, her palm bomb followed suit and, once again, adopted the tranquil status of a non-threatening palm light.

"It is like a speckled hó, but smaller," said Elva, her eyes thoroughly examining the bird. "It is so very beautiful."

"It would seem that your natural touch with the animal kingdom stretches across into the Human Realm, Finwe," said Varis, who was also admiring their visitor. Finwe gave the shy grin of one who is modest, and yet chuffed with themselves. In true fashion, Lucan abruptly brought everyone back on task.

"While I too find this hó-like bird beautiful," he said, "we have no time to indulge in such discoveries."

With a big sigh, Finwe spoke softly to the owl in old elvish and, in the next moment, it had soundlessly ascended from his arm, and back into the cover of the summer's night.

The hunt for the Labradorite Amulet immediately resumed.

Frustratingly, the hunt wasn't bearing any fruit. Annie thought about the TV dramas she had seen that showed search parties forming a close, human chain to scour an area of ground more thoroughly. She stopped and turned once again to face her friends.

"When I was spotted that night, I couldn't have been any farther away from my portal than this," she stated, pointing to the ground at her feet. "I think it would be best if we spread out from this point and gradually make our way back to my portal while scouring the ground."

"Right," announced Lucan. "we shall form another of Annie's daisy chains, but this time we shall be side by side."

Annie couldn't repress a fond and amused smile at Lucan, the career soldier, and gruff commander of the Sun Elven Army, adopting her terminology. Apparently oblivious to her amusement, Lucan continued with his instructions.

"We shall take small steps in unison so as not to miss a single ichné of ground."

The others had not missed Annie's amusement and wrestled with their face muscles to keep them in something approximating neutral expressions. When in instruction-giving mode, Lucan's already naturally limited and stilted sense of humour tended to reduce to nothing. He would not in the least bit appreciate any lightheartedness at this juncture.

Inching their way back towards her portal gravestone, Annie was starting to lose hope of ever finding the Labradorite Amulet again. She was beginning to wonder if she had dreamed the whole thing up, when she spied something in the grass. It glinted in the magical beam of her palm light. Creeping towards it as if it were a roe deer that would spook and run if it got wind of her, Annie tiptoed closer. She tried to hold her excitement in check as the familiar, rich and unusual blue hue of the stone shone.

"Here," she whispered horsely to the others. "I think I've found it."

Her four companions immediately sprang to either side of her and peered intently to where the palm light's beam alighted on the piece of ancient-looking jewellery, the size of Annie's fist. It was dazzling and practically glowing, amongst the wild summer flowers.

Elva noted that it was carefully cemented into a low plinth at the base of a modest gravestone. She passed Annie a small hammer that tapered to a point at one side of its head.

"You will need to do this, Annie," Elva explained in answer to Annie's look of confusion. "Only the hand of Meredith the Thief can hold the Labradorite Amulet. And since your ancestor is long gone, yours is the nearest we will ever have to her hand."

Disguising her wince at being reminded that she was related to the thief who had put all the realms in such terrible danger, Annie took the hammer and crouched beside the tiny plinth. Before making contact with the amulet, with her free hand, she pulled away the weeds and wildflowers that surrounded, and masked it.

Now fully exposed to Annie's palm light, the Labradorite Amulet revealed its true, almost mesmerising beauty. The large stone in the centre of the piece was a luminous and rich cyan-blue colour. As with her previous encounter with it, Annie could feel it almost beckoning to her. It made her face beam broadly. She felt a surge of energy flow interwoven with expectation, as she approached it with Elva's hammer. Like her first encounter with the amulet, she was like a lioness creeping up on her prey.

"You need to be very careful," hissed Lucan, just as Annie swung the hammer back a little, readying herself for making her first strike. He made everyone jump and four pairs of eyes glowered at him. As was his wont, Varis soothed the intensifying situation.

"I, for one, am confident that Annie is acutely aware that great care is required, Lucan," he said affably. "Perhaps we ought to turn our backs so that Annie is not unnecessarily pressured by the intensity of all our gazes."

Annie gave Varis a small smile of gratitude and the four elves moved as one to turn, and face outward. Annie resettled herself to the delicate task in hand. Once again, she looked all around the plinth that held the amulet, in an effort to ascertain the best point at which to start chipping away.

Having chosen what she thought was a promising weak spot, she hesitated, concerned that in making contact, something might well spark, or shock her — or worse still — set off a chain reaction that could harm her friends, or bring the whole of Glasgow and beyond to rubble.

Her golden fleck swished impatiently.

All right, I know, she thought in reply to her fleck. *Getting cold feet now simply isn't an option. The elven realms are depending on me.*

Her golden fleck made short stabbing motions as if to chastise her.

Okay, Okay, she admitted. *And, if I were to be selfish, Carric is depending on me, and I am depending on me.*

She was grateful that her friends couldn't see that her palm light was becoming more bomb-like in response to her internal struggle. Roughly sweeping her mental torture and guilt firmly under the carpet of her mind, Annie focused once more on making her breathing slow, and steady. Once she had successfully calmed her palm light, she gently swung Elva's hammer, closed her eyes, and made first contact.

There was a supremely, anticlimactic *chink*.

Okay, she thought, while cautiously opening one eye a smidge. *So this isn't going to be an Excalibur moment of 'one touch and it's yours', then.*

Deciding the freeing of the amulet from its 'plinthy prison' was going to be all about practicalities rather than magic, destiny, and elven myths etcetera, Annie rolled her shoulders to loosen the tension that had been building up there. She then settled to her task in a decidedly more down-to-earth manner. She set about teasing the amulet away from the concrete with a series of nibbling strikes all around the edge of it. On her third trip round the plinth, the Labradorite Amulet came away and fell silently among the flowers.

Annie gasped and, as one, the four elves swung round to see that the freed amulet was now fully caught in the palm light's beam. In the pool of light, it was radiating its cyan-blue colouring in all directions. Elva quickly pulled the small velvety pouch from her belt and handed it to Annie.

"Here you are, Annie," she said, her awe and excitement clearly evident in the tone of her voice. "Once you have picked the Labradorite Amulet up and quelled its immense power, you can slip it into the bag that the Wise One gave to us."

Absorbing the sheer beauty and joy of the stone, Annie reached for the pouch in a slightly bewildered daze. But then her astute mind quickly snapped back to its usual razor-sharpness.

"Wait, what did you say?" she asked, feeling a spiking surge of alarm linked to the natural need for self-preservation. "What do you mean "once I've quelled its immense power"? How am I supposed to do that, exactly? And what happens to me, to all of us, if I can't?"

What the hell's this? she thought, her alarm finding no reason to abate. *Are these amazingly brave and noble warrior elves actually kicking imaginary pebbles with their toes, and navel-gazing right now? How dangerous can this be? What are they not wanting to tell me?*

"What happens if I can't quell its immense power?" she repeated firmly, staring hard at each one of them in turn. Eventually, Varis relented.

"Well," he started, clearly uncomfortable with whatever piece of knowledge he was about to impart. "*If your hands are able to touch the Labradorite Amulet, but prove not to be as fundamentally at one with those of Meredith the Thief, well...then... then...*" He petered out, perhaps in the hope that one of the others would take up the baton of explanation.

But, no one did.

"Well then what, exactly, Varis?" Annie demanded, running out of patience and running into ill-disguised annoyance.

Seeing none of the others were going to help him out, Varis sighed and opened his mouth to speak once more.

"Well, we will be all right, but you will simply be atomised to your most fundamental components, and blown to the four winds," Lucan chipped in matter-of-factly, finishing Varis's sentence for him.

Varis shot him a tacit "Thank you," and looked back at Annie apologetically.

Annie's face blanched to whiter than virgin snow, and her golden fleck instantly recoiled and shrank to a pinprick. Neither she, nor it, were particularly thrilled with the possibility of being atomised.

"Oh, well that's just bloody marvellous," she exclaimed indignantly. "And you didn't think to mention this until I've practically laid my paws on the thing?"

Agitated, Annie jumped up and paced back, and forth, back and forth.

"Do you have paws?" Finwe asked, joking.

But he was promptly shot down by a seriously withering look from his twin. Evidently this was absolutely not the time for lighthearted cajoling.

"*When*," Elva said with repeated, placating hand gestures. "I should have said *when* you have quelled its immense power. We all have complete confidence that you are the hands of Meredith the Thief." She pointedly looked to Varis and Finwe to help her out.

"Yes," Finwe chimed in. "You grow increasingly masterful of your magical powers too. If anyone can do this, that anyone is *you*."

"Yes, yes" agreed Varis in suspiciously overly positive and warm tones. "Elva and Finwe are absolutely right, Annie. We have *complete* and *utter* faith in you."

Unsurprisingly, Lucan was clearly running out of patience.

"Look," he barked in his no-fluffy-bunnies-or-rainbow-unicorns style. "We do not need to have faith or confidence in you. The Wise One was absolutely certain that you and Meredith have the same blood. The Wise One is called the Wise One for a very good reason. She is incredibly wise. You will have no problem with the amulet. That is a fact. You need to grab it and get it in the pouch, and you need to do it right now."

Funnily enough, it was Lucan's direct, logical and steely approach that spurred Annie into immediate action. With the mantra, "it's now or never" running through her head, Annie took one last deep breath and plunged her hand down among the foliage. Before she wrapped her fingers firmly around the amulet, she hesitated with her fingertips less than half an inch away from the object.

She was ready and willing to overpower a resistant, magic-infused object, although she wasn't at all sure as to how. She was primed to absorb the immense power that this amulet could wield. She was ready for anything — or, at least, she hoped she was.

Except she absolutely wasn't. And neither were her companions.

They weren't ready for what actually happened when Annie finally took the plunge and held the Labradorite Amulet.

What happened?

Nothing.

Absolutely nothing.

It was a thoroughly disappointing anticlimax.

"Well, that was nice and easy," said Annie, holding the Labradorite Amulet aloft in triumph. The four elves exchanged confused glances and expressions of deflated disappointment.

"What now? What's the matter?" she asked, irritated at their distinct lack of celebratory behaviour. "I've got hold of the Labradorite Amulet, and with not so much as a flutter of resistance or heat. Why all the glum faces?"

They all came to sit on their haunches beside Annie, shoulders slumped and discouraged.

"There is a very real problem here, Annie," explained Elva. "There should have been some sort of a struggle at the very least. At the moment that you touched it, the amulet should have instantly glowed white hot and vibrated violently."

"But, I am definitely the hands of Meredith the Thief," Annie protested, throwing her hands in the air. "I *have* to be. Otherwise, wouldn't I have been atomised to my most fundamental components and blown to the four winds?"

She couldn't believe that she had come so much closer to saving Carric, only for it to feel like she was now even farther away.

"This *is* the Labradorite Amulet. I'm *sure* of it," she insisted with desperation noticeably leaking into her voice. Varis placed a large, soothing hand lightly on her shoulder.

"This is *a* labradorite amulet," he said quietly. "But it is clearly not *the* Labradorite Amulet."

"We have all been fooled, Annie," offered Finwe empathetically. "This amulet looks exactly like the one that we are searching for. But, it is not our amulet. This one will not save our realms. This one will not save anyone or anything."

Utterly gutted and swiftly working her way towards distraught, Annie looked down at the dud labradorite amulet, that nestled inertly in her palm. Ominous clouds appeared making the moon and stars disappear.

"And so we're left with no enchanted amulet and no way of finding it," she said, simply, in the small voice of one who has something that they were so sure of, only to have it cruelly stripped away.

I have no way to save Carric, she thought. "I have no way to save the elven realms," she added aloud while she switched out the light that was sat in her other palm.

Chapter Three

For many minutes, the unlikely group of friends sat in the dark in complete, dejected silence. It was so very frustrating to have come this far, through all their trials, certain of the Labradorite Amulet's whereabouts, only to be saddled with this useless dud.

Annie had angrily tossed the useless amulet into the grass in disgust. Moments later, without uttering a word, Elva suddenly sprang to her feet and went to retrieve the amulet.

"Be careful, Elva," Finwe warned, worried that some harm might come to her.

"It is absolutely fine, Finwe," Elva replied as she reached down and confidently scooped up the amulet. "This is not our amulet. It can neither repel nor injure me."

While nonchalantly tossing the amulet up and down from one hand to the other and back again, Elva came back to sit crossed-legged next to Annie.

"I have had an idea that I think will get us right back on track with our mission," she said, brightly, nudging Annie out of her sorrowful reverie.

"It's no use, Elva," she replied, not bothering to look up. "Nothing is going to change this dud into the powerful, life-saving, life-giving amulet that we need." But, true to form, Elva was not one to be easily deterred.

"I know that, Annie," she said, unable to conceal the hope and excitement in her voice. The others had heard her optimism and excitement, and leaned in closer to hear what Elva had to say.

"This "dud amulet", as you call it, Annie, is like Finwe and I," she continued. "This amulet looks exactly like our amulet. Perhaps this could be our Labradorite Amulet's twin." Spurred on by the looks of encouragement from the others, Elva went on. "Finwe and I have a particularly strong bond because we our twins and, unlike the amulets, we are not even identical."

"So," Finwe interjected as he caught and surfed on Elva's wave of thinking. "We are usually able to divine each other's whereabouts and state of health, and maybe this amulet can do the same."

"Do you mean to say," asked Varis, "that you think this amulet could reveal the whereabouts of its twin? That is to say, our Labradorite Amulet?" The Mexican wave of excitement had made its way round to Lucan.

"It is certainly worth a try," he agreed, with unusual eagerness. "How do you propose we do it?"

"We do not," said Elva, nudging Annie once more. "It is all down to our Annie here."

Annie wasn't feeling the sense of hope, excitement, and anticipation that had infected the others.

Well, quelle surprise, she thought, while pitifully wallowing in self-absorbed disappointment and bitterness. *Yet again, it all comes down to little old me.*

"Okay," she sighed, not daring to raise her hopes for them just to be dashed to nothing all over again. "So, how am I going to get this thing to reveal to me its twin's whereabouts?"

Elva securely pressed the dud amulet back into Annie's hand and, one by one, curled each of Annie's fingers around it.

"Here," she said. "I am not at all sure about how you do it, but I think it is going to need you to focus all your magical energy into it before you ask it any questions."

"Sorry, what?" Annie protested, still yet to catch the wave of hope. "You're saying you want me to converse with a piece of jewellery?"

Finwe calmly placed his long, strong fingers around both hers and his sister's.

"Think back to the cave of crystals, Annie," he encouraged softly. "You were unsure of how to handle and manage your powers then, yet you managed to more than clear the barricaded exit to save us all. This may well be much the same."

"Open your mind to imagine the completely improbable," Varis chipped in, while placing his hands on Annie's narrow shoulders. "You have met so many strange and unusual things head on and not shied away from any of them. And this? This is no different."

All these words of encouragement simply served to make Annie feel guilty about how she was planning to deceive them all. Unlike his companions, Lucan thought that all this softly, softly, warm, and fuzzy encouragement was getting them nowhere. So, his contribution to spurring Annie into action took its usual form of being clear, blunt yet pointed, and masterfully authoritarian.

"You need to stop indulging in all this self-pity right now," he ordered. "Stop this defeatist attitude, and pull yourself together, immediately. We have a critical mission, probably the most critical mission in elven history, and we are going to get it done. So just get on with it!"

Once again, it was Lucan's straight-talking, no-messing-around approach that kicked started her into action. Without another word, Annie took herself a little way off from the group. She felt more than a little self-conscious at the thought of trying to chat with a piece of jewellery in front of an audience. She sat on the ground with her back to her friends and held the dud amulet, nestling it in both her hands.

As with the creation of her palm light, she decided that slowing and deepening her breathing was a really good place to start. She figured that, if she could let go of her frustration, worry and guilt, even just briefly, it might just open the door for her to apply her powers, and enable a 'conversation' with this amulet to take place.

Breathe in... two... three... four, she coached herself again. *And out... seven... six... five... four... three... two... one.* The ominous clouds had dissipated again to reveal the moon and stars above. On her next, deep inhale, Annie felt her magic brew and swirl in the depths of her stomach. A vision of Carric suffering at the hands of Tathlyn popped into her mind's eye. As a result, her magic threatened to erupt, and the night air instantly dropped a couple of degrees.

This isn't helping anyone, she chastised herself sternly as she shivered a little.

But still her magic threatened to erupt. In an effort to calm things down, her golden fleck swished calmly in a figure of eight.

There's no need to chastise yourself, she thought. *You are doing the best you can with what you've got and, in this moment, right here and now, the only thing that matters is communing with this amulet. Dial... everything... down.*

And with that, Annie successfully resumed maintaining a focus on her deep, slow breathing.

Gradually, her magic downgraded from a potential eruption, to a calm, slow-moving, convection-like current in the bottom of her belly. She fluttered her eyes open and softened her gaze as she looked at the amulet to the exclusion of all else. She softened her gaze so much that she felt as if she were looking right into the amulet.

Almost imperceptibly at first, the blue-cyan of the labradorite stone began to swirl languidly. As soon as Annie noticed it, the swirling immediately halted, as if caught out in a game of "What time is it Mr Wolf?".

Okay, she thought. *I've got to sort of look at you and and into you, without actually looking at you at all, do I? Well, I think I can do that.*

She settled back down once more, re-softening her gaze and softening it further still, to the point where she could no longer see where the labradorite stone stopped and the air around it began. She slowed her breathing further still as the stone resumed its lazy, languid swirling. Soon her hands and the labradorite pixelated, and merged with one another. She was it and it was her. She wasn't even surprised when striking up communications felt like the most normal thing in the world to do.

My friends and I desperately need your help, she whispered with her inner voice. *The elven realms are in the most grave danger. The worst danger that they have ever faced in their entire history. They are dying. Soon, I fear everyone in the realms will be dying too.*

The swirling changed direction as if to say, "Go on."

Only the matching labradorite amulet to yourself, your twin, can save the realms, and all who dwell within them, Annie continued.

"And so what do you want from me," the stone asked. Annie was amused by the fact that this jewel speaking with her now felt like a normal, everyday occurrence. But she didn't allow it to distract her.

Please reveal to me where I can find your twin, she pleaded. *Your twin, who has been lost for some twelve hundred elven moons.*

There was silence and stillness, as if the stone was pausing to think.

"And what will become of me if I do?" it asked. "Will I be once more imprisoned in the man-made rock in this place of utter melancholy?"

How interesting, she thought, hoping it was out of the amulet's 'earshot'. This inanimate item has feelings, wants and desires. Who would have thought?

A new and quite probably better solution pierced Annie's mind. A solution that would serve both her and this gem. If they ever managed to retrieve the enchanted amulet and get back to the Sun Elven Realm, she could use this dud amulet as a decoy while she took the enchanted amulet to Tathlyn, and saved Carric. She wouldn't dare to take the dud to Tathlyn, for fear of him finding out and instantly killing Carric.

Once Carric was safe, she would, somehow, steal back the real Labradorite Amulet and replace it without the Sun Elven and Woodland Elves ever being any the wiser.

Quite the feat, if you can pull it off, she sneered at herself.

She turned back to address the dud.

I promise that I will bring you back to the elven realms with me, she thought to the stone, and then tightly held her breath while she waited for its answer. There was no response. Don't you go all quiet and coy on me now, she huffed. Then, thinking the better of it, she added a desperate and placatory, please.

"Very well," said the stone at length. "Providing you take me with you, I shall reveal my twin's whereabouts."

Experiencing a mixture of relief and anticipation, Annie held the amulet more firmly, and agreed to the deal.

So, tell me about your twin's whereabouts, she thought, trying to prise the information out of this artefact while, at the same time not appearing too pushy, and causing it to clam up. Somewhat irritatingly, this amulet was proving to have rather a 'flouncy diva' vibe.

"You will need to travel to here," the amulet explained, while showing Annie visions of its twin's current resting place. As if looking through her own eyes and walking through the visions, she could see a modest-sized church. On the south front she noticed a blocked priest's door, and on what she guessed was the southwest corner of the nave roof, there was a sundial dated 1718. In her mind, she turned to look at the sign outside the church. It read "Saint Mary's Church". Suddenly, the vision rapidly zoomed her out, as if she were using a maps app on a mobile, in street-view mode. Looking down on the area she could see that the church was in the centre of a small village called Newchurch In Pendle. Zooming out further still, the vision revealed that Newchurch-in-Pendle was near Pendle Hill.

Pendle Hill, she thought. She was daring to get excited now. She knew exactly where Pendle Hill was. *We need to go to my home county,* she thought. *We need to go to Lancashire!*

Thinking again, she supposed that it shouldn't have been much of a surprise that the sacred Labradorite Amulet was where she had grown up. After all, it was her ancestor of so very long ago, who had stolen it in the first place.

"There," the amulet asserted. "Having been donated to the church when it was being built, you will find my twin hidden among the various religious artefacts."

Annie jumped up and happily dropped the dud amulet into her pocket. Before striding back to the others, she suddenly thought better of her actions and gently pulled the amulet from her jacket.

Thank you, she thought, with genuine gratitude. Thank you.

And with that, she slowly and carefully slid the amulet back into her pocket, and zipped it shut to keep the dud safe. Having concealed her newly discovered accomplice, she marched over to her friends and sat among them.

"I notice there is a springing confidence in your step, Annie," said Varis. "Are we to take it that you have some welcome news?"

All four elves leaned in with raised hope and intense interest. Annie nodded in confirmation. She told them of the enchanted Labradorite Amulet's whereabouts and how it was, not so surprisingly, close to where she had grown up.

"Well that is most excellent news, Annie," Finwe affirmed, jumping up and punching the air in triumph.

"Where is, what you called, the 'dud amulet' now?" Elva asked. Hoping that no one noticed her nanosecond of hesitation or her golden fleck squirming in the discomfort of a lie, Annie said,

"I returned it to its resting place on top of its concrete plinth."

Not wanting anyone to notice that the conviction in her voice didn't ring true, or that the dud amulet wasn't actually on its plinth, she, too, jumped up, adding,

"We really do need to get out of here before the security guards discover us." And as if right on cue, a little way off, a narrow beam of torchlight could be seen strobing back and forth along the lines of gravestones.

Without another word, the five friends grabbed their soft leather satchels and silently made their way to the entrance of the Necropolis, by way of a convoluted route that circumnavigated the reach of what they took to be the security guard's beam of light. As there were no headstones behind which they could duck, the entrance to the Necropolis left them exposed. But they had no other option. It was too risky to remain in the graveyard and, in addition, Annie didn't want to risk the others discovering that she had lied, and the dud wasn't actually back on its plinth at all.

Annie's elven friends stood on the Necropolis side of the Bridge of Sighs and ogled at the road which lay beneath.

"What in hellé's name is this river?" Varis hissed. Acutely aware that now wasn't a good time to start explaining about the Human Realm's road links, traffic, street lighting, and the like, Annie hissed back,

"In the Human Realm, not all bridges span water or valleys. Here, we have many stretches of manmade tarmac on which our favoured mode of transport — that is to say, cars, among other vehicles — transport us."

"Oh, I see," Varis replied, nodding his head, clearly not really seeing at all, but at the same time aware that further questions could wait until a more appropriate time.

Crouching very low either side of the bridge, in order to remain below the height of its wing walls, they silently crept along, making their way over Wishart Street, and towards the dark silhouette of Glasgow Cathedral.

Their attempt to remain incognito was suddenly and completely dashed as a drone seemed to drop out of the sky, buzzing and flitting above their heads like an angry wasp. Instinctively reaching for their favoured weapons against this metallic skéity dragon-like creature, the elves frustratingly came up empty handed. Without hesitation, Annie released a diminutive palm bomb, which adeptly smashed into the drone and sent it spiralling towards the ground. Seconds later, they heard it come to an abrupt and sorry end as it smashed into a nearby monument to the long deceased.

"Drama averted," she confirmed, trying to sound confident and maybe even a little nonchalant, but not really feeling either. Waving her arms, she urged her friends to make haste across the bridge. Regrettably, however, their troubles were far from over. Two sets of police van headlights flicked on, silhouetting the figures of approximately two dozen police officers with batons drawn.

Then came the order that was barked over a loud hailer:

"Stop, this is the police!"

Chapter Four

Varis and Elva spun round to go back, only to find that three dog handlers had appeared to block their way, and were firmly holding their all-too-eager Alsatians. Finwe, Lucan, and Annie remained facing the dazzling lights of the police vans.

"What are 'police'?" Elva called to Annie.

"They are like... like Lucan and Varis, who protect the safety of their realm," Annie replied, racking her brains for a quick and simple explanation in this terribly dry tinder-box situation. She was acutely aware that the slightest spark, which would most likely come from Lucan, would set the whole situation ablaze.

"We are without our preferred weapons," called Lucan to the others, "And yet, we may still be able to take these... these police humans and their pets." And with that, all four elves adopted a wide, bent-legged stance in readiness to pounce.

"No! No! No!" Annie shouted to them. "It's all a mistake. They can't want us. They didn't know we would be here and we've done absolutely nothing wrong. And these dogs really aren't pets!"

The police and dogs started to advance across the bridge towards them. The Alsatians were very much aware of the rising tension and their alertness, and keenness to get stuck in, made them jiffle and bark in eager anticipation of being let loose.

"You four stay right where you are," instructed the policeman with the loud hailer. "We are arresting you on suspicion of dealing significantly large quantities of drugs."

"What are they saying, Annie?" Varis asked over his shoulder, while still keeping his stare fixed on the officers in front of him. Apparently, unlike Annie's ability to speak Elvish in the elven realms, the elves had not, in travelling through her portal, gained the ability to speak English in the Human Realm — or any human language for that matter.

"They think that we dealing large quantities of drugs," she replied, again searching for a concise explanation. "That is to say, selling dangerous, hallucinogenic and illegal powders, and concoctions to humans."

"Well, we have clearly not been doing that!" Lucan blustered, maintaining his defensive stance. "Only the Wise One deals with anything of that nature." Elva gave a little cough. "Well," he corrected, "mainly the Wise One and sometimes Elva, under the Wise One's tutelage."

"And there is nothing about it that is against the law," Elva chimed in.

"What kind of bloody gobbledygook language is that?" Annie heard an officer sarcastically mutter to his neighbour, as he moved past her without even looking in her direction.

"Yeah, and they're a really weird-looking lanky bunch too," said his fellow officer.

Hang on a minute, she thought. *You four? There's five of us. Can't they count? Can't they see me?* Her golden flecked swished with smug confidence. *Wait. Am I invisible to them? Like, literally invisible?*

Annie was abruptly brought out of her musings by another barked instruction from close by.

"I said," the police officer repeated, clearly becoming rather annoyed by her friends' lack of compliance, "drop your bags to the floor."

"What is this police human saying? What are we to do?" Finwe called to Annie. "This is your realm. You need to guide us."

Confident that she was both unseen and unheard by the police, Annie nipped around the side of them to come closer to her friends. As she moved, she noticed other movement among the monuments and gravestones, a little way back from the Bridge of Sighs, where they currently stood. Her golden fleck thrashed with another seed of an idea.

These must be the real drug dealers, she thought as, once again, the idea seed took root and grew.

"He wants you to put your bags on the ground," she said.

"But, at the very least, we need our supply of the Wise One's strength potion," Elva protested.

"I know," Annie assured her. "That's why you're going to stay perfectly still until I give the word to move, bags and all."

While the police and elves were at an increasingly tense stalemate, Annie continued to swiftly move past the humans undetected. Although the dogs did take notice, their handlers dismissed the dogs' signalling, sine there was clearly nothing there. Annie didn't know how long the police or the elves would remain at a stand-off, so she had no time to waste on whether her idea could, or would work. It just simply had to.

Just lean on the confidence Elva has always had in me to 'use my intention', she thought as she made her way up to the four real drug dealers. She found them lurking in the shadows, keenly watching the drama playing out on the bridge. Their plan was to let this group of strikingly tall, weirdly dressed people keep the police busy, and then make their own exit from the Necropolis once these others had been taken away in the police vans.

Unbeknownst to them, Annie had a very different plan in mind.

Realising that she needn't take measures to conceal herself any longer, she strode up to stand directly behind them. Recalling her newfound technique, she created a palm light in her right hand. Silently, she focused on it. First, she willed it to rise up out of her hand and hover above the dealers. Thankfully, the palm light dutifully obeyed. Next, she ramped up her magic energy and let it surge into the light, causing it to take on floodlight capability. Suddenly, the drug dealers were brightly illuminated and she could hear the police below her exclaim their surprise at this sudden revelation.

Panicked by their unanticipated exposure, the drug dealers scattered dropping their luggage bags of 'product' and trying to take cover among other gravestones. The police had now split ranks, with half of them advancing in pursuit of the real dealers, and half remaining on the bridge with her friends.

Now for phase two, she announced to herself, and she could have sworn her fleck jiggled in childish delight. Had it had hands, it would have surely been rubbing them together with glee. She began releasing palm bombs relatively close on the heels of the various dealers, frightening the life out of them, and driving them down towards the police. Soon, she was able to narrow her attention when she saw that two of the police dogs had apprehended one of the dealers, and had deftly taken him to the ground, while he squealed like a little girl.

Two more of the dealers were taken to the ground by officers. It was as if the dealers were actually relieved to be caught — like they were seeking safety in the open arms of the law.

Making herself invisible once more, Annie made her way back towards her friends on the bridge, while causing as much chaos as possible, with her palm bombs exploding behind her as she went. Soon there was only a skeleton staff of police still with the elves on the bridge.

Suddenly, someone barged past Annie with such force that she was nearly sent sprawling to the ground.

It was the last remaining dealer.

Confused by having been sent off balance by some unseen object, the dealer staggered sideways towards one of the bridge's wing walls. In an effort to allude the remaining police, he sprang up onto the wall and made to run along it. Not wishing to cause him to fall, the police dropped back a little.

All eyes were on this dealer as he attempted to flee with a smug, self-satisfied look on his face. A smug, self-satisfied look that instantly disappeared as he lost his footing and plunged down onto the busy Wishart Street below.

There was a sickening screaming of horns, brakes, and the dealer, as he made fatal contact with an unsuspecting truck. Everyone, including the elves, dashed to lean over the wing wall.

Below was utter carnage.

Multiple vehicles had crashed into one another and had come to a halt at crazy angles. Many drivers and passengers had exited their vehicles, trying to gain some sort of understanding about what had just happened. Those who could, were giving immediate assistance to those in need. Others were on their phones calling for help or calling loved ones.

Those police not directly handling the other three dealers swiftly turned their attention to getting down to Wishart Street where they could assist those in need, while everyone awaited the arrival of both the fire and rescue, and ambulance services.

There were virtually no police with the elves now and Annie saw the need to seize their opportunity, and make their escape. Sprinting past everyone on the bridge and pointing at the cathedral, she shouted,

"Run and meet me in the shadows of the largest doorway of that dark, old building with the spire!"

Discussion and debate were not necessary. As one, the four elves took a lithe leap backwards and dashed away in different directions so as to split the attention, and chase by any police humans, should they opt to pursue them. They were so fast that, within seconds, they were already gathered in the shadowy doorway of the cathedral by the time Annie got there. There was no time for celebration at their getaway, since they had not yet completely got away.

Instead, there was a quick check to make sure they had all their necessary provisions, to put on their capes, and redistribute their satchels, in order to roughly change their appearance, before they headed away from the cathedral. To disguise themselves further, Annie remained visible to increase their number to five, so as not to be identified as the group of four that had been temporarily detained at the Bridge of Sighs.

They also moved away from the cathedral's site at a casual tourist's speed, since nothing said "guilty" like running away from a scene.

<><><><><><><><>

"I see your carriages require no horses," Varis commented to Annie, as various vehicles passed them and came to a standstill as a result of the traffic accident. "They are fascinating."

Since Annie knew Glasgow like the back of her hand, she guided the group southwest along High Street. They then cut a left up London Road, a right onto Charlotte Street, and didn't come to a halt until they were on the banks of the River Clyde in Glasgow Green, not far from the Nelson Monument.

Once by the Nelson Monument, Annie wasn't the least bit surprised to find that she was quite out of breath. The whole episode had been more than enough to make anyone's heart race. Her companions, while looking a little shaken and somewhat perplexed by some of what they had seen in the Human Realm, were breathing easily. Elva embraced her.

"You were absolutely amazing," she mumbled into Annie's hair. "Vanishing and flushing out the real quarry was a real stroke of brilliance."

Annie admitted that she hadn't realised she could vanish but, having done so, had decided to make the most of it while she had. All her life she had made herself unnoticed and unseen so as not to attract unwanted attention.

Perhaps I've been literally disappearing all along, she pondered.

Finwe was taking in their surroundings.

"It is curious," he said finally. "The trees that you have are obviously healthy, and yet you have so few of them. How does your realm breathe?"

"That," Annie replied. "Is a very astute question. One that humankind have been debating and battling on a daily basis, for years."

"I have no wish to be disparaging," Elva said, "but with this lack of trees and other plant life, and with all these horseless machines', filth and noise, and the harsh, drab buildings, I am wondering if this Human Realm is far more mortally wounded than our elven ones."

Annie gave Elva a wry smile.

"I'm not offended Elva. I can appreciate why this realm would appear rather sickly to elves, and Woodland Elves in particular."

Lucan had been prowling up and down, clearly agitated.

"We *must* leave this place this very night," he said. "Those police humans will be hunting us before long and we have very little with which to defend ourselves."

"Those 'police humans'," said Annie, horrifying herself that she'd used her hands to create air quotes, "are going to be tied up with the dealers they caught, the traffic collisions below the bridge, and the death of a suspect while they were in pursuit."

"And we need to be 'tied up' with reaching our Labradorite Amulet," retorted Lucan, also deploying air quotes, much to Annie's amusement. He growled and spun away in frustration.

"Look," said Annie, more kindly. "I know you want to get the real Labradorite Amulet as soon as possible. All of us do. But, to get where we need to go, we will need to take a train and there are no trains running at this time of night."

In the beam of the street light, Annie could see that her friends didn't understand. Using a stick from the grass, she started to draw in a patch of soil and explain what trains were.

"From what I can tell," said Finwe, "these trains move on wheels, and yet you tell us that they run."

"But not this late at night," grumbled Lucan, arms folded tightly across his broad chest.

Annie couldn't help smiling once again. Gruff and starchy though he was, Lucan had really grown on her.

"I am guessing that having a wheeled vehicle that runs, is a figure of speech," Elva offered by way of explanation to Finwe. "Like when we say that time flies, but it does not literally do so."

"Exactly," said Annie. "And we cannot catch... I mean travel on one of these trains until the early morning."

Ever the voice of reason and calm, Varis suggested that they take cover among the little copse of trees and get what rest they could. As they spread their capes from their satchels out on the ground and lay down, Elva realised that their appearance was not going to help their quest.

"We are far too conspicuous as we are," she said into the night. She could not see the twinkle in Annie's eye.

"You leave that with me," she said, adopting her favoured foetal position in these all-too-familiar surroundings, and settling down for what remained of the night.

<><><><><><><><>

At first light, Finwe put his Woodland hunting skills to work and caught some salmon and sea trout, for breakfast. So as not to attract further unwanted attention to themselves, there would be no fire on which to cook them.

Trying hard not to wretch, Annie joined the others in eating the fish raw.

I'm going to have to steal us something more palatable than this, she thought as she engaged in agitated negotiations with her stomach, to allow her to swallow and retain the raw flesh. Not wishing to offend Finwe and his efforts, she arranged her face into what she hoped would vaguely pass for a smile as she forced herself to chew.

With breakfast completed, and feeling reasonably confident that the raw fish would remain within her stomach, Annie headed out via Greendyke Street, Mart Street, and Osbourne Street to her favoured charity shop — the Shelter Scotland shop on Stockwell Street. There, she set about browsing the many rails for suitable clothes that would enable her companions to blend in. Having chosen several items, she went into the changing room under the ruse of trying some of the items on. She purposely had many more clothes than were needed.

She had considered vanishing herself, in order to go about her task, but she wasn't yet sure quite how it worked, and she didn't want to terrify the shop assistant with clothing that seemed to be floating itself through the air.

Once inside the changing rooms, she rolled the items for her friends up tightly, and packed them into her and Elva's leather satchels. Feeling a pang of guilt with regard to depriving her fellow homeless community of support, she decided to leave her leather jacket behind for Shelter Scotland to sell. The elven cloak in her satchel would more than suffice should the weather turn colder.

When she came back out of the changing room, she still had an armful of clothes that she wouldn't be buying. As she passed them to the shop assistant, she paused and caught him in her softened gaze.

I wonder, she thought. Feeling her magic swirl gently and her golden fleck dancing a kind of jig, she said quietly,

"You are going to take these clothes and not notice that there's only half of what I went into the changing room with. When I get to the door and the bell rings, you're going to thank me for the leather jacket, and then forget I was ever here." She held her breath for a moment before making her way to the shop door.

Well, this is either going to go really well or really badly, she thought as she closed her eyes and opened the door.

"Thanks for your leather jacket," he called after her, and Annie grinned broadly.

"She reminds me of someone I used to see on the streets here," said the next customer, who had crossed paths with Annie as she had left. "Who was that?"

"Who was who?" asked the shop assistant. "I haven't had anyone in here in over an hour."

<><><><><><><><>

Having changed into their new clothes and been rather bemused, and amused by the phenomenon known as zips, the elves nearly looked like they could blend in with the general populous.

Nearly, but not quite.

"Here," said Annie, as she distributed a variety of hats. "I know it is summer, but it's your turn to cover your ears. It's okay to have folk wondering why you're wearing them at this time of year, but we can't have those perfect points drawing unwelcome attention to us."

For a moment, she was transported back to being on the Shoreland Elf ship, crossing the ocean to the Sun Elven Realm. She could see herself with her hair braided to cover her human ears so as not to spook the superstitious crew. She chuckled to herself as she remembered how green around the gills she was and how Finwe and Carric took care of her as she tried to overcome her seasickness.

Carric, she thought, and her chuckle instantly disappeared to be replaced with acute, leaden heartache. Her memory jumped to see her firing off palm bombs in an attempt to prevent Carric being dragged off the ship and below the waves by the swarm of Shadow Elves.

Her memory jerked forward again, to when Tathlyn visited her mind while she was alone in her room in the Sun Elven palace. Remembering the anguish of seeing Carric suffering made her body feel the pain in the now.

Thank all available gods for Finwe coming in to console and contain me, she thought. *If he hadn't absorbed my grief, I could have accidentally brought the whole palace down around everyone's pointed ears.*

"Are you all right, Annie?" Finwe asked. "I was asking if I looked dapper in my hat, but you seem to be... how did you put it? ... away with the fairies, again."

At the mention of fairies, Lucan and Varis visibly shivered like something nasty had crawled down their spines.

"Ugh," said Varis, performing another exaggerated shiver. "Let us not make mention of those devious creatures again."

Annie had been warned about the treacherous fairies in the elven realms and, although she knew they gave the elves the creeps, she was still curious to meet at least one.

Elva was as perceptive as ever.

"Were you thinking about Carric?" she asked.

Annie nodded and then shook her head as if to clear her mind, and refocus on the present. She appraised their head gear favourably and suggested that they head out to walk through what she now saw as the concrete jungle of Glasgow, to the Glasgow Central train station.

<><><><><><><><>

Not long into their walk, Annie smiled as she led her comrades past the Shelter Glasgow shop where she had acquired their clothes. There, on the manikin in the window, was her old leather jacket. Finwe spotted it and drew her attention to it.

"Annie, is that not your leather jacket?" he asked, pressing his nose up to the glass and pointing. Spotting the shop assistant giving her a curious look through the open door, she grabbed Finwe by his denim lapel and dragged him away.

"Yep," she said. "But let's move on quickly before the shop guy recognises half his stock for taller men is walking down the street!"

As they all moved on, Annie's blood suddenly ran ice cold, her golden fleck went into flits of panic, and the summery breeze turned nippy.

The dud amulet, she shouted in her head, metaphorically shaking herself by her metaphorical lapels. *The bloody shéatting dud amulet is in the zipped pocket of my leather jacket that's now adorning that bloody schteelcün manikin!*

Without a word to the others, she about-faced quick smart, and marched back into the charity shop, nonchalantly lifting a man's wallet from his back pocket as she went.

"Are you looking for anything in particular?" the shop assistant asked, clearly sensing he should recognise her, and yet having absolutely no memory of seeing Annie only forty-five minutes before. "I noticed you admiring that leather jacket in the window. It was new in this morning."

"Yes, how astute of you," Annie replied, turning on the charm, or as she preferred to call it, ramping up her woo. She took out a twenty pound note and told him to keep the extra five quid as a further donation to the charity.

As luck would have it, the victim of her pick-pocketing had stopped a few shops down and was patting himself down in a failing attempt to locate his wallet. Having put on her reacquired jacket, Annie was able to assuage her guilt, at least partially, by dashing over to him and holding his wallet aloft.

"Is this what you're looking for?" she asked. "I spotted it on the pavement."

The man was grateful for Annie's keen eye and honesty. Annie could feel her golden fleck screw itself up in discomfort around her deceit, and she swiftly made her exit before the guy could discover that he was twenty pounds short.

From the Shelter Glasgow shop, Glasgow Central Station was only a twelve minute walk away, via Howard Street and Jamaica Street. However, it took them longer as Annie was brought up short by a tatty and faded picture of herself fastened to, not one, but three different lamp posts. Under each picture was a hand written message:

Have you seen Annie Harper?
She is eighteen and went missing on her birthday.
Please give any information to
Hunter Street Homeless Services (0141 552 9287)
The homeless community miss her

"They are missing me," she said in an almost inaudible, emotional whisper.

"Who?" ask Elva, putting a comforting hand on Annie's shoulder. "Who are missing you? Your family?"

Annie gave an ironic half smile and shook her head vigorously.

"No, not my family," she answered. "Not my biological family at least. My mother wouldn't know to search here and, even if she did know I had been here in Glasgow, she wouldn't have come searching anyway." Annie was experiencing a cocktail of sorrow, anger, and disappointment, and was turning a blue-sky sunny day into one that was rapidly clouding over.

"I ran away from home when I was just under sixteen and there was no mention of me in the local newspapers or any posters on lamp posts, even then. Absolutely nothing, zip, nada."

No, it was her "homeless family" that had been missing her. Missing her, despite the fact that she had very much kept herself to herself. Members of her "homeless family" must have made the posters themselves. She wondered how many of them had been put up around the city. A tiny flickering, warm glow ignited within her and the cloudy sky returned to blue as she realised that she had mattered, that people had cared about her. She had mattered to her family forged through circumstance.

She teared up a little.

Three other hands joined Elva's on Annie's shoulders and she teared up a little more as she gave her friends a slightly soggy smile. Then a thought struck her.

How come these posters are so tatty and faded? She thought back to her realisation in the Necropolis, that the seasons had moved on while she'd been away. *But these posters look much older than a few months.*

Pulling away from her friends' comforting hands, she hastened over to the R S McColl newsagents and cast her eye over the papers on the shelves.

The Times — 2 June, 2023
The Sun — 2 June, 2023
The Daily Mail, The Express, The Telegraph — all of them said 2 June, 2023.

It hadn't been just six months since she'd first travelled through her portal to the elven realms. It had been over eighteen months!

The newsagent's gruff and nasel voice burst through Annie's reeling thoughts.

"We're not a chuffin' library, you know. They're not there to read for free. Are you gonna buy somethin' or what?"

"What? Sorry?" Annie replied, while hastily backing out of the shop. "Erm, I'm going to 'or what'." And with that, she turned on her heel, and performed a pseudo-confident flounce off to return to her friends, that papered over the fact that she felt more than a little shaken.

"Come on," she ordered ignoring their questioning glances. "We'd better get a wiggle on, if we're going to catch our train."

"We have to catch the train?" asked Lucan, looking rather alarmed, yet willing to give it a go. With a smile and a mischievous wink, Finwe added,

"I think we would get there faster if we ran rather than wiggled!"

Welcoming the light relief, Annie burst out laughing.

Chapter Five

Although there had been a lapse of around one and a half human years since she had been in the Human Realm, Annie found no change in how busy and bustling Glasgow Central Station was. If anything it was busier and more bustling than ever. Bright sunlight shone through the glass roof that was held in place by a complex web of thick steel girders. Annie had always found the juxtaposition of the past and the present here rather pleasing to the eye — the modern shop fronts and huge, computerised train arrival and departure boards, rubbing cheek by jowl with the curving fittings in the concourse, dating, if her memory served her, to the late nineteenth-century. And then there was the classic clock with its Roman numerals. It had been one of her favourite daytime haunts when she was living rough.

The elves were starting to feel less shocked about all the alien sights and sounds around them. If they were to have any chance of succeeding in their mission, they would simply have to take everything at face value and not think too much about it.

"Now that I am experiencing your world, Annie," said Varis mesmerised, by the seemingly magical, ever-changing, arrivals and departures board, "I humbly admire how well you assimilated and adjusted to our elven realms."

"And we must aspire to do the same with regard to this Human Realm," ordered Lucan, while dragging Varis out of the way of a stampeding crowd of people whose train's platform had, just that moment, been announced.

Suddenly, Annie belched and was horrified to taste the raw fish from breakfast.

I've got to get something less gopping to eat for our time here, she thought, and eyed up the unsuspecting Starbucks coffee shop. *Time for a little more invisibility*, she decided and she told the others to wait in the seats in the middle of the concourse, while she went to do some hunting and foraging "Annie-style".

Within five minutes, she had returned with a veritable smorgasbord of muffins, cheese and ham, and vegan deli sandwiches, gingerbread men, and smoothies, all stuffed into her satchel. Thinking she was still invisible and soundless to all but her companions, she began to brag about her cache of goodies.

"Oi!" came a staccato shout from the direction of Starbucks. "Yes, you there!" It was one of the coffee shop's baristas. "You're gonna need to pay for all that, you bloody witch!"

"Does he know you?" asked Finwe with a mixture of innocence and mischievousness. Annie didn't even register Finwe's quip.

"Shéat!" she exclaimed. "I must have 'switched off' my invisibility too soon."

Shifting her satchel strap to rest across her chest, Annie took off at speed, in the direction of the platform barriers and shouted over her shoulder,

"Run!"

Needing no further instruction, Elva, Finwe, Lucan, and Varis instantly sprang out of their fixed seats, and hared after her. Unlike Annie's ungainly, yet well practised, vault over the platform barrier, the elves easily cleared it within their normal running stride.

Previously, Annie had taken note that their train would be departing from platform two. As the elves didn't know where they were going, they quickly fell into formation behind her. The whistle warning that their train was departing, was being blown, and the elves only momentarily hesitated to leap onto the last carriage before the doors electronically shut behind them, and locked.

Relieved to be continuing their quest in earnest, all five of them laughed in relief as they flopped into neighbouring seats. Annie shared out the spoils of her hunt and Finwe, who, Annie thought must share at least some DNA with a gannet, immediately started to tuck into a large apple slice, cardboard packaging and all. Annie burst out laughing at Finwe's exaggerated expression of disgust and, without a word, released the hot apple slice from its packaging for him to eat.

"While this... this train... transports us," said Lucan, assuming control once more. "we should get some rest. We know not of what is yet to face us."

The others wholeheartedly agreed and shuffled in their seats so that they could lean their heads on the headrests to snooze, and recharge.

<><><><><><><><>

Just twenty-five minutes later, Annie's repose was rudely interrupted by the muffled yet distinct and dreaded announcement from the rear door of the carriage in front of theirs.

"Tickets please."

While Annie was now convinced and confident that she had, in the past, successfully travelled on public transport without paying for a single ticket because she was literally invisible, there was now the added complication that she was not on her own. Now she had four, noticeably tall, lithe accomplices, who would not be at all easy to hide.

"Come on," she whispered, while shaking each of them out of their dozing. "Silently move to the back of the carriage with me."

Without debate, each of the elves did her bidding.

"What is the matter?" Elva asked, in hushed tones that matched Annie's. "Are we to dismount the train while she is moving?"

"I am sure it will be very much like dismounting our steeds mid-gallop," Lucan asserted, while adjusting his satchel, ready for the jump.

"What?" hissed Annie. "No! We're not jumping off any trains. First off, the doors are locked until the train is at a standstill —"

"We can squeeze through the lowered window," enthused Finwe, cutting Annie off in mid-sentence.

"Again, what?!" Annie hissed louder, while spreading her hands in a 'let's just all stop for a beat' motion. Taking a deep, somewhat exasperated breath she added, "Secondly, the train is travelling far faster than your horses, and we would most likely get killed."

To Annie's frustrated amazement, her companions were now discussing between themselves, whether or not the train was travelling faster than a lintië haron.

Whatever the hell that is, she thought while rolling her eyes.

"Stop! Stop! Enough!" she asserted, rather louder than she had intended. Everyone was instantly taciturn and all eyes were fixed back on her. "Look," she said, pointing down the carriage. "That guy there in uniform, is working his way down the train checking people's tickets."

"But Annie, we have no tickets," said Elva, looking worried. Annie noticed that the usually stiffed-shirt, honest-to-a-fault Lucan was not in the least bit squeamish about cheating their way onto the train. Neither had he quibbled about the stealing of clothes or food.

You're an upstanding pillar of the community when it suits you, sir, she thought and turned her attention back to Elva.

"Precisely," she replied. "Now we know that *I* can disappear at will, but I have no idea what to do with all of you. Had I not been spotted stealing the muffins etcetera, I would have acquired another wallet and bought us tickets."

"We can easily take this ticket human," said Lucan, loosening his shoulders and neck in anticipation of a tussle. "He is but one human and we are trained, and experienced warriors."

"Again, stop," Annie insisted. "Nobody is going to 'take' anybody. He's just a guy doing his job. He doesn't deserve being mobbed by warrior elves."

While Lucan, Elva, Annie, and Varis had had their gaze fixed on the slowly approaching, and blissfully unaware train conductor, Finwe had been deep in thought. Had the others been looking at him, they would have realised that he was forming a plan.

"But, why not just make us all invisible," he said quietly. The others whipped their heads round to look at him questioningly.

"Please listen to my reasoning," he continued, as Lucan opened his mouth to debate his idea. "Annie, whenever you have been invisible, your clothes and satchel have been invisible too. When you first stole the food and placed it into your satchel, it was also invisible."

"And so," Varis encouraged, as he started to get the drift of Finwe's thinking. He was also acutely aware that the conductor would be with them soon, and was trying to speed Finwe along.

"So, if Annie goes invisible and holds all of us, we may all go invisible too," he said, simply. "Just like Annie's clothes. Just like the satchel. Just like the food."

The ticket inspector was already over halfway down the carriage, and the group were not going to be able to remain hidden in the vestibule at the back of the train, for much longer. They all looked at each other and nodded in agreement.

In the next moment, the four elves huddled around Annie as tightly as they possibly could. Each of them was touching her, and she was touching each of them.

So, thought Annie again. *This is either going to work brilliantly or, spectacularly not work at all.* She didn't let her mind think anything of what could well happen if it didn't work. If she had, her mind would have instantly conjured up a scenario where the innocent and unsuspecting ticket inspector was ambushed by these tall, strong elves, and unceremoniously bundled out of the door window to his certain death. And that, quite frankly, would not do.

Slowing her breathing by at least half, Annie allowed her golden fleck to be the catalyst in igniting her magic to turn her invisible. She just hoped that she was turning the others invisible too. There was no way for any of them to tell. As with being on the Bridge of Sighs and on the station concourse, she could still see her companions and they could see her. The only way they would know she had been successful was if the ticket inspector came through and thought the vestibule was empty.

The ticket inspector passed the last seats and, finally, entered the vestibule.

They all held their breath.

All, that is, except Annie.

For her magic to remain under her control and effective, she needed to continue breathing, slow and steady. Very slow and very, very steady.

The unsuspecting ticket inspector stepped further into the vestibule. He was now less than a couple of inches from walking into Finwe's back. Finwe could feel the inspector's presence through his recently acquired faded denim jacket. Unwavering, he looked at Annie's upturned face with her eyes closed. He stood stock-still with his hands on her upper arms and softened his gaze until there was no peripheral vision, and all he could see was, Annie. Had anyone else seen, they would have seen a wanting and a yearning, coupled with a sadness.

Unexpectedly, the train jerked roughly to the side and back again. The motion threw them all with it, but the inspector, with no additional ballast from any friends, toppled sideways and, thankfully, backwards. Catching the handrail, he thought better of lingering in the empty space any longer, and turned to make his way back through the train.

With the inspector's back to them, Annie lost her focus on remaining invisible and they were all brought back into view. They all gave a long, slow, and quiet exhale of great relief.

<><><><><><><><>

Approximately three hours, seven more stints of invisibility, and one change of train at Preston later, the Labradorite Amulet rescue party's train finally pulled in at Blackburn Station. In an effort to minimise attracting unwanted attention, the elves loitered on the benches at the farthest end of the platform, while Annie sought out their next connection.

Having found that their next train was being prepared for its next journey, they all slipped down the side of that train and onto the track in readiness for leaping on at the very last moment. Varis was utterly fascinated by what he saw.

"It really does have wheels," he announced in surprise. Annie was astonished.

"Well yes," she said. *Duh!* she thought. "Of course it has," she continued, "I drew it out for you in the soil. What did you think it moved on?"

"Well, fair Annie, I did not know," he replied, with the excitement of discovery in his voice. "When we leapt upon, and then dismounted our last train, the doors and the ground were almost on the same level. And yet here, we see that there is almost as much train below the ground as there is above it, and it is primarily wheels. Lots and lots of wheels!"

With a prickly poke from her golden fleck, Annie instantly realised that she had been unkind. Her depiction in the soil had only shown the train from the platform upwards, so Varis's comment was fair enough. Also, she'd had to cope with all manner of peculiarities in the elven realms and yet, only initially, had there been any mild ribbing from Lucan. Not once had she really been made to feel stupid or ridiculous. It was now incumbent upon her to afford her friends the same level of kindness. These elves had become her friends. One of them had become her lover and was currently suffering god-only-knew-what at the hands of Tathlyn.

That's odd, she thought. *I've had no cruel 'visits' from Tathlyn to remind me of Carric's suffering and our dreadful deal.* She surmised that while she was in the Human Realm, Tathlyn was unable to literally get inside her head. She had no doubt that, once she and her companions had returned to the Sun Elven Realm, Tathyln would be swift to re-engage her in conversations within her mind.

Before long, the travellers on this train started to board. It was time for the comrades to surreptitiously crawl out from under the train and do the same. Once again, they took seats at the very rear of the last carriage. From their vantage point, they could see that among the final people to board, was a young teen girl in smart school uniform, and a group of six, rowdy, boisterous young soldiers who had, Annie guessed, recently completed their initial training and had, in celebration, got close to steaming drunk on a mix of lagers and jägerbombs. The only seats available for all of them were those in the middle of the carriage. Varis, Lucan, Annie, and Elva sat, closely observing the scene. Without enough seats, Finwe had opted to stand in the rear vestibule.

The journey from Blackburn to Clitheroe was only twenty-six minutes and promised to be completely, and thankfully, uneventful. The likelihood of a ticket conductor necessitating yet another period of invisibility was virtually nil. However, when the friends made a swift exit from the train at Clitheroe, they left behind them an exceedingly grateful young teen girl, a number of startled members of the general public, and six, semi- and completely unconscious young soldiers.

<><><><><><><><>

From the moment the train had left the station at Blackburn, the rowdy, and significantly inebriated, squaddies had spied the attractive young teen, in her crisp school uniform. They clearly saw her as a source of laddish entertainment, and a means by which they could display a perverted kind prowess, and pecking order among themselves.

It all started small-scale, with stupid twittering among themselves. One would whisper something to his mates while pointing at the girl and they would then all guffaw loudly, elbowing each other at some banal, and coarse double entendre. The teen was obviously, at the very least, uncomfortable and embarrassed, but as the carriage was full, she was pretty much trapped in her current position. She clearly felt that she couldn't move away.

Annie was quietly seething. She had both seen and experienced this kind of diabolical behaviour before.

"What is going on?" asked Elva, picking up on Annie's brewing anger. "What are they saying?"

"I'm not going to dignify their bullying ways by translating what they are saying," Annie replied, her eyes fixed on the obvious ringleader, a lad referred to as Tiny. Her golden fleck had started to fizz angrily. As per the norm in such cases, the ringleader was not the one issuing the smut and filth — oh no. He was simply the one encouraging the weaker ones to amuse and impress him. He was deftly exploiting their need to be accepted and liked by him.

It was clear that the other passengers were uncomfortable with what was going on, but every single one chose to look down or out of their windows, rather than take any action.

Cowards, Annie seethed. *Typical*. And she paraphrased a well-known saying, making it her own. *Evil flourishes where good people do nothing.*

A particularly needy member of the group, who was clearly desperate for the approval of his leader, precipitated the downfall of them all.

Much to the tawdry delight of his comrades, he touched the teen's hair and, ignoring her flinch, and fear, he proceeded to rub is groin against her shoulder. Annie had seen more than enough. She jumped out of her seat and shouted,

"Oi, you! Back right off her, right now!"

She was about to stride right up to confront them, but was beaten to it by Finwe who, standing head and shoulders above the prime miscreant, snarled viciously into his face,

"You, déchwoot, will step away from this youngling and take yourself, and your fellow shiedaits to the other carriage."

While none of them had a clue what Finwe was actually saying, they all grasped the gist via the cutting intensity of his tone and stare. Elva and Annie motioned to the girl to come over and sit between them on their double seat. The girl didn't understand Finwe's seething Elvish either, but she totally recognised that someone was stepping in to help her, and for that, she was extremely relieved, and grateful.

Tiny, rather foolishly, decided to stand face to face with Finwe. He was a strikingly tall young man, falling only an inch or so short of the Woodland Elf.

Of course you're called Tiny, Annie thought. *You and your moron minions obviously couldn't think of something more original.*

Tiny foolishly thought the six of them could easily take this deeply tanned beanpole and his diminutive yet gobby, and clearly feisty, sidekick. Tiny's adoring entourage encouraging him to "land the bronzed bastard on his arse", turned out to work horribly against him.

Tiny didn't get to land anything, anywhere.

Finwe easily and artfully dodged Tiny's fist as it made to connect with his jaw. In the same moment, he took hold of Tiny's thumb and proceeded to bend it backwards beyond its natural position. This caused severe pain, and Finwe took him to the floor, as Tiny whimpered, pitifully. Finwe then rolled him onto his stomach and twisted Tiny's whole arm such that it was held at ninety degrees to his shoulder blade. Not one for holding back, Annie joined Finwe and dropped down onto the backs of Tiny's legs. She wrapped her arms around his ankles to render him completely helpless.

Stepping on the back of Tiny's head, Lucan hammered Tiny's face into the hard floor and knocked him out. A puddle of red added to the smorgasbord of questionable stains that already adorned the grubby, grey carpet. Seeing that their illustrious leader was out for the count, the others' eyes became disbelieving saucers.

In the next instance, Lucan took hold of two of their number by the throat and applied constant pressure until they simply passed out, and slumped in their seats. While Lucan was taking them enthusiastically by the throat, Elva had vaulted two sets of seats, and their occupants, to land in the aisle. From there she took out two more of the soldiers: one by means of her knee and foot, and the other by means of her elbow and fist. The last soldier standing was prevented from running away by Varis, who had grabbed him by the collar.

"Running from your comrades as they are soundly thrashed, is a pathetic display of cowardice," he said conversationally, as the young man hung like a curing kipper, his feet several inches off the floor. Varis screwed up his face as a wet patch started to spread outward from the soldier's groin. "And now your pathetic display has reached an all time low." As if wanting to put him out of his misery, Varis delivered a sharp jab of his fist to relieve the lad of consciousness.

"We need to get away immediately before any of these rambunctious, naxa nalantas recover enough to raise the alarm," Varis urged, as they hastily alighted onto the platform. "We do not want to be delayed more than is absolutely necessary."

"Agreed," said Lucan, striding across the platform to put a sizeable distance between him and the train. The others followed suit.

"Wait," called Annie while halting in her tracks. "There's no need for us to flee."

And with that she hopped back on board the train. She took the girl's hands and placed them on her own shoulders. Stunned by what had just happened, the girl simply left her hands where they had been placed. Annie then placed her own hands flat on the body of the carriage.

Please make this work, she pleaded with herself. It had worked with the guy at the charity shop, so why not with a carriage full of passengers? She shrugged her shoulders to herself and then addressed everyone in the carriage.

"You have all just witnessed these inebriated and bullish, bullying young men harass a very young woman." She hoped that her voice was commanding enough. She didn't realise that her magic was making her voice sound like all the occupants' voices speaking in unison. "A fight broke out among them and they have managed to knock seven shades of shit out of each other. You will report these young men to the police and give witness to their terrible behaviour towards... towards..." Annie's expression tacitly asked for the teen girl's name.

"Freya," said Freya, filling the blank.

"You will report these *young men* to the police and give witness to their terrible behaviour towards Freya," Annie concluded.

Taking her hands off the inner walls of the train, Annie now looked into Freya's searching eyes.

"You, on the other hand, Freya," she said firmly yet quietly, so only Freya could hear, "I want you to remember it all. Every moment. Remember it, so that you know that you need *never* put up with such appalling behaviour, ever again."

And with that, Annie released the grateful Freya from her hold and darted from the train to join the others.

<><><><><><><><>

In order to get from Clitheroe to Newchurch In Pendle, the friends would have to finally take a bus. This didn't really seem like a viable option. It would be harder to blag a lift on a bus, and besides that, Lucan had got his fill of Human Realm public transport for one human day and, quite possibly, for an entire elven lifetime.

"I cannot spend another wretched moment of this day cooped up cheek by jowl with obnoxious humans, in a juddering metal box on squeaking wheels," he declared.

He's going to have to suck it up for our return trip to Glasgow, thought Annie. But, based on the jaded expression set on Lucan's face, I'm going to leave that conversation for the last possible moment, when we have the enchanted amulet in our safe keeping.

"So, what do you prefer as an alternative, Lucan?" Varis asked. As his soulmate, only Varis had the knack for smoothing off Lucan's somewhat sharp and prickly edges. Lucan released a long exhale, relaxed his shoulders, and then shrugged them.

"Obviously, I would ideally opt for my stallion," he said. "But I accept that particular choice is not available to me here."

"I very much feel the need to stretch my legs," Finwe commiserated. "I think that I have never sat in such uncomfortable seats, for so long, in all my life."

Elva, Lucan, and Varis nodded in vigorous agreement. Having witnessed how naturally fluid and physical the elves were in their own realms, Annie could also see their point of view. She even admitted that she preferred the initially bum-numbing saddle and trot of Yavanna, the trusty, and unflappable mare she had been loaned while in the elven realms.

Between them, it was decided that they would traverse across country on foot, to the village that had been home to the Labradorite Amulet for some twelve hundred elven moons. The distance they needed to cover was just over seven miles. They would cross over the lower tail-end of the ridge that swept up to form Pendle Hill, and then up a steep climb into Newchurch In Pendle itself. The elves could have travelled the estimated two-and-a-half hours in just under forty-five minutes. However, they accepted that they would need to accommodate Annie's non-elven, and somewhat shorter than average, human legs.

They would be travelling at the pace of the slowest member of their group and Annie was embarrassed about holding her friends back.

And wasting precious time that could see Carric freed that bit sooner, she thought. *If only there was a way I could keep up with the elven pace.*

Seeing and reading her embarrassment, Elva set Annie straight.

"You are not holding us back," she assured her. "You must remember that, without you, we would not have had the remotest chance of retrieving the Labradorite Amulet and saving our realms."

Annie's embarrassment was assuaged and the group set out together down King Street. Even at the slower, human pace, they would reach Newchurch In Pendle by mid-afternoon.

The spirits of the companions were running high and they were full of hope.

Chapter Six

As the final leg of their journey to Saint Mary's Church was to take some time, and the June weather was treating them kindly, the companions took the chance to relax and recharge as they went.

Annie indulged the elves' curiosity about the Human Realm, doing her best to give a particularly potted history of her county's evolution, from the period of the Romans, through the War of the Roses, the Industrial Revolution, and on into the present day.

Had she known her future, the younger Annie, who regularly hid away in the local library, would have made more of an effort to 'gen up' on such things.

"I am not sure that everything has been an evolution," said Varis thoughtfully. "I believe that evolution is about improving things over time, and yet, I am not sure that all these fumes, and the substance you refer to as tarmac, are an improvement on what your realm naturally provided."

Annie was about to delve deeper into their discussion, to explore which particular factors one might take as measures of progress, when she was roughly pulled up short in her tracks. She made such an abrupt stop that Finwe pitched into the back of her, bumping her a number of involuntary steps forward.

"What is it, Annie?" asked Elva, concerned that Annie had suddenly paled to be as white as a sheet. Remaining stock-still for fear of drawing attention to herself, Annie whispered her reply:

"It's Lisa. It's my mother."

There, across the street and a little way ahead of them, was a painfully thin and terribly unkempt woman. Her forty-one years looked extremely hard won, as she shuffled along the pavement to poke about in the bin outside the Doe Bakehouse on Market Place street. Intent on finding something sweet and less than half eaten, Lisa was unaware that she was being closely observed.

While she'd always thought that Lisa had been less than useless as a mum, it still tore at Annie's heart to see that her mother had been reduced to these sorry circumstances. Like a rabbit trapped in headlights and unable to turn away, Annie observed children crossing the street to avoid Lisa as she intermittently shouted out phrases like, "Woodland Sun Realm," "I've got to save my baby," "I love you, Adran," and "It's in my eye, you see. Do you see?"

As Annie experienced conflicting feelings of sorrow, love, pity, and anger, Finwe placed a consoling hand lightly on her shoulder. She realised that she'd been holding her breath and Finwe's touch enabled her to exhale much of the tension that had firmly frozen her to the spot.

Trying and failing to disguise their alarm, Lucan and Varis exchanged knowing glances. Finwe immediately quizzed them.

"What is it?" he asked. "Do you two know something about Annie's mother?"

Annie wasn't listening. She was solely focused on her mother and the tragic scene playing out before her. With a twitch of her golden fleck, Annie came to a decision. While her mother was clearly in need of support and care, the needs of her friends, the elven realms, and — most importantly to her, the needs of Carric — were far greater.

What is the saying, she thought, *the needs of the many outweigh the needs of the few?*

Well, except for the one named Carric, she scolded herself. *It would seem that the needs of the many can go to hell in a handcart where he's concerned.*

Annie visibly winced at this deep-thrusting, self-inflicted cut to her moral compass.

It would appear that Carric is a powerful magnet that's been held far too close to your moral compass, the chastising inner voice continued.

"Oh shut up!" Annie blurted aloud, leaving her taciturn friends to exchange questioning looks. And with that, Annie settled and deepened her shallow breathing to make herself invisible. She couldn't avoid passing her mother, but at the same time, under no circumstances did she want to be seen by her. Sensing that this was no time to press Annie for an explanation regarding her most peculiar behaviour, the elves simply followed.

With her head down and eyes averted, Annie intended to hold her breath until she had passed by her mother. She was taking no chances and would remain 'cloaked' until she and her friends had rounded the corner, and were well out of Lisa's view. Lisa was weaving down the pavement now, and was more than a little unsteady on her feet. Her limbs moved in a jerky fashion, like a puppet in the hands of an unskilled puppeteer. When Annie and the elves were just a few steps past her, Lisa stared straight in Annie's direction, and shouted out. Completely shocked and horrified, Annie took off at a sprint, not daring to look back. Lisa looked down the street where Annie was running and shouted out again,

"I see you, Annie Harper! I. See. You!"

<><><><><><><><>

Annie was running almost blind, with large, streaming tears obscuring her vision. As she trotted next to her, Elva placed a kind and caring hand on Annie's shoulder. Instantly, Annie's magic surged and she unexpectedly accelerated to a humanly impossible speed. Sensing the shift in gear, her friends matched her and urged her to go faster still. They only tried to bring her to a stop once they had run out of the town, and into the expanse of the countryside beyond.

"Annie, stop," Elva insisted. "It is just us now. You are safe."

As Elva's hand lifted off her shoulder, Annie's speed rapidly decelerated to that which one would expect of an average eighteen-year-old, young human woman. Although her body had slowed down, Annie's mind had not. As her mind was frenetically racing with layer upon layer of unanswered questions and ruthlessly painful mind chatter,

Annie was unable to hear or register anything that was outside her head.

"Leave her to me," said Finwe, simply, with an uncharacteristic solemnity in his voice. Without waiting for a reply, he sprang to stand in front of Annie. As he had done so in the palace bedchamber, when Annie was being tortured by Tathlyn and the visions of Carric's suffering, Finwe enveloped her in his arms, and held her firmly to his chest.

Just as in the bedchamber, Annie initially, violently struggled to resist. She flailed her arms and punched with her small, tightly clenched fists. Walking calmly backwards, as she attempted to storm forwards, Finwe, unabashed, enveloped her all the more. After a few more moments of angry resistance, Annie, emotionally exhausted, slumped into him and sobbed loudly. Still saying nothing, over the course of a few more steps, he gradually slowed them to a complete standstill. The others formed a protective, outward-facing circle around them and waited quietly for Annie's tears, and cries to abate.

"We shall take a few moments to gather ourselves before we press on to the church," instructed Lucan. "By that, of course, I mean a few moments for Annie to gather herself."

Varis gave him a hard stare and Lucan, looking a little sheepish, rethought his communication.

"We shall allow Annie the... time she needs to... to be ready to resume our mission." Varis nodded his approval of Lucan's effort, ignoring his stilted and clumsy delivery.

"It would appear," mused Varis, "that you do have a means of running with us elves at our speed after all, Annie."

A muffled reply came from somewhere in Finwe's chest. After Varis confessed to not understanding a word she'd just uttered, Annie held Finwe's upper arms, stepped back, rubbed under each of her eyes with the heel of each hand, and faced the others.

"I said," — she wiped snivelling snot from her upper lip with the cuff of her jacket's sleeve — "that I now realise I've done something a bit like that before. It was when I was first attacked by Shadow Elves and was running to the palace from The View. I didn't realise it at the time, but I travelled across the gardens far faster than I could have purely under my own steam. I think my magic may have helped me."

She looked to each of her friends. The fact that they didn't doubt her claim and simply believed her was a double-edged sword. She was so grateful to have such trusting, caring friends.

And yet, came the inner voice, *we will be throwing that trust in their faces once we're back in the elven realms.*

"I wasn't anywhere as fast as I've just been with Elva, though" she continued, trying to override her self-reproach.

"Perhaps, once you are running, the touch from one of our kind acts like a booster of some sort," Elva suggested.

It was agreed by all, that this latest development in Annie's magical skills was bound to be of great benefit to how they could travel as a group from now on.

<><><><><><><><><>

As they were preparing to move on, something that Finwe had said earlier came back to Annie, front and centre.

"What made you ask Lucan and Varis if they knew my mother?" she asked him.

"That," said Finwe, as he pointed to the ill-disguised look of alarm and discomfort that was passing back, and forth between Lucan, and Varis.

"Well?" Elva and Annie chorused, both with hands on hips. Lucan gave Varis an almost imperceptible nod to go ahead and explain. Taking the deepest of breaths and then sighing heavily, Varis set about explaining on behalf of them both.

"We were actually present when the second human was sent back to the Human Realm. The human was a woman called Lisa."

Annie's eyes widened in surprise and shock. Her golden fleck dilated like a droplet of oil carefully placed onto the bluest water, and she was rendered speechless.

"Go on," Elva instructed.

Varis awkwardly shifted his weight from foot to foot, like a child who had been caught out doing something he absolutely shouldn't.

"We were there in our capacity of guarding the king," he continued. "In truth, I think the king was particularly cruel. Without warning, he stole the human's... I mean, Lisa's, memories of her time in the Sun Elven Realm, just at the moment she was entering her portal."

"Until we heard you call her Lisa," Lucan chipped in, "and heard her speak of the Woodland and Sun Realms, and of Adran, we had absolutely no idea that you were the daughter of the second human visitor to the elven realms."

Annie was simply stunned.

"And the baby that Lisa was talking about?" Elva asked quietly.

Varis, his eyes skyward and darting left to right, was obviously doing some mental calculation before giving his answer.

"From what we have learned about the movement of time in the elven realms compared with the Human Realm, I would guess that the baby Lisa spoke of was, most probably, you, Annie."

Silently, Annie slowly sank to her knees.

It was as if a torch had been lit and her view of her mother took on a completely new light. Perhaps her mother hadn't been selfish, cruel and weak at all. She had been living a heartbreaking, desperately fractured life, and her addled mind was, apparently, serving up snippets of her time in the elven realms. The cruelty of stripping Lisa of her memories for them only to serve as a source of humiliation and distress when they surfaced, must have been a constant, unbearable torture.

She must have thought she was losing her mind, thought Annie. *Perhaps she actually did lose her mind. And who wouldn't in those circumstances?*

While the anger and disappointment that she had felt towards her mother, for as long as she could remember, didn't evaporate completely, it did move over a little to allow in some understanding, sympathy, and compassion. She had a strong urge to go back to her mother and tell her that she understood. She wanted to tell her that she could see herself coming to a place, maybe in the not-too-distant future, where she could even forgive her for being her present, yet absent parent. However, her golden fleck assertively twitched Annie back into the present.

But not yet and not now, it seemed to say. *Right now, it's all about getting the Labradorite Amulet back into the elven realms. It's all about rescuing Carric and then the realms.*

As she came to agree with herself, she looked up from where she knelt and found four concerned, and enquiring faces looming down on her from their great height.

"Are you ready to go on, Annie?" Lucan asked in an uncharacteristically gentle voice. Annie unhurriedly rose to her feet and nodded.

Elva placed Annie's right hand on her left shoulder, and the five of them took off at an elven speed.

Saint Mary's Church of Newchurch In Pendle and the Labradorite Amulet, were now only a handful minutes away.

Chapter Seven

Pendle Hill was a locally famous and untamed place. It was steeped in mystery and was known as the home of the Pendle Witches, who were tried, and executed for witchcraft in 1612. This beautifully rugged hill was the highest point in the Ribble Valley and on clear days, it offered up spectacular views over the Lancashire countryside, and across to Yorkshire.

Far less widely known, were the Silver Banshees of Newchurch In Pendle.

Tales of these tall, silvery skinned, and cruelest of cruel creatures, first appeared back in 1624. The story was that a Meredith Harwood, who had inexplicably gone missing for four years, presumed dead, had quite suddenly, and quite literally, reappeared — chased by the six Silver Banshees. As she appeared, Meredith was almost trampled to death by a Suffolk mare ridden by Thomas Glover. Thomas, a local blacksmith, had swept Meredith up onto his horse and carried her away from her pursuers. Not long after, Thomas and Meredith were married and despite their many efforts, the banshees' attempts to capture Meredith were always foiled. It was later postulated that this was most likely because of Meredith's abilities with magic — a widely feared and despised set of skills at the time, that Meredith worked to keep hidden from those outside her immediate family.

Over the last four hundred years, the Silver Banshees had made quite a name for themselves and had become the stuff of legend, and nightmares, among the locals. While there were many accounts testifying to the their existence across the ages, these historical narratives were generally accepted as being fanciful and exaggerated, incorporating details of supernatural skills, and other such mystical phenomena.

These Silver Banshees were, in fact, six of King Tathlyn's Shadow Elves who had managed to hitch a lift on Meredith's skirts as she travelled through her portal, back into the Human Realm. What were thought of as fanciful tales — exaggerated by the Chinese whispers effect of storytelling across the area and down many generations — were, in point of fact, completely true.

The Shadow Elves had been hell-bent on retrieving both Meredith and the Labradorite Amulet for their king. What they hadn't at all bargained for was that Meredith would not only escape their clutches, but would go so far as to place a highly effective and invisible dome of protection over herself and Thomas.

For almost half a millennia, Codila, Folca, Invu, Ubsu, Druguth, and the female, Moto, had been trapped in the Human Realm. They had also been cursed with knowing the precise location of the Labradorite Amulet, but being unable to acquire it. To top it off, they weren't even able to return home. Instead, for all this time, they had loitered in and around Newchurch In Pendle, and Saint Mary's Church, always watchful for an opportunity to seize a descendant of Meredith, and force them to acquire the Labradorite Amulet for them.

Over time, they had deduced that the hand of a descendant would be able to hold and make off with the Labradorite Amulet. However, they had no way of knowing that the person who was able to hold the amulet would also needed to have inherited the golden fleck that was the key and catalyst to magical capability. This descendent would also need to know the location of their own, personal portal to the elven realms, and would also need to have the wherewithal to open, and travel through that portal. The chances of all these pieces aligning were extremely slim.

Even their many attempts to seize a descendant of Meredith had been foiled, time and time again. The clever and quick-witted Meredith had also worked out that her descendants would, most likely, be able to touch the amulet. She had realised that this, therefore, would make them vulnerable to the Shadow Elves' attacks. To mitigate against this, despite this period in history being highly treacherous for those with 'the gift' — or perhaps in this period, 'the curse' — of magic, she gradually learned how to infuse her blood with a spell of protection. She had successfully woven this protection into, what in centuries to come would be known as, her DNA.

Over many generations, as the branches of Meredith's family tree expanded, farther and wider, this spell of protection came to act as a double-recessive genetic allele, at best. As a result, over time and generations, the protection was increasingly watered down to next to nothing. Had the history of humans not meant that members of families became far more geographically widespread and far flung, the Shadow Elves may have stood a chance of commandeering the assistance of a 'Meredith' to at least take hold of the Labradorite Amulet, well before Annie or her mother, Lisa, had been born.

For the Shadow Elves, it had been the most testing and frustrating four hundred human years of their existence.

To while away their time in the Human Realm, they learned the English language and took great relish in mischievously, and often cruelly, toying with both locals, and visitors alike. Their antics ranged from the incredibly petty to the down-right petrifying.

They stole washing off lines and placed the items of clothing on other people's lines to stir up bad feeling, and conflict between neighbours. They drove scientists and conspiracy theorists to utter distraction by creating mystical, and increasingly elaborate, crop circles in hay fields. They snatched and ate farm livestock, leaving bloody entrails in very public locations. They even committed several macabre and unsolvable murders. And all of this was just for fun, to while away the years, the decades, and the centuries.

Lucan, Varis, Finwe, Elva, and Annie knew nothing of the presence of the Shadow Elves. No one from the elven realms knew of Meredith's unwelcome hitchhikers.

But all that was about to change.

Chapter Eight

Although it was mid-afternoon and the sun was beating down on an unusually dry June for Lancashire, there was no one around Saint Mary's Church. It appeared that the generally preferred dead of night for such an incognito mission as theirs, was not necessary.

To be on the safe side, the group dipped behind gravestone after gravestone as they progressed towards the church itself.

"I find it interesting," commented Varis as he dodged behind another headstone that leant at a precarious angle, "that your places of religion, prayer, and devotion are embattled."

"They are em-what-tled?" Annie asked, joining him behind one of the more elaborate headstones.

By way of explanation, Varis pointed to the top of the tower on the west end of the church. Looking up to the top of the tower, Annie could see what Varis was referring to. The very top edge of the tower was like the classic children's depiction of a castle or fortress wall.

"Ah," she said, now grasping Varis's use of the word, 'embattled'. "I think that's more about the aesthetics than being a feature for defence."

Satisfied with Annie's answer, Varis hopped to the next gravestone. Annie admired how such a heftier-built elf as Varis was still able to move so lightly — gracefully, even.

In the meantime, Lucan's warrior senses were heightened and prickled by potential threats. He had noticed strange shadows behind the waxy leaved trees at the far end of the graveyard. The shadows were clearly moving unnaturally. He alerted Elva and Finwe.

"Do you see that movement over by the trees?" he asked.

Keeping their heads still, Finwe and Elva used their peripheral vision to search for the movement of which Lucan spoke.

"Yes," Finwe agreed. "There are shadowy movements that are not in harmony with the motions of the trees' branches and leaves."

Both Lucan and Finwe nodded agreement as Elva said,

"I have a nasty feeling that we are not the only elves in the vicinity and, as we have none of our preferred weapons, we may be vulnerable."

<><><><><><><><><>

Varis and Annie noticed that the others were not keeping up with them. Varis shot Lucan an enquiring look. Lucan signalled for them to continue heading into the church. Elva, Finwe, and Lucan also made their way to the church, all the while keeping their peripheral vision homed in on the trees, and the unnatural shadows.

A few moments later, all the friends were huddled inside the south porch. Seeing their concerned faces Annie asked,

"What is it? What's wrong?"

True to form, Lucan didn't waste time mincing his words.

"We strongly suspect that there are other elves here. Shadow Elves."

Annie's eyes widened and her body tensed. Plainly, she was troubled.

"But, how can that be?" she asked with more alarm in her voice than she would have liked to show.

Her friends theorised that the Shadow Elves were most likely to have come to the Human Realm by catching a lift from Meredith the Thief as she absconded with the Labradorite Amulet.

"But that was twelve hundred elven moons ago," said Annie. "Are you saying these elves have been here for all that time?" Lucan nodded. "But what have they been doing for all that time?" she continued.

"Waiting," Lucan replied, simply.

"If that is the case," added Varis, "they will not have given up their mission to retrieve the Labradorite Amulet for Tathlyn."

Annie flushed and her golden fleck cringed. She hoped that her friends hadn't noticed, or, if they had, she hoped they would mistake her guilty discomfort for concern. Turning away from them to further mask her thoughts, she tried the door and found it to be unlocked.

"Well, Shadow Elves or not, we have to get your Labradorite Amulet," she said, and without waiting for a response, she slipped through the door into the comparative darkness inside the church.

As soon as the others had followed into the building, the posse of Shadow Elves slunk out of the shadows and silently made their way to the church porch. Druguth moved to open the door but, as his hand touched the handle, Moto laid a halting hand over his.

"Wait," she instructed. "We need this Meredith lookalike to take possession of the amulet, then we will take possession of it and her."

"But what of her Meredith blood?" Folca asked.

"Could you not smell it?" Moto asked with an evil, exultant glint in her eye. "There is next to no protection in her blood. Her link to the original Meredith is watered down by the passing of many Human Realm years and generations."

Pleased at this, the others grinned hungrily, bearing their razor-sharp and pointed teeth. Their opportunity for the triumphant retrieval of the Labradorite Amulet and to return home, was finally here. They had already waited four hundred years in isolation and hiding. They could easily wait a few human minutes more.

<><><><><><><><>

The interior of Saint Mary's Church was fresh and understated. The dark wooden pews and pulpit matched the arching beams, and were in stark contrast to the plain walls, which were painted cream. The stained glass window above the altar, looked relatively modern. It depicted scenes in bright colours of cornflower blue, cyclamen, and apple green. The cool colour scheme of this interior was a pleasant relief from the heat of the afternoon outside.

"Where will we find the amulet?" Annie asked.

"Your guess is as good as ours," Varis replied while looking up and admiring the craftsmanship in the windows.

"I think Annie's guess will probably be better than ours," Elva chimed in. "She is of Meredith's blood afterall, and will better understand the thought process of a fellow human."

The elves hung back to, quite literally, give Annie room to think.

Okay Meredith, what did you choose to do with the Labradorite Amulet? she thought as she looked around the church. *Well,* she asked herself, *what would I do with it?*

She let her eyes rove freely while she pondered her question. As she softened her gaze, she realised that she, herself, would most likely have hidden the amulet in plain sight. *Perhaps on something that was bejewelled.* But everything in sight was modest, almost plain. Annie's train of thought was rudely interrupted as a single, elderly voice pierced the quiet. Annie spun round and the elves instantly adopted defensive stances.

"Can I help you, dears?"

Before them stood a particularly short, elderly lady, possibly in her mid-eighties, with cut flowers in one hand, lethal looking secateurs in the other hand, and an impish twinkle in her eye.

Of course, thought Annie. *You're the reason the church is open.*

"I'm sorry to disturb you with your flower arranging," Annie said. "I was wanting to show these... these... foreign students, the beautiful artefacts that we often have in our churches."

"Oh I'm sorry dear," the old lady apologised. "I'm afraid our cross, plates, and chalices are locked away during the week. They are only brought out for our services on a Sunday, or for particularly important days in our Christian calendar."

"Oh that's such a shame," said Annie, feigning disappointment while thinking, *now I just need you out of the way while I break into your secure store and take a particularly close look at your cross, plates, and chalices.*

Thinking on her feet, Annie quickly suggested that the old lady — who, it turned out, was called Alice — might show her 'foreign friends' how she went about arranging the flowers so beautifully for the church. Alice said she'd be delighted to oblige and shepherded the somewhat bemused elves to the back of the church. Once there, she proceeded to explain, in very slow and very loud English, what she was doing, and how the colours of flowers she chose were to reflect the current period of the church calendar.

Annie couldn't help smirking at Lucan as he threw her a hybrid look of confusion and aggravation. Confident that Alice was now completely absorbed in expounding the ins and outs of religious-based floristry, Annie slipped away to the locked door that stood to the left of the cloth-draped altar.

The locked door didn't require an application of Annie's magic. Her skills at picking locks, honed over many years, were more than adequate. Within moments, she was inside the locked room and staring at the various bejewelled artefacts that were housed at Saint Mary's. There was no need for Annie to check over each item, for the enchanted Labradorite Amulet powerfully drew her to it.

And there it was. She had been right. The quick thinking and cunning Meredith the Thief had hidden it in plain sight.

It was nestled at the centre of the cross that was carried before the vicar and choir at each, and every service. The light through a high window caught the labradorite stone at the perfect angle to reveal its luxurious blue-green colour. Just like its twin, the Labradorite Amulet brought an instant and broad smile to Annie's face.

As with its twin in the Necropolis, Annie could clearly feel the stone beckoning to her. But this beckoning was far stronger. There was the familiar surge of energy flow, interwoven with expectation, as she approached the cross that held it. Once again, she was like a seasoned lioness deftly creeping up on her prey. She approached it hesitantly, as if reaching for something that might spark, or shock her. This time, she fully understood what made her both curious and, at the same time, reticent.

Annie thought back to the consequence of being atomised should she not turn out to be the hand of Meredith the Thief. However, deep, deep down, she knew for certain that she and Meredith were kin, and the fear of such a consequence quickly evaporated.

Her golden fleck jiggled in unbridled excitement and her magic confidently bubbled in the pit of her stomach. Not wanting to waste another moment, Annie boldly seized the Labradorite Amulet.

The instant that her fingers grazed the labradorite itself, she was surprised to find herself in an intense battle of wills — hers against the amulet's. The cyan-blue stone turned white hot and it took all Annie's determination, and downright bloody-mindedness, not to let go. The hotter the stone became, the more determined she was to grip it all the tighter.

Having failed to repel the human's hand, the labradorite vibrated violently — so much so that it and Annie's hand, together, became a blur. But still Annie held fast. Nothing and nobody was going to stop her from acquiring this gem. Not even the amulet itself.

As if finally acquiescing to a greater power, the amulet stopped vibrating as suddenly as it had started, and it instantly cooled to room temperature. Annie had won. She was mightily relieved that she had mastery over this much coveted, enchanted amulet.

Just as her fingers prised the Labradorite Amulet from the religious cross's hold, she heard shouting.

Lots of shouting.

Before going to see what on Earth was going on, she slipped the enchanted Labradorite Amulet into the deep, aubergine-purple, velvety pouch provided by the Wise One. She then slipped the pouch into the safekeeping of her leather satchel. At the same time, she fondly patted the dud amulet that was still housed in her zipped pocket, as if to reassure the dud that she had not forgotten her promise.

She jumped out of her skin when she heard, as an accompaniment to the uproarious shouting, the sound of large, heavy items being violently tipped over. With no time to dwell in the joy of having both amulets in her possession, Annie emerged from the side room and into utter carnage.

Chapter Nine

There were now nine distinctly elven figures in intense combat, hefting over pews and tackling each other to the ground in a manner that would have impressed the professional rugby community, worldwide. Annie figured that, since 'her elves' were not in possession of their preferred weapons, and double the number of Shadow Elves were very much in possession of theirs, her friends were coming in close to minimise the usefulness of anything other than short daggers.

Looking over to the back of the church, Annie could see that Elva was shielding poor Alice.

Wait, no, thought Annie. *Elva's not shielding Alice. She's holding the secateurs-brandishing octogenarian back so she doesn't get hurt while trying to stab, or possibly fatally prune, an elf!*

Seeing that Lucan, Varis, and Finwe were holding their own in a two-to-one ratio, Annie decided to help Elva by getting Alice to safety before she accidentally stabbed the Woodland warrior or herself. Swapping places with Elva,

Annie quickly summoned her magic to sooth and calm the raging Alice down. She managed to bring Alice down to at least five notches from being a wrinkly SAS commando, and then applied her recently discovered persuasion technique. Firstly, she wanted to ensure that Alice left the building before she got hurt and, secondly, she wanted to ensure that Alice would only be reporting a group of vandals to the police. Annie decided Alice would report five young males and a female. For good measure, Annie installed brief descriptions of the vandals that were an accurate description of each of the Shadow Elves. With the gentlest nudges from Annie, Alice left the church unharmed, yet mightily annoyed by the 'wicked vandals'.

In the meantime, Elva had started to make her way to join the melee, with rampant zeal. While Annie was wholly focused on getting Alice to leave the church safely, she didn't see Ubsu break away from his comrades and approach her. He was intent on seizing this descendent of Meredith and the precious amulet that he guessed was in her possession.

Creeping upon her with catlike stealth he, with confident nonchalance, tossed his short dagger from hand to hand. He had no notion of Annie's skills or her pluck. At the moment his fingers reached out to grasp Annie by the arm, a short arrow whistled through the air and forcefully lodged in his brain by way of piercing the side of his skull. Death was so swift that Ubsu had no time to register what had happened, or to change his facial expression from that of a hungry wolf bearing down on its prey. He immediately crumpled to the ground, his lifeless fingers grazing Annie's forearm as he fell.

Shocked, Annie whipped round to see Elva grinning and waving a small crossbow in her hand.

"I know I could not bring my favoured weaponry, but surely you did not think that I would come to this Human Realm with only a dagger as my limited arsenal," she called from four upturned pews away. The twinkle in her eye led Annie to believe that Elva was thoroughly pleased with herself for secretly stashing more weapons about her person. Puffing out her cheeks while breathing a sigh of relief, Annie was also exceedingly pleased.

With Elva and Annie joining their friends, and with Ubsu dead, the fight was now even with five against five. At first, it was difficult for Annie to engage and release her palm bombs. With the others in such close and intense combat, she was in fear of harming or even killing her friends. Deciding against striving to make direct hits on the Shadow Elves, she instead opted to give her friends the advantage where she could. Calling out to Varis to dodge to his left, she released a palm bomb to hit at his opponent's feet, causing Invu to startle and jump back. In Invu's moment of alarm and confusion, Varis seized his moment and drove his dagger home through Invu's ribs, and up in, to pierce his heart. As the lifeless form of the Shadow Elf collapsed to the ground, Varis took Invu's sword, bow, and arrows for himself.

The Shadow Elves were now outnumbered, five to four, but this didn't deter them in the least. For Druguth, the altered odds simply served to further fire his desire to put these 'brùkling Sun and Woodland Elves', and their pet human, to the sword. With a macabre grin adorning his face, Druguth took his fight to Elva. Before she could ready her one-handed crossbow, he was upon her. At such close quarters as these, her crossbow was rendered useless. Throwing it to one side, she whipped her short dagger from where it had been tucked at the back of her belt. But Druguth's lightning speed and fierce intent meant that his blade was about to go through her shoulder before she could adopt her fighting stance.

A split second later, before making his attack on Elva, the Shadow Elf was gone. Finwe had wildly launched himself at Druguth and slammed him sideways to the cold, stone floor. The two elves rolled over and over each other as they landed, and came to an abrupt halt as they careened into the far wall. Druguth ended up on top, with his blade buried deep in Finwe's side.

Joyous, victorious bloodlust spread across Druguth's face as he slowly removed his blade and took in Finwe's expression of agony, and anger. He was about to dispatch Finwe with a killing blow, when the joyous, victorious bloodlust was wiped clean off his face by a palm bomb that was accurately delivered between his shoulder blades. It caused Druguth to arch his back in agony as his clothes and flesh were melted away to reveal the snowy white bone beneath.

In the next second there was a sickeningly squelching thud as another short arrow was released from Elva's crossbow and embedded itself to the left of Druguth's exposed spine, and straight into his heart.

Together, both Annie and Elva ran over to Finwe, releasing him from the hefty weight of Druguth's lifeless body. Finwe groaned, partly from having the surprisingly heavy Shadow Elf lifted from him, and partly because of the searing pain from his deep wound.

With the loss of half their posse and having been divested of most of their weapons, Moto ordered the remaining Shadow Elves to fall back. Turning tail and darting out of the church, Annie shouted after them,

"That's right, you brùkling cowards. Go run and lick your wounds!"

Lucan looked at her sternly.

"That is not the last that we shall see of them," he warned. "They will have fallen back in order to regroup. Am I right in assuming that you have the Labradorite Amulet?" Annie confirmed that his assumption was correct. "Then they will, most definitely, pursue us as we journey back to your portal," he added matter-of-factly.

"The Labradorite Amulet is still very much their mission," Varis added. "And, after all this time in your Human Realm, you will be perceived as their ticket home, and a means for them to get the amulet to Tathlyn."

There was a long, guttural groan from the floor and they all came to kneel beside Finwe. Blood was rapidly seeping between his fingers, where his hand clutched his side. Elva was preparing a makeshift pressure bandage which, with assistance from Varis, she wrapped around Finwe's ribs and over the opposite shoulder to his knife wound.

"We need to be on our way now," Lucan urged, while helping Finwe to his feet. The five friends made their way to the church door.

"Wait," said Annie. "Come in close to me so that I can cloak you all while we leave the church." But Elva shook her head.

"Your cloaking will most likely be of no use to us against the remaining Shadow Elves," she explained. "They will still be able to see us."

"Ah, but it's not them I'm hiding us from," said Annie with a cunning smile, while drawing her finds close to her. "Our fate is all in the hands of feisty Alice now."

<><><><><><><><>

Outside the church a considerable crowd had gathered. They had initially been drawn to the place by the noise of the crashing pews and Annie's palm bombs. Now Alice shouting at 'the vandals' was drawing even more people in. Someone had decided to call the police, and their sirens hailed their imminent arrival.

On seeing Annie and her friends exiting the church, the Shadow Elves had come out of hiding from behind the trees, only to be subjected to Alice's extremely public, and intensely raging, fury.

"That's them there," Alice shouted, pointing wildly with secateurs still in hand. "Those bloody hoodlums have caused all sorts of damage in there. I think there are three more of them still in there. They all scared me out of my wits. Me. A frail and harmless woman in her eighties!"

Frail and harmless woman my arse, thought Annie while wearing a fond grin.

"She is a most impressive elder," Lucan observed admiringly, as the invisible group sneaked around the side of the church and out of sight of the Shadow Elves.

The arrival of the police and the sheer volume of humans that stood between the three remaining Shadow Elves and their enemies, made pursuit across the graveyard nigh on impossible at that moment. With a word from Moto, the three of them scarpered in the opposite direction. They would have to run a large arc around the village and use their tracking skills to pick up their quarry's trail.

They may have lost half their number, but this game of cat and mouse was far from over.

Chapter Ten

Lucan and Varis knew only too well that they had only temporarily lost the Shadow Elves.

As they prepared for Annie to reach elven speeds, Finwe winced loudly and sagged towards the ground.

"You need to go on ahead without me," he said through gritted teeth as he clutched his injured side.

Everyone could see that blood was seeping through the bandaging. Simultaneously, all four of his companions, each in their own way, stated that there was no way in héllè, he was going to be left behind. They would never leave him to either the fate of the Shadow Elves or to an existence trapped in the Human Realm alone, until such time as Annie *might* be able to rescue him, or he died of his injuries — which ever came first.

Finwe smiled weakly as he realised that his friends saw the situation as absolutely non-negotiable.

"But I cannot reach our elven speed or endurance while I am in this poor condition," he protested with more energy than he could readily afford. The group fell silent, dreading the thought that they may have to leave him after all. Then a thought struck Varis.

"What if you could, in some way, 'gift' your speed and endurance-acquiring powers, to Finwe, Annie?" he postulated.

Annie thought for a moment, as did her golden fleck, while it paced up and down across her iris.

"Could you do another of your daisy chains?" Lucan asked. And even the pained Finwe raised a smirk at the commander's adoption of Annie's terminology into his everyday lexicon. They gave each other a knowing and amused look, yet said nothing.

Annie realised that Varis and Lucan could be right.

"I think you've nailed it, Lucan," she exclaimed. Lucan, who still found the human's turn of phrase perplexing at times, wondered what it was that he had nailed, but thought the better of asking her at this time.

"I shall hold onto Elva with one hand and then hold onto Finwe with the other," she continued. "Through touch alone, I should be able to share my ability to run at your elven pace."

"But will it work?" Finwe grimaced. No one liked this 'half-empty', doubting Finwe. He was nothing like their usual 'half-full, if not full to the brim and overspilling' version of the optimistic and jovial Woodland Elf.

"Well, there is only one way to find out, my friend," said Varis as he took Finwe under his armpits and hauled him to his somewhat unsteady feet.

Before Finwe could protest any further about slowing them down and endangering the mission, Annie had firmly grabbed his hand, and interlocked their fingers for good measure. She then placed her free hand on Elva's shoulder. In the next instant, to the naked human eye, there was a blur of movement and all five of them disappeared.

Now that all five had the ability to travel far more swiftly under their own steam, it was decided that they would run directly to Preston in order to catch the direct train to Glasgow. The less time they had to spend loitering around in train stations, waiting for connections, and drawing unwanted attention, the better.

<><><><><><><><>

The three Shadow Elves, led by Moto, had picked up the rescue party's trail. Annoyingly, the presence of a throng of Newchurch In Pendle residents and police officers had slowed Moto, and her comrades, down. The detour they had been forced to follow had taken them approximately thirty miles out of their way.

Since they had no idea as to where the gifted human and the elves had entered the Human Realm, they had no means of divining their route, and cutting them off. Their only option was to follow them.

The three Shadow Elves were beyond furious. While such elves weren't typically known for being schmaltzy, the extraordinary circumstances that they had found themselves in, and four hundred human years of only each other for company, had proved to supply a rich compost for affection to take root, and grow. They had lost Druguth, Invu, and Ubsu in a matter of minutes and, on top of aspiring to getting their king what he vehemently desired, they were hungry to avenge their friends.

On the outskirts of Clitheroe, Folca noticed that the elven trail had taken on a different and distinctive quality.

"They must have switched to their brisk mode," he observed. "From here they are noticeably more fleet of foot."

"Then we shall do the same," Moto asserted and indicated that Folca, with his particular mastery of tracking, should take the lead. Within moments, their speed had also made them a blur to any humans eye that may have been watching.

<><><><><><><><><>

Without a break, Annie and the elves sped through the open countryside: past Bashall Town, over the River Hodder, along Birdy Brow, past isolated farm buildings, along side the Dilworth Upper Reservoir and the Alston Reservoir Number 2, out of Longridge New Town, through Red Scar, over the M6 motorway, through Grange, and into the heart of Preston itself. What would have take a regular human over six hours to walk, had taken just sixty-six minutes at their elven speed.

It was almost ten to nine in the evening, and the train that would take them to Glasgow would be leaving in just five minutes. There was no time to stop and admire the Victorian period features, like the wrought-iron, white and red foot bridge that gave passengers access to opposite platforms. Without needing to say a word, the elves huddled around Annie, and she turned them all invisible to gain access to the train without any interruptions by humans wanting such things as mundane as valid, off-peak tickets.

With less than a minute to spare, they re-emerged on platform three and boarded their train. As it departed the station, three exceptionally tall, lithe, and silvery-skinned figures easily straddled the barrier, much to the consternation of commuters, and leaped onto the tail-end of the last carriage. Huddling together in the doorway that currently connected to nowhere, Moto, Folca, and Codila figured out what their next move would be.

They decided, or rather Moto instructed, that they would locate their quarry and observe them, incognito, to ascertain their final destination. By biding their time, they would conserve their energies and take the human, and the Labradorite Amulet, as they neared that final destination.

"It will be our best chance of freedom and absolute glory," she declared. Folca and Codila needed no convincing.

As the train rattled and juddered along the line at speeds of up to 125 miles per hour, the Shadow Elves, slowly but surely, made their way along the roof of the train. They soon realised that it was best to keep their bellies close to the train and slither like a retpoilè, lest they lose their heads on bridges, and other train-related structures, they knew not the purpose of.

Having managed to traverse the disconcerting couplings between carriages, the Shadow Elves located Annie and her friends in the sixth carriage from the front of the long train. With their elven ears pressed to the relatively thin skin of the train's roof, and tuning out the commotion of the train itself, they listened intently.

<><><><><><><><><>

Inside the carriage, Varis, Elva and Annie were chatting away in Elvish. Their spirits were high and the Shadow Elves weapons that they had acquired, were held low under the table between them. The human commuters around them knew that they were foreign, but no one had the foggiest idea about their country of origin. Finwe was eerily quiet, simply because he was hurting so badly, and was trying to conserve his energy. Lucan's quiet was of a very different nature. He was quiet because he didn't believe that they had seen the last of the Shadow Elves, and he was remaining constantly alert for the slightest sign of them.

Just over halfway through their journey, as they pulled in at Carlisle, his patient vigil was proved astute. In the relative quiet of the train, as it paused and powered down briefly to allow commuters off and on, Lucan heard unusual movement overhead. He then saw, from the corner of his eye, an unnatural shadow-like movement slipping into the vestibule behind the last commuter to board.

Catching an almost imperceptible shift in Lucan's stance, Varis was also immediately on his guard. Within a few more seconds, Elva, Finwe, and Annie were also alerted. As nonchalantly as the cramped seating would allow, all five companions moved to stand at equal distances along the aisle, weapons in hand. Surprisingly, the commuters were none the wiser and not the least bit perturbed. To them, the ornate, retro weapons looked like something one would use for role play or re-enactments, or some such. For the first five minutes after leaving Carlisle, nothing happened. The companions were tensed and ready. In contrast, the commuters went about their usual travelling habits of listening to music, podcasts, or audio books, reading newspapers, e-books, or actual books, chatting with each other, or chatting at an annoying volume to someone on their phones. All the while, Annie and the elves remained stock-still, listening intently, and observing their immediate area by using their peripheral vision.

Ironically, one annoyingly loud phone caller was just saying how incredibly uneventful the journey from London had been, when all hell let loose.

As per his modus operandi, Codila took a battering-ram approach down the aisle of the carriage, with his double-edged axe in one hand and a ten-inch spike in the other. Folca, remaining crouched, deftly leapt across the tops of backs of seats and people's heads, to the centre of the carriage. His long sword was completely useless in the close quarters and, therefore, remained strapped to his back, while his double-edged dagger was held tightly between his teeth. At the other end of the carriage, Moto appeared, and her nickel-coloured eyes greedily alighted on her nearest foe-cum-prize, Annie.

The listening, reading, daydreaming, and chattering of the commuters ceased abruptly. Unable to comprehend what was unfolding before them, their mouths fell open and slack, much like dead cod.

Mistaking Annie for easy pickings, Moto raised her small, single-hand crossbow to take aim at Annie's leg. She needed to hobble Annie rather than kill her. Annie was going to be her ride home and part of her gift to her king. At the very moment her finger squeezed the trigger, Annie unleashed a palm bomb, deflecting the arrow such that it forcefully embedded in the ceiling. As Annie was about to unleash a second palm bomb directly at Moto, the Shadow Elf grabbed an alarmed young man by the shoulders and dragged him in front of her to form a quaking human shield. She was well aware that, while such a shield would be useless against a fellow Shadow Elf, other elves and these sickeningly sentimental humans, wouldn't dream of harming such an innocent. It was clear to all combatants that only the Shadow Elves had no regard for avoiding at least injury, much less death, to the human passengers. It was tacitly understood that Lucan, Varis, Elva, Finwe, and Annie had the double task of overthrowing the Shadow Elves while also preserving the lives of the other passengers.

Annie's general lack of faith in humankind was slightly redressed, when a youth in an "Evolution of Skateboarders" hoodie and over-sized, colourful cargo pants, deployed the nose of his skateboard to deliver a swift, sharp jab into the left side of Moto's ribs. The attack from such an unexpected quarter both surprised and winded her, and she let go of the young man immediately. Needing no other prompting, the quaking young man dove down and slunk back as far in his seat as he could.

Now unshielded, Motto had laid herself open. Realising that her palm bombs were ordinarily lethal, Annie let loose a toned-down version, somewhere between a full-on palm bomb and a palm light. She didn't want any human fatalities on her conscience. The blast hit Motto squarely in the chest, lifting her off her feet and slamming her hard into the overcrowded luggage rack.

By now, the majority of the commuters had, with self-preservation at the forefront of their minds, ducked down on the floor and shoe-horned themselves in the spaces between their seats, and the back of the seat in front of them. No amount of nasty old chewing gum, sticky wrappers, spilt drink, and God knows what else could be as bad as being on the wrong end of who, or whatever these individuals were.

All they knew, almost for sure, was that the silvery-skinned ones were the "baddies" and the others were the "goodies".

Seeing Motto struggling with her bomb-punched chest and the luggage that was raining down upon her, the skateboarder guy jumped up and, with all his might, struck her around the head with his board. She wasn't going to be rejoining the fight any time soon. Annie and the skateboarder exchanged broad grins, and nods of mutual respect.

Meanwhile, in an exchange of powerful blows with Varis, Codila's axe had been successfully jammed in between the two seats where Varis and Lucan had been sitting. Finding that he was too weak to offer much up to the fight, Finwe had thrown himself into the seat in front with the dual purpose of holding onto Codina's axe and shielding two younglings, and their mother, with his body.

Varis skilfully swerved his substantial torso so that Codila's ten-inch spike missed him completely. As Varis head-butted Codila, Lucan grabbed the spike and rammed it, point downward through Codila's foot, and through the floor of the carriage itself. Codila's booming roar of pain reverberated throughout the train. A final throat punch from Varis cut Codila short, and he fell backwards with his foot still gruesomely pinned to the floor. As his hulking body hit the floor, several of the braver passengers saw, and took, the opportunity to lie on him, using their combined body weight to ensure he remained incapacitated.

Having deftly leapt across the tops of seat-backs and people's heads, Folca unfurled himself from his crouched position, and came face to face with the magnificent Elva. Thinking he had the upper hand against this voluptuous

Woodland Elf, he smiled with a mix of sordid intent and lust in his eyes. While his double-edged dagger was still held between his teeth, Elva took hold of the handle and the point, and pushed back hard, and as quickly as she could. The sharp edge of the elven metal sliced into his cheeks like a hot knife through butter. It opened up his mouth, making it look like some horrifying, bloody flip-top lid. His scream of pain was turned into a hideous gurgle as he struggled and choked on his own blood. As he staggered backwards, a burly young man stuck out his leg. Folca haplessly windmilled his arms in an attempt to remain upright, but was tipped over the leg and onto the floor by the burly guy's girlfriend, as she grabbed his collar, and yanked him downward. Elva and the couple exchanged tacit appreciation of each other's resolve and collaboration.

As the train slowed into the station, much to Annie's surprise, Lucan addressed the carriage:

"I have always been informed that humans are feeble and not ever to be trusted. My visit here has proved this to be largely untrue. Earlier today, I witnessed the bravery and unbridled pluckiness of one of your female elders. Here, in this tin tube with cramped, scratchy seats and dubious stains, I have seen examples of keen self-preservation, quick-wittedness, and gung-ho mettle from both males, and females alike. You have impressed me and I shall tell of your heroic contributions to our cause, until my very last breath. On behalf of the Sun and Woodland Elven Realms, I thank you."

Not the least bit understanding a single word he had said, or who the elves really were, but grasping the importance of the occasion nonetheless, everyone in the carriage erupted into applause and whoops of triumph. Though they didn't know what it was, they all appreciated that they had done something truly significant and good today — a feeling not often enough shared between humans in their Human Realm.

The moment the train stopped in Glasgow Central, Lucan, Varis, Elva, Finwe, and finally, Annie, leapt onto the station platform. Somewhat dazed, Moto hauled the bloody mouthed Folca to his feet. Roughly throwing passengers off their comrade, they freed Codina's bloody foot and the three of them followed. They left behind them two-dozen passengers either squeezed under seats, readying themselves for further hostilities or sprawled prostrate in the aisle. All of them, however, were elated and full of joy — even the quaking young man.

Much to the confusion of those waiting on the platform, the passengers all spontaneously erupted into more hearty applause and whoops.

There was absolutely no time for Annie to ransack and remould their memories. They would just have to deal with what had just happened as best they could, and Annie suspected that their stories to their friends, and loved ones would be exciting, animated, and enthusiastic in the telling.

So why would I want to mess with that? she thought as she ran from the scene.

Chapter Eleven

Wasting no time in checking if they were being followed, and simply assuming that they most definitely were, Annie held onto Elva, and Finwe. Together, they powered up to elven speed and led the way back to the Necropolis.

It was now past eleven at night, and Lucan was acutely mindful that the Shadow Elves, though injured, would have a sight advantage in the dark of the graveyard. As the friends reached the far side of the Bridge of Sighs, Annie let go of Elva and used her spare hand to create the same kind of palm light that she had made to illuminate the drug dealers, just the night before.

"This should give us a more level playing field," she said to Lucan.

"This is no game, Annie," he said reproachfully, misunderstanding her completely. "But it will give us a more equal chance, if we can see them just as clearly as they can see us." Choosing not to notice the exaggerated roll of Annie's eyes, he led the group towards Annie's portal.

Elva and Varis walked backwards on the lookout for an attack from behind them. Annie remained in the middle with her palm light hovering above her left hand like a tamed drone, and her right arm firmly around Finwe. He was clearly feeling weakened and was in desperate need of the Wise One's attention.

And there's absolutely no way you're going to be left behind, she thought with out-and-out determination.

"Thank you," Finwe whispered, squeezing her hand and causing her to start.

Can he read my mind? she wondered. *Let's hope not,* she taunted herself. *We're not wanting him to cotton onto our plans for the real, enchanted amulet, are we.* A flash of guilt caused her palm light to glitch as she wrestled to corral her thoughts back into focus on the here and now.

"Are you all right, Annie," Finwe asked with concern.

"I'm a lot more all right than you are," she quipped, not registering the tenderness in his voice.

They were so tantalisingly close to her portal now, but during the glitch, when her light was off, the Shadow Elves had capitalised on the moments of darkness. As Annie's light flickered on again, Moto, Folca, and Codila were upon them.

Finwe shook himself free of Annie's hold and pushed her towards the position of her portal. Fighting with Codila, and using his short dagger, he managed to deliver a critical wound to Codila's thigh, causing Shadow Elven blood to rapidly pump from a major artery. In doing so, Finwe lay himself open to Codila's spike that had been retrieved from the train carriage floor, and he received a second, deeper puncture to his side. Growling through his teeth like a wounded grizzly bear, Finwe sank to his knees. Both the Woodland Elf and the Shadow Elf were incapacitated, and very close to death.

Varis was engaged with Folca, and Lucan with Moto. Elva rushed to her twin's side, as did Annie. As Annie reached them, she was unceremoniously picked up around the waist by Lucan who, leaving Varis to engage with both Folca and Moto, quick-marched back to her portal position.

"You *must* remain on mission, no matter what," he ordered in harsh, staccato tones. "If we lose you and the amulet, all *this* will be for nothing."

"But —" Annie protested.

"But *nothing*," Lucan interrupted fiercely, gripping her jaw in his long, strong fingers and piercing her eyes with his stare. "Make your portal and get back to our realm. Now!"

And with that, he turned away to rejoin Varis in keeping the remaining Shadow Elves at bay. With a lead-heavy heart, Annie had to admit that Lucan was right.

Having created her portal twice now, Annie knew exactly what she needed to do. Recalling the cocktail of her extreme emotions from the past twenty-four hours, she summoned her magic and put her golden fleck into action. There was the shock of losing Varis and the joy of having him returned to them. There was the guilt of how she was planning to deceive her friends and the realms, and her yearning for the safety of her love, her soulmate, Carric. There was her exponentially growing worry for the mortally injured Finwe. There was the embarrassment of seeing her mother and the sorrow for not having understood her for all those years. There was the anger she felt towards the bullying squaddies and the posse of Shadow Elves, and the warmth she felt towards the feisty flower lady, Alice. As all these emotions ran high and served her well. Her portal sprang into being, easily.

She looked back at her friends who were fighting so hard, so that she could get back to their realms and save their communities.

She couldn't leave them. She just couldn't.

"Quickly," she shouted. "I don't care what you say. I'm not leaving you here. Make the daisy chain. Make the daisy chain. Make. It. Now!"

With a growl of utter and resigned frustration, Lucan barked his orders.

"Fine," he shouted. "Elva, get yourself and Finwe to Annie. Varis you are to be next, and you had better follow the orders of your commander this time, or I shall end you myself!"

Lucan and Varis kept Folca, and Moto engaged in order to allow Elva to help Finwe get to Annie, and start the daisy chain. When Lucan gave the nod, Varis moved quickly to join the chain. Now Lucan was in close combat with the two combat-capable Shadow Elves. Had there been less at stake, it would have been impressive to watch. Annie suddenly realised that Lucan had no intention of going with them. He was committed to fending off the Shadow Elves and ensuring their safe passage — their safe passage *without him.*

Not on my brùkling watch you over-starched shirt, she thought fiercely.

"You'd better get your schteelcün warrior arse over here, Lucan," Annie hollered, as she wrestled to hold her portal stable. "We're not going without you!"

Growling yet again, Lucan acquiesced, knowing better than to question this particular human's unrelenting mulishness. Secretly, he had admired how it could match his own, though he doubted that he would ever tell her. So, while furiously thrusting and parrying, he made his way backwards to join the others. As soon as he had got hold of Varis, he slashed Folca across the chest and shouted,

"Go, Annie! Go!"

Annie literally dove into her portal and, as she made contact with the viscous surface of it, her vision swirled fast before her. As Lucan, on the tail end of their daisy chain, was about to bring his second foot into the portal, something took a tight hold of his ankle.

It was Folca.

The daisy chain had increased in length, by not one, but three, as the hand of the mortally injured Codila clasped Folia's hand, and Moto took hold of Codila's thick belt.

<><><><><><><><><>

Instantly, it was as if Annie and the rest of her daisy chain had, once again, been unceremoniously thrust into a roller-coaster carriage that was midway through an inverted loop. They were steeply rising, falling and somersaulting. Yet again, they were completely out of control.

Annie, her companions, and the three Shadow Elves, saw momentary flickers of memories pass before them. Once again, these visions were not shared. Each experienced their own memories. Sometimes they were observers looking down on themselves, sometimes they were looking through their own eyes, reliving these past events in the here and now. All of the moments evoked strong, and sometimes, overwhelming emotions.

As each member of the party lingered at different moments, the daisy chain became elongated and stretched to the point of almost breaking.

Lucan was stubbornly ignoring his personal memory trail. He was laser focused on working to actually break the tail-end of the chain. He was hell-bent on ensuring that the unanticipated hangers-on would be trapped in the portal, like Varis had been — only their entrapment would be permanent and ultimately lead to their evaporation.

But it was no use. Folca had a vice-like grip of Lucan's ankle. Lucan took a deep breath and came to the conclusion that, in order to be rid of these damned Shadow Elves, he would have to sacrifice himself, and remain in the portal corridor with them.

He loosed his hold on Varis's arm.

This action violently ripped Varis from his personal trip down memory lane that, sadly didn't include his mother, and he instantly re-snatched Lucan's wrist into his hand.

"We have the schteelcün brùkling Shadow Elves with us," Lucan called out. "You have to let me go, Varis."

"Never!" Varis asserted with a growl that easily matched the ferocity of Lucan's.

He underlined his insistence by gripping Lucan's large wrist all the more tightly. There was nothing Lucan could do. He had more chance of prising a pletim off a nigrate rock. All he could do now was pray that he, Varis, and Elva would be able to finish off the Shadow Elves once they landed in their Sun Elven Realm.

Everyone's images before them slowed down. There was a brief moment of relief before there came the now familiar, deconstruction of everything.

The distinct edges and boundaries between objects, surroundings, and the individuals in their visions, started to evaporate. Everything, everywhere, became pixelated and reverted to their atomic level components. Folca, Codila, and Moto were absolutely terrified, but no less committed to their mission.

It was impossible for any of those in the daisy chain to process the information. There was just so much of it. They could see everything, smell it, taste it, and hear it. Their senses were completely overloaded. None of them could tell where one thing ended and another started. Looking down they could see that their bodies were pixelated too. They couldn't see where they ended and everything else started.

There was a brief moment of tar-like blackness, where the sounds, smells and tastes simultaneously stopped.

There was nothing.

Nothing at all.

Then Annie hit the cold, unforgiving earth. She hit it hard.

<><><><><><><><>

In his very much weakened and extremely pained state, Finwe simply flopped down on top of her, completely enveloping Annie in the process. Elva came next and managed to nimbly dodge to one side, so as not to add to Finwe's injuries. A significantly less nimble Varis lurched after Elva, spinning them both around to face the portal. As Lucan joined them, he and Varis, adopted a defensive fighting stance. Not knowing why they were doing this, but trusting them implicitly, Elva did the same.

Then came the Shadow Elves.

Elva's eyes widened to saucers and her jaw went slack. She shook herself to refocus. Now was not the time to question how this had happened.

Folca fell onto his hands and knees, and was immediately held in place by Varis's acquired sword. Codila landed like a large sack of potatoes, face down. He was a dead weight. More accurately, he was a weight that was dead. He had finally taken his very last breath while exiting the portal corridor.

Lastly there was Moto or, rather, there was less than half of Moto.

Unbeknown to Annie, this daisy chain had contained one too many. As the seventh elf in the chain, Moto had been sliced in two, just below her ribs. Unbelievably, with her cauterised guts spilling out and trailing behind her, blackened blood pooling out around her, and her breath coming in increasingly shallow gasps, Moto managed to drag herself towards Annie.

"Tell me you have got it," she wheezed. Annie instantly stiffened beneath the unconscious Finwe and her blood ran cold.

She knew this voice.

This was the voice of Tathlyn.

"Confirm that you will bring it to me," he continued. "Tell me that —"

The inhabited Moto said no more, for Annie had wriggled out from underneath Finwe, grabbed Lucan's sword and swung the Shadow Elven blade across Moto's neck, neatly separating Moto's head from her shoulders. She couldn't afford to allow Tathlyn to speak another word through Moto. She was fearful that perhaps the others could hear him and he would give the game away.

Annie, Elva, Varis, and Lucan almost jumped out of their skins at the uproarious cheer that then erupted around them. While they had been utterly focused on their emergence from the portal and dealing with the Shadow Elves, they had failed to notice the huge crowd that was gathered all around them.

"How can all these elves have known when we would return now?" Annie asked her friends, panting from the effort she had just expended on despatching Moto.

"We did not know when you would return," replied the familiar, syrupy voice of the Wise One. "You only left but a few moments ago."

<><><><><><><><>

The large crowd, who had given the amulet rescue party a hearty sendoff, had only just turned their backs to return to their daily lives, when the rescue party, plus some unexpected — and unwelcome — hangers-on, had returned.

Generations to come would recount the tale of how they were there when the human, Annie, had brought the Labradorite Amulet, her comrades, and two-and-a-half Shadow Elves back from the Human Realm, just a matter of moments after they had departed.

Palace guards stepped in quick-smart and took the bleeding Folca away while Lucan, Varis, Elva, and Annie turned their greatly concerned attention to Finwe. He still hadn't moved since he'd landed on Annie, and they were desperately fearful that they may have already lost him. His beautifully bronzed skin had been replaced by a deathly white pallor that had taken on a puttylike texture.

"Out of my way," the Wise One ordered, assertively pushing them aside. She took one look at Finwe and had him removed to her rooms where she would work her skills and potions to, hopefully, heal him. The crowds deferentially parted to allow for Finwe to be carried by six soldiers of the guard into the palace, and on to the Wise One's rooms.

As he passed, the crowd filled back in to surround the remaining rescue party.

Annie looked to each of her friends.

"What happens now?" she asked.

"Now," came a refined and booming voice from the back of the crowd, "now, assuming you have *my* Labradorite

Amulet, we celebrate its return, put it in its rightful place and begin to thrive once more."

It was King Peren.

The crowd parted once more to allow him, astride his stallion, to trot to the front.

Annie tried not to allow her distaste of him to show on her face as she remembered what this sour king had said.

What was it? she thought. *Come back with the amulet or don't come back at all.* Then she immediately thought, *You utterly bitter and evil, old, déchwoot goat... no offence to goats.*

With a haughty flick of his hand, Peren indicated that Annie, Elva, Varis, and Lucan were to follow him.

Typical, thought Annie, struggling to keep her thoughts inside as opposed to letting them loose, and blurting them out for all to hear. *You literally sit on your high horse having done nothing, while we who have risked everything, and slogged our guts out, have to meekly follow behind you on foot, with only a horse's backside for a view... no offence horse.*

Chapter Twelve

Once King Peren had reached the top of the broad palace steps, he skilfully turned his flighty stallion to address the crowd.

"This is a great day indeed. Perhaps it is the greatest day that will ever go down in our history," he announced, looking prouder than Punch. "I have retrieved our Labradorite Amulet."

The crowd was ecstatic. There was none of the polite, reserved, and almost delicate clapping that Annie had heard when she first landed in the Sun Elven Realm. This was more akin to the noise that had accompanied Scotland beating England at rugby, to claim the long contested, Calcutta Cup. There was a tidal wave of unadulterated relief, joy, triumph, and hope.

Lucan and Varis worked hard to keep their faces in a noticeably stiff expression of neutrality. Truth be told, they were angry at, disappointed in, and embarrassed by their king. Elva, who had no such allegiance, was clearly exasperated and utterly offended. Annie was straight up enraged and her golden fleck was furiously strutting around the circumference of her iris.

What the absolute brùkling héllè? You have done diddly-squat. I and these fine elven friends have done it all.

She intensified her thought, as the previously cloudless sky clouded over and the temperature dropped noticeably by a few degrees, to the point where members of the crowd that were nearest to her, pulled their cloaks tighter around them to fend off the unexpected chill.

Casting her mind back and digging into one of her favourite library reads — Shakespeare's *All's Well That Ends Well* — she added, *You really are the owner of no one good quality.*

"There is not a moment to lose," Peren continued, completely unabashed.

He was clearly ignorant of, or ambivalent to the rescue party's response. Annie just couldn't decide which. "This night, a grand ceremony will take place to return our Labradorite Amulet to its rightful place, where it shall nourish us all once more and forever!"

Very few of those present in the huge crowd would actually attend the grand ceremony, by dint of their lowly station. However, despite this, everyone erupted once more into deafening cheers. While the cheering was still at full volume, Peren turned his horse and continued into the palace. Annie and her friends followed, exchanging looks that needed no one to voice their thoughts out loud. She could have sworn the horse was arrogantly swaggering.

"I am going straight to Finwe," said Elva while peeling off to make her way to the Wise One's rooms.

"I'll come with you," said Annie making to follow her.

"You will do no such thing," Peren barked and three guards blocked her way. Frustrated, Annie turned to Lucan and Varis for support.

"While we also wish to go to Finwe's side," Lucan explained. "We must focus on the ceremony. Our mission is not yet complete. The amulet is not back in its rightful place."

And its not going to be, Annie thought while screwing her face up in what looked like pure annoyance, but was actually that mixed with a hearty slug of guilt. Varis ventured to ease her mood a little.

"Between the Wise One and Elva, Finwe is in the very best of hands," he said. "With luck, he will be well enough to join the ceremony."

Annie's shoulders fell and she snorted out a long, hard breath of extremely reluctant acceptance. She allowed herself to be guided back to the bedchamber she had used before she had set out to the Human Realm with her friends. There, she waited to be summoned to the blasted ceremony.

<><><><><><><><>

Her recent time in her Human Realm had been so short that there hadn't even been time for anyone to make her bed from the night before. The silky satin sheets were still rumpled and the numerous pillows were scattered, with some still bearing the imprint of her head.

Across the large room, on the fine-legged dressing table, she saw a platter of what looked like citrus fruits and dainty cakes that were all the colours of the rainbow. Next to the table, hung an undeniably beautiful gown. It was the exact same shade as her skin that acted as a background to the structured lace which ran up the length up her dress like sky-blue ivy that exactly matched her eyes. The lace edged with gold that echoed her golden fleck, wrapped around the bodice and created high-arching netted web that stood proudly across her shoulders. The front of the neckline plunged to enhance her bust and from the structured bodice the skirt flowed to the floor in a fit-and-flare style that meant that every step Annie took once in it, would cause the bottom of the dress to billow, and swirl around her feet. The fabric was so soft that it almost felt like it wasn't even there. Beneath the dress, a pair of heavily beaded satin-like pumps peeked out. Evidently, this was what she was expected to wear to the ceremony.

Realising that she was ravenous, she sat before the platter and started to devour all that lay before her. The stupid glamorous gown could wait.

A sudden cold, razor-sharp voice from somewhere in her head, caused Annie to spray the mirror before her, with crumbs of what she had just identified as, a delicious parsnip and ginger cake. Her golden fleck retracted to be a pinprick speck.

"You never answered my question," said Tathlyn with more than a hint of sulky pouting. Whether it was the satiation of hunger, the worry for Finwe, her contempt for the pompous Peren, or a combination of all three, Annie was feeling rather emboldened.

"It wasn't exactly the right time or place," she quipped sarcastically. "But, in answer to your question, I do have the damned Labradorite Amulet. I shall be bringing it to free Carric, so he had better be in good health when I get there."

"Ah," Tathlyn replied. "*Good* health may be rather a stretch, but I can assure you that he is in some sort of —" Annie was seething with unchecked anger now, and she cut Tathlyn off in his tracks.

"Now you look here," she spat, and was instantly delivered a fierce counter interruption.

"No," Tathlyn snapped. "*You* look *here*."

And with that, the crumb-covered mirror before her revealed Carric, still chained to the wall of Tathlyn's tower. Annie gasped in horror. Carric was thinner, gaunt almost, and there were fresh cuts and bruises all over his body. She desperately wanted to avert her eyes, but found she simply couldn't.

"So," Tathlyn continued in his threatening whisper, "bring the Labradorite Amulet to me and you can have your precious prince. Fail to do so and... well..." Tathlyn's voice petered out. A moment later he was gone and the mirror revealed only her weary, teary reflection.

Once Annie was sure that Tathlyn had left her mind, from the bottom of her satchel, she dug out the velvety bag that contained the enchanted amulet. She wondered — would simply making a run for it right now work? No. She would need to use her cunning and guile. With the velvety bag in one hand, she patted the zipped pocket of her coat with the other.

She perched on the end of the large bed. She took the enchanted Labradorite Amulet from its bag and held it in her palm to examine it. But for the addition of the enchantment, this amulet was exactly the same as its dud twin.

So how come you are twins in all but this one way? she wondered. Holding the amulet firmly in her hand, she created a calm, slow moving, convection-like current of magic in the bottom of her belly. She opened her eyes and softened her gaze as she looked at it to the exclusion of all else — just like she had done with the dud amulet at the Necropolis.

How come you are enchanted and your twin isn't? she asked with her mind.

Once again, almost imperceptibly at first, the cyan-blue of the labradorite stone began to swirl languidly. As soon as she noticed it, remembering how the swirling halted if she looked directly at the dud, Annie leaned into her softened gaze to the point where she could no longer see where the edges of the labradorite stone stopped and blurred with the air around it. Soon her small hands and the labradorite pixelated and merged with one another. Once again, just like with the dud, she was it and it was her.

What is your story?

At first there was silence. But the languid swirling kept going, so Annie presumed the stone was thinking of how best to answer. From her conversation with its twin, she knew better than to press it for an answer, and so she patiently waited. And waited. Eventually, the answer came.

"My twin and I came into being approximately four thousand five hundred human years ago," it answered.

"As part of the First Dynasty of Lagash under King Eannutum. It was a significant period in the history of Mesopotamia."

Wow! thought Annie. *You are seriously old.*

"Well, I prefer the term 'immensely antique'."

Of course you do, thought Annie, quickly thinking the better of rolling her eyes for fear of this enchanted amulet flouncing and sulking back into silence. *Please do go on,* she urged.

"We are set in hardened clay that is adorned with precious fragments of gold leaf. We were dazzling, and still, even after all this time, we maintain our glowing quality."

Thankfully, the amulet didn't notice Annie pulling a face that communicated something along the lines of, 'love yourself much?'

"Our initial custodian was a wealthy Mesopotamian merchant's wife called Nammu," the amulet went on, clearly enjoying being centre stage. "Unbeknown to Enkidu, her husband, or the rest of her family and friends, Nammu had her own portal to the elven realms, just like you."

Just like me! Annie wasn't expecting this at all. *Please, do go on — again.*

"Nammu accidentally passed through her portal and into the Sun Elven Realm. There, she fell madly in love with the elder Sun Elven prince, Prince Álváró. And he also fell deeply in love with her. He was the older brother of the current king, King Peren."

This morsel of information shocked Annie and she very nearly dropped the amulet. *So, there weren't two humans in the elven realms before me. There were actually three. Why has no one felt the need to mention this?*

"Because it is before the time of the elves who are your companions," the amulet explained. "This all happened when King Peren was not much more than a youngling. He was originally destined for a life of great privilege and no responsibility, but Nammu and Álváró changed all that."

Does anyone else know? Annie wondered.

"The Wise One is the only other one who knows the whole truth," the amulet confirmed. "Everyone else was brought to believe that Prince Álváró had died in a gruesome hunting accident."

Why? asked Annie. *What really happened?*

"King Adran, Álváró's father, was incensed beyond belief with regard to the prince and the human's relationship. He flatly refused to allow the human to stay and he certainly was not going to have his heir to the throne be wedded to one. In an attempt to separate the soulmates, King Adran had his son placed under close guard, trapped in his chambers, while the human was forced back to her realm. Thinking he had Álváró severed from the love of his life successfully and permanently, Adran released his son from what had amounted to the closest house arrest. King Adran was completely confident that he had triumphed. But he was so very wrong. Nammu returned and brought me with her. At great personal expense to herself, she had stretched her magical powers to their limit in order to infuse and enchant me. While I am in the elven realms, I am endowed with the gift of giving and sustaining premium wellbeing, health, and prosperity to all around me for hundreds of miles."

Extending across the Sun Elven, Shoreland and Woodland Realms, Annie figured.

"Exactly so," replied the amulet.

Annie could see that there was more to the amulet's story, and she waited patiently for it to continue.

"Nammu thought she could perhaps appease the king with such a magnificent gift of me, to these elven realms. She hoped she may be allowed to remain and be with Álváró after all. But she was so very wrong. King Adran tricked the lovers by taking me with the promise that they could be together. I was placed in the Great Window with the understanding that, if I were ever removed, all the surrounding realms, and those within them, would wither and die. But, instead of keeping to his word, King Adran gave the order to have Nammu killed. Realising that there was no future for himself and Nammu in the elven realms, Álváró helped her to get to her portal before she could be executed. This time Álváró travelled through Nammu's portal with her, and was never seen again."

Wow! Annie thought, while ending the conversation with the amulet. Her mind was racing to piece together all this information in light of what she already knew. This information gave her new insight into why King Peren was so extremely bitter, sadistic, and somewhat of a wizened husk. It didn't in any way warm him to her, but it gave her greater understanding of the current elven king.

And now all I have to do is find a way to fool the wizened husk, the Wise One, the courtiers, and my friends, she thought ruefully.

A light fluttering of her fleck and the magic in her stomach confirmed her hatching plan as being the one most likely to succeed. It would mean using her friends and abusing their trust. It would mean betraying her core value of integrity far more than she had ever had to do before, and she hated herself for it.

But what else can I do?

You could put the amulet in its rightful place and give Tathlyn the dud, she suggested to herself.

I couldn't risk him realising I'd given him the dud, she debated. *He'd kill Carric instantly.*

There was an uncomfortably pregnant pause in her thoughts.

You could, of course, leave Carric with Tathlyn, sacrificing the one for the many, she finally countered. The thought of losing the soulmate she had only just recently found in Carric, was too much to bear.

No, she argued with herself. *That is not an option for me. My plan is to save Carric first and then save the dying realms by stealing the enchanted amulet back once Carric is safe, and well clear of Tathlyn.*

If you say so, came the sniping retort.

I do, very much say so, she then asserted acidically.

Emotionally thoroughly torn and tortured, she sank down deep into the soft pillows on the bed, to seek some tiny morsel of comfort. She was surprised at just how terribly tired she felt. Not knowing or caring when the blasted ceremony was to start, Annie closed her eyes and, within moments, was fast asleep.

Not that her sleep afforded her any real rest, respite, or recuperation.

Visions of Carric and Finwe, both severely wounded, swirled around inside her head and intermingled until all she could see were the hideous injuries themselves.

She was liberated from her deeply disturbing visions when Varis came to fetch her. He demurely turned his back as she wriggled into her gown and slipped on the shoes. He then frowned when he saw that she was wearing her worn leather jacket over the top.

"It is really not my area of expertise," he said, trying to be tactful, "but I am not sure that your... much-loved jacket sets off the beauty of your gown."

"You're absolutely right. It doesn't," Annie replied flatly. "But, as you say, it's my much-loved jacket and so, wherever I go, it goes." And, she thought, *more importantly, I need the dud that's nestled in the pocket of my much-loved jacket.*

And with that, she stomped past the mildly amused Varis and headed towards the great hall.

Chapter Thirteen

As the Labradorite Amulet rescue party had been gone from the palace and its grounds for only a few brief minutes, everywhere was still adorned with the rousing send-off paraphernalia. If anything, even more trappings of pageantry had been dusted off and brought out in the last few hours. The garlands of tired flowers and ferns adorning the foyer, and the entrance of the palace, had been further embellished with golden ribbons, twinkling crystals, and pearls. And now the corridors, royal courtroom, and banqueting hall had also been similarly festooned.

The palace was abuzz with unconstrained excitement and anticipation. While courtiers, guards, and servants had twittered among themselves before the rescue party's departure, they now engaged in loud, openly celebratory chatter and laughter, like joyous birdsong hailing the rising of the suns.

Gently taking Annie's elbow, Varis guided her along the high-ceilinged, marble corridors, and pillars carved with folds that perfectly mimicked delicate linen. They paused outside the royal gallery, where the ceremony itself was to take place.

There, they were joined by Lucan and Elva. The three elves were decked out in their finery. Lucan and Varis were in their full ceremonial uniforms. Their tailored tunics were of the deepest navy blue and provided a beautiful contrast to the heavy, gold brocading that sat across their broad shoulders, around their waists, and diagonally across their chests. Lucan's seniority was demarcated by the addition of a large and ornate embroidered sun over his left breast, that was heavily encrusted with shining, precious stones.

Elva was also in a ceremonial uniform.

No stupid floaty dress and twinkly shoes for you, I see, Annie thought sulkily, as she was brought to feel even more ludicrous and out of place than she had when she first slipped into her dress.

In contrast to the Sun Elves' colourful and shiny garb, Elva's uniform was more muted and clearly reflected the Woodland Elves' connection with the nature in their realm. Her close-fitting tunic and britches were a patchwork of leaves in every colour of each season, all stitched together with golden thread. Around her waist, Elva wore a broad belt with a bronze buckle and her hair was swept back and intricately braided.

Looking at Annie, Elva and Lucan could see that she was feeling, at the very least, self-conscious and awkward. They took note of her well-worn jacket and took her wearing it as an understandable assertion of her own identity. Lucan searched for something encouraging to say.

"The juxtaposition of this light, elegant gown and your... your sturdy... robust jacket is... is striking, Annie."

Appreciating Lucan's effort, Annie gave him a warm smile and, holding the skirt of her dress, performed a deep, and slightly wobbly, curtsy.

"The dressmaker has matched the colour of your dress to your eyes and golden fleck, perfectly," Elva added as she took Annie's elbow to ensure her curtsy didn't morph into an undignified flop to the ground. Annie shared a smile with Elva and coupled it with a nod of thanks for saving what little dignity she had left.

As she regained her balance, Annie noticed that there was another figure standing close behind Lucan and Varis, as if he were part of their group.

Wait, she thought. *It can't be...* and yet it was. Grinning sheepishly, was —

"Finwe!" Annie shouted, enthusiastically throwing her arms around him in relief and joy, and not caring if her dignity had been lost altogether.

"Oowff," Finwe replied as he staggered backwards slightly to soak up the impact of the exuberant Annie. His side still hurt like héllè, but he wasn't going to let that curtail this joyous reunion. Annie became aware that he was clutching his side and so she wriggled free, apologetically.

"Oh, I'm so sorry Finwe," she said, tentatively touching the hand that held his side. "You've made a miraculous recovery only for me to set you back again!"

"It was no miracle," Finwe laughed, instantly regretted it. "It was the fine and masterful skills of the Wise One and my amazing sister that steered me away from death's wide open and beckoning door."

Annie smiled at Elva, to find her actually blushing coyly.

Coy and blushing? she thought. *I wouldn't have said being coy, or even blushing, were in Elva's repertoire.*

A moment later, they all came round Finwe to embrace him — very carefully and gently. Finwe held Annie at arm's length and looked at her in earnest.

"Even with your well-worn jacket, you look beauti —"

The end of Finwe's sentence was brusquely cut short as a senior official curtly informed them that the formal ceremony for the return of the Labradorite Amulet, was about to start.

Quickly straightening up, they fell into a formal formation with Lucan and Varis at the front, Annie in the middle, and Elva, and Finwe bringing up the rear. There was a fanfare played on some sort of ancient brass-like sounding instruments, from somewhere high up in the rafters, and the large, ornate doors to the royal gallery slowly opened.

<><><><><><><><>

The royal gallery was absolutely crammed full with elves of all kinds. Annie presumed by all their jewels and finery, that they were dignitaries, royals, and the like, from the Sun Elven Realm, the Woodland Realm, and even the Shoreland Realm.

They stood, for the most part, reverentially, to face the incoming party. The intricately woven rug cut a powder-blue, silk stream down the centre of the gallery for the five friends to slowly walk down, unhindered. The initial fanfare had now morphed into a rousing, yet ethereal, choral piece that accompanied them all the way down to the ornate and opulent throne upon which, King Peren was waiting.

Unlike everyone else in the room, Peren remained seated.

Typical, thought Annie. Knowing more about the origins of his misery really hadn't laid any kind of cooling balm on the disgust and repugnance that she felt towards this elven king.

As someone very much used to the pomp and circumstance of pageantry, Lucan timed their progress perfectly, such that they arrived in front of the throne as the choral piece reached its climatic, and triumphant conclusion.

King Peren took his time to stand and addressed the hall.

"I have ensured that the Sun Elven Realm, the Woodland Realm, and even the frustratingly *neutral* Shoreland Realm are saved," he announced with — what was that? — feigned modesty?

Oh please, not this again, thought Annie, her magic frothing and her fleck pacing with a mix of indignation and anger. *You have done absolutely nothing of the sort.*

Above everyone, the chandeliers began to quiver and only stopped as Elva and Finwe each laid a settling hand on her taught shoulders. They knew what she was thinking and completely agreed with her. However, they also knew that shattered chandelier shards raining down on everyone, wouldn't be good for anyone.

Annie reluctantly allowed their hands to have their desired, settling effect and refocused on the job in

THE WORST DECEIT

hand. She needed to perform her most important ever sleight-of-hand and bring everyone to believe she had retuned the enchanted Labradorite Amulet to its rightful place.

"The Labradorite Amulet," Lucan hissed. Annie suddenly realised that she'd been so engrossed in her own thoughts, that she hadn't been listening to any of the ceremony. She looked at Lucan quizzically.

"Sorry, what?" she asked, realising that all eyes were on her, including the particularly stern, ice-cold eyes of Peren. Lucan rolled his eyes in exasperation and Varis calmed him with a subtle hand signal.

"The Labradorite Amulet," Lucan repeated, clearly wrestling to remain calm. "Where is it?"

"Oh," she replied taking the velvety bag from her pocket and offering it to him.

"No, no," said Lucan, holding up his hands in surrender and physically retreating. "Only you can touch it. You have the hands of Meredith the Thief, remember?"

Now it was Annie's turn to roll her eyes in exasperation.

I do wish people would stop calling her Meredith the Thief, she thought. *I'm sure she had her reasons, and many good qualities.*

As she held the velvety bag containing the amulet, some monk-like chanting began from another unseen source in the rafters. Annie couldn't understand the words and presumed that they were singing in an ancient Elvish, not used today. When the chant began, the Wise One appeared as if from nowhere at Annie's side and, ever so gently, guided her past the elaborate throne to the heavily embroidered curtains that were a good few feet behind it. Annie had never really noticed the curtains before. She'd been either running from her initial Shadow Elves attack or arguing with King Peren about saving his son — her Carric. She assumed that they hung to decorate an otherwise drab wall.

She couldn't have been more wrong.

With the monk-like elves still singing their chant, the Wise One swept open the curtains with a swift yank of a cord, to reveal the most enormous stained-glass window Annie had ever seen. She gasped and held her breath. It was absolutely stunning, standing 140 feet high, and thirty feet wide. Or at least it would have been stunning if the colours of the glass weren't so very faded to being somewhere between insipid and virtually colourless.

"You need to place the Labradorite Amulet here," said the Wise One while pointing, at arm's length, to a piece of the window that was missing. Her elven arm's length that is. Being short of stature, even for a human, never mind a lithe and lanky elf, Annie had no chance of placing the amulet without some assistance. What she need was some sort of a leg up.

As, for the sake of dignity for all parties, a leg up was out of the question, on the Wise One's orders, two servants hurried away to bring a plush footstool for Annie to stand on. However, this proved to not be enough and, therefore, stable hands were summoned to bring a mounting block used by youngling elves when first learning to ride.

While they waited, the monk-elves valiantly chanted on. They had sung and re-sung the chant so much that Annie, while she didn't understand them, was starting to know the words, and was singing along with the monk-elves under her breath.

It was now King Peren's turn to dramatically roll his eyes. The Wise One recognised that his foul temper could rise up and burst forth at any minute, and so, she intervened by addressing the room and busking it as if her life depended upon it — which, looking at Peren's facial expression, it possibly did.

"We have waited more than twelve hundred moons for this auspicious moment, so it is nothing for us to wait a moment or two more," she said, projecting her voice all the way to the back of the gallery. "It will make the moment of our Labradorite Amulet rejoining us, all the more sweet."

A polite tittering wave circulated around the room and, when it had died down, the Wise One valiantly continued.

"We will be forever in the debt of our extremely brave and tenacious rescue party." She ignored the blatantly peeved look on Peren's face, and pressed on. "The commander of our army, Lucan, his steadfast second-in-command, Varis, our revered Woodland Elves, Elva and Finwe, and our most unexpected hero, the human, Annie."

With her back to everyone else, Annie was glad that no one would be able to see her cringe and colour up with the shame of being referred to as a hero. After all, she was about to perform an atrocious scam upon them all.

Just then, the stable hands, in conspicuously less flamboyant attire then that of the rest of the room, arrived with the tallest mounting block that they could find. Annie noticed the slightest twitch of relief cross the Wise One's face, as she was released from the need to ad lib in the most significant ceremony in elven history since the Labradorite Amulet was first bestowed upon them.

Picking up the skirt of her chiffon-like dress in one hand, Annie climbed up the steps of the block in what she hoped was a dignified and befittingly theatrical manner. To the relief of everyone present, it was clear that she would now be able to reach. The monk-elves abruptly ceased their singing mid-stanza.

Everyone, even Peren, was staring intently.

Annie let the skirt of her dress fall to cover her feet and, more importantly, leave her with both hands free. Keeping the deep purple bag in plain sight, she plunged her hand in and pulled out the enchanted Labradorite Amulet. There was a collective gasp of awe from everyone. As she moved her hand across her stomach, she unzipped her pocket and swapped the enchanted amulet for the dud twin. Annie then raised her hand to make an elaborate show of what only she knew was the dud, Labradorite Amulet's twin. Everyone gasped again and held their collective breath in eager anticipation of its reinstatement.

Eat your heart out, David Copperfield, she thought as she swept her arm through a dramatic arc and confidently pressed the dud into its place in the window.

The royal gallery erupted with clapping, cheering, and whooping. It was so loud that another fanfare on the brass-like instruments was all but drowned out.

Nothing changed.

Nothing happened.

Nothing at all.

Of course, only Annie knew why.

To Annie, it felt as if those present were attempting to kick-start the Labradorite Amulet with their vociferous, celebratory noise. Not wanting to draw any more attention to herself, she slowly climbed off the mounting block and rejoined her friends. She was finding it really hard to breathe. It was like a knowing, annoyed, and deeply disappointed elephant had sat on her chest. She was suffering an almost suffocating fear of being found out.

What if they question as to why there's not an instant change in the window, in the gardens, in the wider realms? What if they figured out what I have done?

She put all her attention into her breathing to calm her nerves, calm her golden fleck, and calm her magic. The very last thing she wanted or needed was for her magic to go feral and burst out uncontrollably.

With a flick of her hand, the Wise One signalled for the monk-elves to resume their chant. This time the words and melody were different. Annie could understand the lyrics and assumed they had been written more recently, perhaps in the hope that the amulet would be returned to the elven realms. As the chant radiated from the front of the throneroom to the back, the congregation settled down to a respectful silence once more. The Wise One spoke again:

"We can go forth to our celebratory banquet secure in the knowledge that this will be our last frugal feast, ever. For, as our Labradorite Amulet takes hold, re-energises, and re-nourishes us, our animals, and our lands, we can look forward to a lustrous future with no end."

And with that, the monk-elves' chant crescendoed to fortissimo and came to a close with a rich and densely harmonised, triumphant passage more in the style of the twentieth-century Shostakovich than an ancient Gregorian Chant.

"All rise," boomed a senior servant at the back of the gallery. He was prevented from saying anything more by a brusque interjection from the king.

"Stay right where you are," Peren demanded, each word fired like a round from a revolver, his harsh voice ricocheting off the walls. Annie was terrified that he had sussed her game, and she didn't dare look at him for fear of giving herself away completely.

"I have one further announcement before we continue our celebrations," he continued. *Only he could make the word 'celebrations' sound like something unpleasant and... and rancid*, she thought.

"The self-proclaimed king of the Shadow Elves, Tathlyn, has demanded that his elves we have captured be released in exchange for Prince Carric's safe return."

Annie's heart did a dance to hope, joy and relief.

This would mean that I don't have to betray everyone after all, she thought. *I can replace the dud amulet with the enchanted one before anyone can doubt or suspect a thing.*

Her golden fleck didn't dance. Had it had a face, that face would have been screwed up in deep, suspicious thought.

But why would Tathlyn do this? she pondered. *This would mean that he would have to come for the amulet rather than the amulet coming to him.*

And then her answer came. With a barely disguised, scoffing tone, Peren continued.

"As if anyone would save a prince at that price. For the heir, quite probably. But for the spare? *Never.*"

Tathlyn knew Peren would never agree to such a deal, she realised. *He's done this to rile me. He's done it to guarantee I'll go through with our agreement.*

And it was working. Annie was incensed that the king didn't care even half a fig for his son and, thinking she couldn't hate him any more than she already did, she discovered new depths to her hatred of him. As she opened her mouth to deliver some visceral piece of her mind, the hands of Finwe and Elva returned to her shoulders, tacitly saying,

"We hear you, we agree with you, and now is not the time." Annie reluctantly held her tongue and her magic, but for how long, she couldn't be sure and certainly couldn't guarantee.

Either blissfully ignorant of Annie's inner turmoil, or completely aware and simply not in the least bit bothered, Peren continued:

"Instead, the Labradorite Amulet Rescue Party, will travel to the Shadow Elven lands as the newly named Carric Rescue Party. They, as the only full-strength elves at this time, will bring the stupid péllopé home. Who knows?" he grinned cruelly. "Maybe stealth and Annie's magic will win the day."

"He is not a stupid péllopé," came the mild, yet assertive voice of Prince Adran. "He is my brother and your son."

An uncomfortable, prolonged, and intensely awkward silence followed as the king and the heir to the throne stared at each other, neither showing signs of backing down. Just as the discomfort for all present was becoming unbearable to the point of painful, the senior servant broke the tension, much to everyone's blessed relief.

"All rise and make your way through to the celebration banquet!"

The news that they were going to head to the Shadow Realm was good news to Annie, for a number of reasons. She wouldn't have to steal away to the Shadow Realm and risk being hunted down. She wouldn't have to make the journey to the Shadow Realm alone. And, her best-case scenario would be that they may be able to rescue Carric without her having to give Tathlyn the amulet at all.

Annie was rudely jerked out of her thoughts by a guard flanking the king as he processed towards the banqueting hall. The guard's head jerked unnaturally to look her straight in the eye and spoke without his lips moving:

"Waste no time in bringing me the amulet, Annie," he said, in Tathlyn's voice.

Annie felt the colour drain from her face and her legs turn to quivering jelly. She hoped against hope that no one had noticed.

Chapter Fourteen

"Are you all right, Annie?" Finwe asked. Evidently he had noticed something was wrong, even if he couldn't guess exactly what it was.

"Hmmm? What?" she replied. "Oh... yes...I was...I was just thinking about..."

"About Carric," Finwe ventured, with a hint of sadness in his tone that Annie, while focused on pulling herself together, completely missed. "We shall recover him for you soon enough," he continued curtly.

Annie turned to thank him, but Finwe had already strode off to keep in step with Lucan and Varis. An arm looped through hers. It was Elva.

"It is all right," she said, nodding towards Finwe. "He never huffs for very long."

"I think he's earned the right to huff after very nearly losing his life in the Human Realm," she replied, mustering up a smile that turned out, to her surprise, to be completely genuine.

Interesting, she thought as she allowed Elva to lead her to the banquet. *I'm not referring to the Human Realm as my realm. I guess that's most likely because I've never felt at home in the Human Realm*, she replied to herself. *And I feel accepted here, by most at least, simply as my true self.* Then, daring to allow her mind to wonder a little further, she thought, *and of course, there's Carric, the elf I love. The elf who loves me.*

<><><><><><><><>

Although the Wise One had referred to this banquet as the last frugal one that they would ever have, there was not even a hint of frugality about it — not in Annie's eyes, at least. Nor in Finwe's either, who had got into a heated spat with Lucan at the food laid out before they'd even made their journey into the Human Realm to retrieve the Labradorite Amulet.

It had angered Finwe that, while most elves in the Sun Elven, the Woodland, and the Shoreland Realms had been surviving off the bare minimum or less, those within these palace walls still had a wide choice of foods and far more of it than they needed, or could ever consume. Annie would have agreed with Finwe even if she hadn't spent just over two years living as a homeless person on the streets of Glasgow, not knowing where her next morsel of food was coming from.

As if to add insult to injury, this banquet was even more lavish than their 'send-off' meal. There were roasted meats and fish of every shape, and size. Some in pies, some on skewers, and some cut into slices, and fanned out on large, gold-edged platters. Pyramids of fresh and dried fruits stood among cakes that stood five layers high. Annie noticed that many of the discarded plates contained half-eaten food. This time, it was Elva and Annie who placed steadying hands on *Finwe's* shoulders.

"Easy, brother," Elva said quietly, yet firmly, under her breath, while smiling to well-wishing dignitaries to her left and right. "Soon, all elves in our realms will be well nourished."

"But they will not be glutinous and wasteful like these spewigs," he retorted through gritted teeth.

One dignitary took a hasty step back in alarm as she caught sight of Finwe's snarl. Ever the quick thinker, Annie stepped in to ease the woman's fear, while still maintaining a firm grip on Finwe.

"I'm so sorry," she cooed in syrupy tones. "I'm afraid Finwe is still in quite some pain from the almost fatal wounds that he sustained in the Human Realm. Please do excuse his grimace." The woman was duly placated and Elva chuckled.

"Your magic is not your only superpower, Annie," she said, and even Finwe managed to laugh a little before wincing and clutching his side where his ribs were still knitting together.

While the food seemed endlessly plentiful and decedent beyond Annie's imagination, she and her companions had little chance to partake of any. The endless stream of dignitaries wanting to be seen fawning over her and the others, made sitting, or even standing to eat, an impossibility.

After what felt like an interminable length of time smiling, nodding, handshaking, rattling off platitudes, and listening to soporific compliments, the group were thoroughly relieved when the banquet gave way to dancing.

However, their relief was short-lived when it was made clear that there was an expectation for the heroic group to start the dancing off. No amount of half-joking that this would be more challenging than crossing into the Human Realm and fighting off the Shadow Elves, could deter the assembled crowd from their insistence.

"It is no good," Varis shouted above the musicians who were striking up a tune. "We shall have to acquiesce to their demands."

The stiff-backed Lucan grimaced.

"If I get through this, stealing Carric from under the Shadow Elves in their own realm, will be a peeshpa," Lucan growled.

Elva laughed, took Varis by the arm, and led him into the middle of the dance floor. Lucan looked at Annie.

"I am starting to feel jealous of Finwe's injuries," he grumbled. "At least he can plausibly abstain from this humiliation." Annie smiled a genuine smile and took him by the hand.

"Oh come on, Lucan," she teased as she copied the hold Varis and Elva were in. "Surely a big brave warrior, and commander no less, can survive just one dance."

"I would not bet my kystralla on it," he replied.

Grumbling and reticence aside, Lucan skilfully lead Annie through the rather restrained, and formal steps of the dance. Half way through there was a tap on Lucan's shoulder.

It was Finwe.

"I think you have suffered enough, my friend," he said, and Lucan, after a brief bow to Annie, made a hasty and grateful retreat to melt into the general crowd.

Despite still recovering from his serious injuries, Finwe's leading in the dance was much more fluid than Lucan's had been.

"No offence to Lucan, but this dance is, quite frankly, much more enjoyable with you," she said. "Although," she continued, "it's still nothing like the happy-go-lucky dancing back in the Woodland Realm, in —"

"In Lilyfire's village," said Finwe, finishing her sentence and smiling at her. He was smiling right into her eyes. She suddenly felt self-conscious, awkward and... and... *what is that?* she thought. *Unfaithful? Unfaithful to Carric?*

Finwe looked genuinely concerned and, with Annie still in his hold, stopped dancing.

"It is all right to feel waves of sadness, Annie," he said softly. "I grieve for little Lilyfire too. We all do, each in our own way."

Annie was feeling overwhelmed about everything. Everything her friends knew about and everything that they didn't. Seeing that Finwe and Annie had suddenly stopped dancing, Varis came to her rescue and addressed the whole room:

"We are all extremely flattered and humbled by the celebrations of this evening. But, as we have much work ahead of us, we must drag ourselves away to rest and recharge for our next pressing mission."

With a flourishing bow that only Varis could pull off with aplomb, he then ushered the others towards the door and concluded, "We wish you all a blissful goodnight."

<><><><><><><><>

Once back in her chambers, Annie gratefully kicked off her fancy shoes, threw off her jacket, and shed the splendid gown, letting it drop and crumple in an elegant heap on the floor. She wriggled back into her jeans and flopped down on the bed. She had never been one for silks and frills. Not that she'd ever had the chance to try them out before. However, much to her surprise, tonight's gown had served to prove to her that, in the right circumstances, something a little fancy could be rather enjoyable.

The next moment, she lurched to sit bolt upright in a juxtaposing cocktail of joy and dread.

"Annie?" came a weak, but familiar voice from the far shadows of her room. "Annie?"

It was Carric. In fear of causing him to spirit away, she slid off the bed and tiptoed towards the voice before answering him.

"I'm here Carric. I'm here, my love." And with that, Carric came into view as a 3D mirage. Instantly, her joy evaporated to leave only dread.

"What has the vindictive dräbssta done to you?"

Standing within an arm's reach of him, Annie could see that Carric's torso was a bloody mess of deep puncture wounds. The whole of his face was a patchwork of purple, blue, green, and yellow bruises. His right eye had disappeared behind a red raw, clam-like swelling. He hung limply from his wrists that were crudely fixed to the dark tower's damp walls by thick and rusty chains. She could see that the ligaments in his shoulders were being painfully and relentlessly stretched. Large, silent tears rolled slowly down her cheeks.

"Can you hear me, Annie? If you can hear me, please... please save me," he pleaded from his cut lips. He then continued to speak in short bursts as breathing evidently pained his ribs. "Death would... be a... relief, but... but... he keeps me on... the precipice to... serve his... purpose."

Tears still freely flowing down her cheeks, Annie reached out her hand in the hope that she might touch and soothe him. Not only did her hand pass right through the mirage, it also merely served to increase his distress, and he cried out in further pain.

Annie immediately retracted her hand and sank down to the floor by Carric's feet.

"I will save you, my love," she asserted in a whisper, realising that he couldn't actually hear her, but hoping the force of their loving connection might somehow get her message through to him.

He struggled to speak again. "I.. love... you, Annie."

"I. Will. Save. You." she asserted more vehemently, laying her head on the cool floor beneath his feet. "I am here with you," she whispered, closing her eyes.

<><><><><><><><>

At sunrise, a young elven maid came into Annie's room and found her fast asleep on the bare marble floor. Annie awoke with a start. She looked up only to discover that Carric was no longer there.

Fresh, salty tears stung her eyes and flowed down her already tear-stained cheeks.

Chapter Fifteen

There was no grand sendoff for the friends' next mission. They may as well been going to do the weekly shop at a local supermarket, for all the notice the palace inhabitants took. Peren had been crystal clear. As far as he was concerned, rescuing the pustid péllopé was nothing to celebrate or even marked as significant. They would either rescue him or they wouldn't, and there was nothing much at all to be gained or lost either way.

There were some concerns being whispered between courtiers, servants, and guards, about the lack of change in the Labradorite Amulet's window. It still remained pale and insipid. Annie hoped that they would be far away before the whispers became heightened worry, or even angry shouts.

As they set out, she asked Varis why they couldn't have simply hitched a ride through a Shadow Elves portal, using one of the Sun Elven Realm's captives. Over the time she had known him, Annie had found Varis to be quite the day-to-day oracle and a mine of useful, and occasionally interesting, yet useless, information.

"Ah, well now," he replied, while settling himself into his answer. "That is because not all Shadow Elves can create the portals to the Shadow Realm."

"Why is that?" asked Annie, with a slight smile, knowing full well that he wanted to be asked for more details.

"Because it has been discovered that Tathlyn only bestows Shadow Elves of a certain rank and above, with the wherewithal to create them. The rest have to hitch a ride to use a portal, like we did with you and yours. Other than that, they simply have to take the long way round, as we are now."

"So, am I right in assuming that we had no such Shadow Elves within the dungeons, or wherever it is that you keep them?"

"Actually no," said Varis, looking somewhat frustrated. "We did have one. Folca who had been trapped and was hiding out near the Labradorite Amulet in the Human Realm."

Annie couldn't see what was frustrating Varis. They had Folca and she knew, from when they had come to rescue her from Tathlyn's tower, that they had the means to force a Shadow Elves to transport them. Although she hadn't ventured to find out exactly what those means were. She urged him to go on.

"So, it turned out that rather than being 'persuaded' to take us through a portal to his home realm, Folca preferred to take his own life — something deeply frowned upon by Shadow Elves in particular. Apparently, he acquired a pleast bone and filed it down to be needle-sharp. He then slipped it into the heart's life vessel in his neck and simply lay down to die. He kept it quiet and low-key to give himself his best chance of success. And, unfortunately, succeed he did."

"Well, that was most uncooperative of him," Annie jested, in an attempt to bring Varis out of his unfamiliarly annoyed state. She was glad when her attempt bore fruit. Being annoyed wasn't a good look on Varis.

"Yes," he said parrying her jest with another. "It was downright mean spirited."

And so it was that the companions had to take the long route back into the Shadow Realm and to Tathlyn's tower.

<><><><><><><><>

Since Annie could, for lengthy bursts, run at elven speed by maintaining contact with an elf, horses were not required to get them to the Shoreland Realm and the sea. At intervals, they stopped for Annie to take a breather, regroup, and go again. She also switched elves each time, as being an anchor for her seemed to take a noticeable toll on the elves over longer distances.

In contrast to the blatant indifference to them at the palace, elves farther afield cheered them on their way. Some even ran alongside and offered to piggyback Annie for parts of the way. Annie felt so lifted, sometimes literally. She felt so appreciative of their enthusiasm, friendliness, and acceptance of her, that she almost forgot how she was actually deceiving them and risking their futures.

Almost.

Questions like, "How long do you think it will be before we start to see and feel the benefits of the returned amulet?" kept bringing her deception into painfully sharp relief.

<><><><><><><><>

By the time the two suns were setting and making way for the two moons, they were within the Shoreland Realm. It was agreed that it would be quicker to sail deep into the Woodland Realm than to run.

"We shall rest up here before setting sail at first light," Lucan instructed as they rented rooms in an inn called The Rùftlan's Tail.

Whatever a rùftlan is, Annie mused.

She had resigned herself to the fact that she would, once more, be traversing the dreaded water. While she had made strides to overcome her childhood fear, the altercation with a bewitched siren, and the swarm of Shadow Elves attacking the ship, and kidnapping Carric, had done little to endear the sea to her.

Once Finwe and Lucan had left to charter a vessel for the morning, Annie asked Elva if she could create a restorative elixir with the ginger-mint leaves that had helped her not to vomit herself inside out the last time they had sailed. Elva smiled broadly and produced from her satchel several small vials of a luminescent, mango-orange liquid.

"I had a feeling that we would be on the ocean once more," she said, "and so, before we left the palace, I worked with the Wise One to produce half a dózer of these in readiness."

Annie let out a huge sigh of relief and hugged Elva tightly.

THE WORST DECEIT

Lucan and Finwe returned far sooner than expected. When asked, it turned out that none of the Shoreland Elves would let them charter a ship.

"Not after what happened last time," Lucan explained.

"I suspect the siren and Shadow Elves attacks only served to strengthen their belief in their superstitions," Finwe added with a wry grin.

Annie smiled. She was so glad to see that Finwe was recovering such that he was becoming more and more like his old self. Her golden fleck swished happily.

Yes, so so glad, she thought pointedly.

Well, he's a great elf and a great friend, she retorted in her defence.

Yes, he is, came her reply, in knowing, conspiratorial tones, heavy with innuendo .

"Oh, shut up," she snapped back at herself, and suddenly realised she'd spat this out loud. Lucan looked extremely annoyed.

"You will not tell me to shut up," he prickled. "And especially when we are hatching a plan to save our prince, who is *your* love."

Annie felt suitably chastised and felt her cheeks blush.

"I'm sorry," she said quietly. "I was... I was speaking to myself." As further proof that he was fully mended, Finwe quickly filled the tacit standoff between Lucan and Annie.

"And just to be clear, Lucan," he said. "Carric is my friend, not my prince."

Lucan huffed and it was Varis's turn to pour oil on the troubled waters of Lucan. He continued where Lucan had originally left off.

"So, I agree with Lucan that stealing the Shadow Elven ship to take us deep into the Woodland Realm is our best, or more accurately, our only option."

"The Shoreland ships are more heavily crewed and moored farthest away from the mouth of the harbour to keep them safer from whatever the sea serves up," Lucan continued. "And, their land-based harpoons could ensnare us before we got to the open sea."

"Also," Finwe added, "by taking the Shadow Elven ship, we would be preventing the enemy from following us."

Elva was looking troubled.

"I have never stolen and, while I would rather keep it that way, I do understand the need for such action at this time. But make no mistake," she warned, wagging a warning finger at the male elves. "I shall not in the least bit enjoy it."

Her friends and her brother barely managed to disguise a collective smirk.

Lucan and Finwe had scoped out the only Shadow Elves ship before returning to the inn, and it was decided that they would acquire said ship in the small hours of the morning. They would need Annie's magic to both furnish them with night vision to match that of the Shadow Elves crew, and also to give them moments of invisibility. As they were back up to full strength in terms of their weaponry, and the Shadow Elven sailors were the least skilful fighters of all the Shadow Elves, Annie and her friends were confident that they would be able to take the ship with minimum effort, and resistance.

<><><><><><><><>

At around three in the morning, the friends met in the blacked out, deserted bar of the inn. Elva had prepared the grothorf-root stew for Annie to conjure up their night vision. Annie harnessed her feeling of calmness and focus to softly blanket her entire being. She acknowledged to herself that she was getting really rather good at this now. Slowly, she positioned her hands into the steam above the boiling pot.

Unlike the first time, she didn't flinch. She knew that the burning and blistering sensations would only be fleeting, and then her hands would feel cool, and alive with crackling, magical electricity. Her skills and control with her magic were improving all the while and, while last time, there was a burst of all manner of meteorological mayhem, this time, she was able to focus all her magic into her task. She slowed her breathing to fewer than three breaths per minute and stared so hard into the pot, that she was almost staring right through it. In this moment, all else was but nought to her.

She centred her imagination onto the affect that she was trying to achieve. She saw Varis and Lucan moving around in the dark with catlike precision. They were moving as confidently as if it were blue-sky, cloudless day. She saw Elva and Finwe readying, and firing their arrows with keen accuracy, each one was finding its mark in the chest of a Shadow Elf, their vision completely unimpeded by the dark.

The stew that was initially a squat, bubbling, and plopping mixture, was now a smooth, freely flowing liquid. It had been altered at an atomic level and those atoms were now moving in such a way as to create a figure of eight without the aid of a spoon. Her golden fleck lay still, curled up at the inner edge of her eye, content that the desired effect had been accomplished.

Thinking back to their first experience with the transformed grothorf-root stew, the elves were a little reticent to tuck in.

"Oh come on, guys," said Annie, lifting the ladle. "You know all the initial discomfort is worth the overall effect."

They all gave Annie a knowing and somewhat withering look.

"Okay, okay," she conceded. "You know all the initial agony is worth the overall effect, so bottoms up." And with that, she downed the ladle of stew.

"I, for one, will not be putting my bottom into such a ridiculous and exposed position," said Lucan with a facial expression of one who had just inhaled someone else's obnoxious fart. "But I do agree that the effect this brutal stew creates is, indeed, worth it."

And he too, downed a ladle of stew. The others sighed and each consumed a full ladle.

"Here we go," said Finwe, while holding his head in anticipation of the impending pain.

And then the magic took hold — like a thoroughly bad-tempered mule, kicking out in all directions.

As before, two bolts of searing pain pieced the backs of their eyes. Squeezing their heads with their palms, they made a concerted effort to ease the pain, and utterly failed. Everything was too, too bright — so bright that they could see nothing but the light emitted from every atom of everything around them. They clamped their eyes shut in an attempt to shut out the light, but it just kept on coming — relentlessly.

Suddenly, their eyes snapped open. Everything was a dense, light-absorbing, and eerie black.

As instantaneously as it had come, the pain evaporated. Fluttering their eyes, as if to break through the sleep of a long, fitful night, the pitch-dark room in which they stood looked as clear as day.

With cloaks on, hoods up, and weapons at the ready, they silently moved out of the inn, and onto the silent quayside.

Against the dim light of the two crescent moons, the harbour of ships bobbed up and down like large apples in a barrel. They were accompanied by the light chinking sounds of metal knocking against metal, as their rigging moved in the strong breeze that was coming off the sea.

Just like the inn, outside was deserted but, for good measure, they dodged from shadow to shadow that were cast by the buildings lining the quay.

Chapter Sixteen

The ship they were intent on stealing was called the Cruel Claut. As Lucan and Finwe had said, it was moored nearest to the mouth of the harbour. Unlike the Shoreland ships, this vessel sat much lower in the water and tapered to what Annie presumed were iron spikes at the bow, and the stern. It was so black that it seemed to absorb any light that the moons and stars were offering around it.

As they neared the ship, their improved night vision revealed to them two Shadow Elves guarding the steep gangplank.

Moving as one, the elves came close to Annie and positioned their hands on her so that she could render them all invisible. Moving like the tortoise formation famously deployed by the Romans of human centuries ago, they were able to creep up on the guards, completely unseen. At the last moment, Lucan and Varis broke contact with Annie, became visible, and rammed their short swords through the throats of the guards before they could register what was happening, or make any sound. Each dead guard was then tightly tied to large barrels on each side of the gangplank to give the impression that they were still on duty, and alert.

Remaining invisible as they traversed up the gangplank wouldn't be possible. It was far too narrow for them all to keep contact with Annie. Instead, they would need to use more traditional means of stealthily boarding. With impressive ease, Elva and Finwe climbed up the ropes that moored the ship to the quay, as the others waited below. Their shadowy figures looked like giant spider monkeys climbing vines. When they reached the top, in one synchronised motion, they swung their legs up and over the rail. Moments later, two Shadow Elves plunged into the water, landing hard and making no attempt to break their entry.

Well I guess they're dead then, thought Annie, and was surprised, and a little guilty at how utterly normal it felt.

The twins both motioned for the others to move up the gangplank. Rather than dashing up it Lucan, Annie, and Varis walked openly, with confidence so, should anyone spy them from a distance, it would appear that they had every right to be boarding the ship.

Once on the deck, Annie drank one of the anti-sickness vials that Elva had given her. She was not going to risk projectile, or even any other kind of vomiting, like she had endured during her previous sailing experience. Just as the last drop slid down her throat, there was a barely audible *zip* sound, and Varis roughly rugby-tackled her to the deck. As he rolled off her, Annie looked up and saw a Shadow Elf's arrow wedged into the railing where she had been standing only a moment before. Its blue-black-feathered fletchings and shaft were still vibrating from the forceful impact of embedding in the rail.

"I thought you said these Shadow Elves wouldn't be that skilled," she said as she and Varis crawled behind a barrel for protection, and to regroup.

"Evidently, they have been practising," Varis replied while leaping to his feet with his long sword in one hand and his dagger in the other.

Before Annie could get to her feet, there was an "ugh" sound and a dead Shadow Elf landed with the dull thud of a large sack of potatoes, right beside her. Protruding from his chest was an arrow that Annie instantly recognised as Elva's. Without any qualms, she wrenched the arrow from the dead elf's chest for Elva to be able to use again.

Yep, she thought as she stood and prepared a couple of palm bombs, *this has definitely become my new normal.*

And with that, she tossed the used arrow to Elva, and unleashed her palm bombs on four Shadow Elves who had come down from the rigging, and were running towards her with obviously vicious intent. So as not to damage the ship, her bombs blew up just before hitting the deck and sent Shadow Elven body parts up, over the railing, and into the sea below.

Annie's golden fleck was performing proud backflips of joy and satisfaction at the control and nuance she now had over this aspect of her magic. However, Lucan needed her to rein it in.

"Annie! We need to have enough Shadow Elves left alive to sail the ship," he shouted, as he disarmed, rather than dispatched, another Shadow Elf.

Varis, Finwe, and Elva then joined them with half a dozen Shadow Elves of their own. These seven Shadow Elves were to be their crew. Annie felt a little sorry for them. They were the least skilful fighters of the Shadow Elves and they had just been ambushed by some of the very best warriors in the Sun Elven and Woodland Realms — not to mention the magically gifted human.

However, her pity for them didn't last long.

Despite being thoroughly beaten, the Shadow Elves were not the least bit cowed and it was highly unlikely that they would comply willingly. Varis voiced a concern that they would most likely attempt to deliberately scuttle the ship, rather than have it take them safely across the waters to deep within the Woodland Realm.

Thinking back to the passengers on the train with Freya, the young teen, Annie thought this would be a good time to redeploy her "magical persuasion". She then placed her hands flat on the railing and rigging of the ship, and focused her attention on just the Shadow Elves. She then allowed the magic within her stomach to radiate through her evenly and with control.

"You will comply and give us safe passage across this ocean."

"Like brùk we will," spat the Shadow Elves nearest to her. Then the elf beside him joined in and the others nodded in enthusiastic agreement.

"There is no brùkling way we are going to do anything for you or your bunch of scriéts, you stinking néate's tongue."

It was no use. These Shadow Elves were a living embodiment of defiance and hatred. The humans she had persuaded hadn't had such vehement feelings towards her. And yet she and her friends still needed them to get across these waters.

As the others were discussing what else they might do to mitigate against being scuttled, Annie caught a glimpse of something familiar in the eyes of all seven Shadow Elves, and for less than a split second, all seven elves' faces became Tathlyn. Annie hastily gathered her wits.

"Leave it to me," she said, gripping the nearest Shadow Elf by the collar. "Again," she added over her shoulder as she roughly marched him below deck.

Once she knew that they were completely out of earshot, she rounded on him.

"Right, you dräbssta," she spat. "If you want this damned amulet, you're going to need to make these sailors comply."

The Shadow Elf's face contorted into that of Tathlyn and wore the familiar mean smirk.

"Well of course," came Tathlyn's voice. "Why else do you think I am here? And at great expense to myself, or at least at the expense of some of my Shadow Elves back here at my tower."

Although she had a sneaking and unsavoury suspicion, Annie really didn't want to think about what he meant by that, and so she pressed on.

"So, you need to instruct them, or whatever it is you do to them, to sail the ship for us, and I need to convince my friends that their compliance is all my doing, despite it not working on my first attempt."

"My part is easy," Tathlyn scoffed. "As for your *friends?* Well, the stupid, trusting pellöts are bound to believe whatever it is you will say you have done. But I rather think that they are going to utterly despise you before too long."

Annie's hackles rose and her golden fleck zigzagged with the combination of hate, self-loathing, and desperation. A palm bomb appeared in her hand and she bared her teeth.

"Now, now," said Tathlyn, with acutely vexing calm. "You do not want to be letting that off in here. You may scuttle the ship yourself, and that would never do."

And with that, Tathlyn disappeared and the Shadow Elf he'd been inhabiting staggered forward looking thoroughly perplexed.

"How did I get down here, captain?" he asked, confused and obviously wary. His manner was meek and a million miles away from the spitting, venomous tone he'd had only moments before, up on deck.

Captain? Annie thought. He thinks I'm his captain? Well, let's see how this works. She set her shoulders back, jutted out her chin, and barked at him like she guessed a Shadow Elf captain would do.

"I have no idea what the brùk you're doing, but you and I both know you shouldn't be in the captain's... I mean... *my* quarters. Now get your miserable brùkling hide up on deck and prepare to set sail!"

Wringing his hands, the elf turned tail and scurried away. Annie gave an impish grin and her golden fleck danced a cheeky jig. She suspected that she was going to rather enjoy this.

<><><><><><><><>

She followed the Shadow Elf up on deck and found Lucan, Varis, Elva, and Finwe looking astonished as he ignored them, and scaled the rigging to release the sail. They then jumped as she bellowed at the remaining elves.

"Stop loafing around. Get to your brùkling stations and set us out to sea!"

All six sailors performed a swift bow and said, "Yes, Captain," then scattered about the ship to do their superior's bidding.

"Captain?" Elva asked as the others still stood with their mouths agape. "Annie, what did you do?"

Yes, she thought, while frantically searching for inspiration. *What can I say that I did when my initial magical persuasion clearly didn't work?*

"I... I adjusted my... my mind-bending," she said, while nodding and hoping that they wouldn't realise she was convincing herself as much as anyone else. She was grateful that her mind had started to serve up a plausible answer, and she hoped she was continuing to mask the fact that she was literally making this up as she went along.

Her fleck remained unusually still, as though it didn't want to distract her mental thread. "I figured that tackling so many with such devotion to hating us so strongly, was too much for me."

She looked from face to face, desperately hoping that her friends would believe her. She silently prayed to whomever, that they had faith in her, and that her past actions would give her at least some credibility.

"Yes," she said more to herself than the others, and then sighed with relief. "I thought that if I could... could convince one, it would... most likely... convince them all."

Lucan didn't look so sure.

"If you say so... Captain," he said.

Annie was worried about his suspicion, but decided that the best form of defence was attack. So, she immediately bit back at him.

"Look," she snapped. "Did you want this damned ship to sail us where we need to go, or not?" Lucan was about to tear back into her, when Varis intervened.

"I understand that you have your reservations Lucan," he said with his hand firmly pressing into Lucan's chest, "but Annie's powers do seem to be evolving and expanding. And, right now, it matters not about how she has achieved the Shadow Elves' compliance. All that matters is that she has it."

"And what about us?" Lucan asked, almost growling while pointing to Varis, Elva, Finwe, and himself. "What do these Shadow Elves think about us?"

"You?" Annie replied, once again rummaging through her mind for another plausible answer. "Why, I told them that... that you are the top Shadow Elves warriors." She held her breath and hoped that this would be enough to satisfy Lucan.

After what felt like an age to Annie, Lucan reluctantly conceded. He muttered something about how before, Annie was in view of all those who she was 'mind-bending' and it had worked, and he stomped away to stare at the harbour as it receded behind them.

As they headed out into open water, Annie fully expected to be regularly hurling her guts out. So, she was pleasantly surprised and hugely relieved that Elva's concoction was working a treat. She even took to strutting about the deck in a manner she felt befitted a Shadow Elf ship's captain, and the Shadow Elves continued to "hop to it" in response.

So as not to fall foul of any sea sirens that might have designs on them, Elva and Annie packed their ears with ocean moss.

"You two very much look like the dérwoodè trolls of the Skarrit Mountains," Finwe shouted, while laughing and pointing at the tufts of violet and drab olive ocean moss protruding from their ears. Even Lucan managed to laugh in agreement.

The seas were clear and calm, the skies were true blue, and the winds were strong, but on the favourable side of being a gale. All in all, the voyage across the seas was going extremely well.

But that was all about to change.

Chapter Seventeen

Despite the suns being at their highest for the day, dense, raisin-black clouds raced in from nowhere to block them out, and created an instant, ill-timed night. These clouds were accompanied by a marked drop in temperature and a sudden raging squall.

"Is this of your making, Annie?" Varis asked, shouting in order to be heard over her moss-filled ears and the powerful wind.

"No," she replied, also shouting, forgetting that Varis's hearing was not hampered by moss. "Why, in any realm, would I create something like this?"

Adopting a much wider stance to accommodate the sudden jerking and rolling of the deck as the ship pitched side to side, Annie grabbed a second vial of her personal seasickness remedy, and swiftly swigged it back.

Thankfully, the settling effect on her hyper-delicate 'sea stomach' was instantaneous. She then hailed one of the Shadow Elf sailors to her side. She realised that while captaining a ship in glorious sunshine and mirror-smooth seas was relatively easy, doing so in such conditions as they now found themselves, was an entirely different matter. The Shadow Elves may believe her to be captain, but that didn't actually, in any way, make her one.

"You there," she hollered.

"Yes, Captain," the Shadow Elf replied, his eyes humbly cast down.

"If you were captain, what would you be doing in these conditions?"

"Me, Captain?" came the question in a tone that was one of surprise mixed with fear for what might happen to him if he were to put a metaphorical foot wrong.

"Yes, you." She was losing patience. She needed answers and she needed them right now. "What would you be doing in these conditions if you were captain?"

"Well... well... I would be furling the sails to prevent them from being torn to shreds by the winds, sir... ma'am... I mean, Captain."

"Good man... I mean elf," she replied, as the sailor looked a little perplexed at this strange term, "man". "That's exactly what I would do. So, don't just stand there. Get it done!"

The Shadow Elves worked together quickly to bring all the sails down safely, and Annie had to admire their work rate, skill, and teamwork. Now they would have to wait out the storm and be tossed about on the swelling, swirling waves, at the mercy of wherever the waves decided to take them.

However, it soon became evident that this was no ordinary storm.

Of course it bloody well isn't, Annie thought ruefully, as she clung onto the ship's tied-fast helm, fully expecting Elva's anti-sickness potion to be stretched well beyond its limits.

Everyone on board, including the Shadow Elves, lashed themselves to the sturdiest parts of the ship. Within seconds, everyone was soaked to the skin and shivering from the unexpected cold.

It soon became clear that the raging sea was taking their ship in ever-diminishing circles. Each revolution was quicker than the last. From his times sailing with his father, Finwe knew that this could only mean one thing.

"Whirlpool," he shouted to anyone who could hear him. Annie decided that this current challenge outweighed the prospect of being lured to her death by a siren, and so she removed the moss from her ears, and threw it down onto the slippery deck.

"Whirl-what?" she yelled back.

"Pool," yelled Finwe. "We are circling a whirlpool!"

"You've got to be kidding me," she exclaimed.

"I can assure you," Lucan chimed in. "There are no infant goats involved here. I believe Finwe is correct in his analysis of the situation!"

Oh my God! Annie screamed internally. *Will Lucan ever take the stick out of his arse?*

I shouldn't imagine so, she replied to herself and, much to the confusion of everyone else, including the Shadow Elves, she began to laugh hysterically. She grappled to regain her composure.

"Why didn't we come across this on our initial voyage?" Annie asked to anyone — all answers welcome at this point. One of the crew tentatively provided an explanation — or at least as tentatively as one could when shouting over a gale.

"I am sure, Captain, you remember that, at this stage of the two moons' cycle, the strängaurd current turns and opposes the brècna current. When this happens over the seabed where there are narrow canyons of considerable depth, they can occasionally produce huge, spontaneous whirlpools."

And of course, this would have to be one of those bloody occasions, she thought, giving the heaviest of sighs. Had it had eyes, her golden fleck would surely have been rolling them dramatically in agreement.

"Ah yes," she yelled back. "Of course you are right. You may become a fine captain yourself twenty moons from now."

The Shadow Elf looked pleased at the prospect of his career's possible trajectory.

The ship's circles were so tight now that it was careening, and the whirlpool itself, with its rapidly rotating vortex, was in close view. Had it not been so immediately life-threatening, Annie would have found it downright impressive. At her best guess, it was about twelve miles wide and its immense power was palpable. It was not anywhere near as large as the biggest whirlpools she had read about in the Human Realm, but it was no less deadly.

Deadly, she thought. *Unlike the sirens, this can't be Tathlyn's work. If we get swallowed up by this gargantuan plughole, his plans will be dashed for good.*

Annie was ripped out of her internal dialogue by Elva.

"Annie!" she shouted. "Can you hear me?"

"Sorry, what?" Annie replied.

"This is no time to be — how did you say it? — away with your fairies, Annie," Varis chided, shuddering at his own mention of fairies, and sounding unusually harsh.

"We are all helpless," Elva continued. "All except you, Annie."

Finwe strained against his bindings to face Annie, and grinned through his sea-soaked hair.

"It is time for you to go well beyond the strength of your palm bombs and mind-bending, Annie," he called out.

They had come dangerously close to the lip of the whirlpool. Within the next two rotations around its circumference, the ship could be consumed inside the vortex of water. The time for Annie to upgrade her magical skill set was now — *right now.*

Fortunately, with necessity being the mother of invention, this situation was the very thing that would allow an instant and significant upgrade. The same had been true of Annie mastering her palm bombs. They had been inspired into being through her rage and anguish over Carric being overrun, and abducted, by the swarm of Shadow Elves during their first voyage across the seas.

Now, Annie intensified her intention into her desired outcome like she had never done before. The ship was sweeping round what looked like its final rotation and tilting dangerously on the precipice of plunging to the watery depths. Allowing the fear and dread to surge through her, she tapped into her internal, magical geyser, squeezing it as tightly as she could. Just when she thought she couldn't apply any more pressure, she "tightened the screw" just a quarter-turn more.

The ship dangerously teetered on the lip of the whirlpool. Its stern was stretched over thin air, right above the deadly well.

In the next instant, there was an almighty, radiating shock wave emanating from its zenith.

The zenith was Annie.

Incredibly, the ship was now completely airborne.

Below, the sea swept outward in a circle from its vortex. It did so with such force that, had anyone on board been in a position to look over the rail, they would have seen that the seabed miles below was visible, complete with the all-important narrow canyons of considerable depth that were a contributing factor to the creation of maelstroms. The draining away of the sea also revealed nigh on a hundred shipwrecked vessels that had come to grief through the ages, because of such whirlpools as this one.

There followed an eerie silence of around sixty unbearable Human Realm seconds. After which, there came the cacophony of sound reaching something approaching half a dozen eruptions of the Human Realm's Krakatoa. It was the roaring, foaming, tumbling seawater as it rushed back to fill the void and once more obscure those watery graveyards nearly seven miles below its regular surface.

And yet still the Shadow Elves ship hovered, like a mighty sparrow hawk eyeing up its prey far below.

Not until the waves had calmed to a relatively settled swell of around sixteen feet, did a magically and emotionally exhausted Annie place the ship back down onto the rhythmically heaving ebb and flow.

As soon as she had done so, despite having consumed Elva's anti-sickness remedy, Annie violently projectile-vomited.

With no need for their captain's orders, the Shadow Elves set to, raising the sails so that they could catch the wind and set them on their way once more. At least they did so once they had established their bearings, having survived the near equivalent of a washing machine on a fast-spin cycle.

The other elves wrestled themselves free of their ropes and immediately came to Annie's aid. Rather than fighting with the knots in the ropes, Lucan ordered the others to step aside as he unsheathed his sword and, in one swift action, slashed asunder Annie's bindings.

Virtually unconscious, Annie sank limply to the floor. But before she literally hit the deck, she was effortlessly scooped up into Finwe's arms and carried down the steps, and below to the captain's quarters.

<><><><><><><><>

Annie's friends took it in turns to sit with her as she recuperated. She drifted in and out of consciousness, staying lucid for mere moments before descending back into fitful sleep.

When she finally came to and managed to remain that way for a little while, it was Finwe who was watching over her.

"Are we at the bottom of the sea?" she asked, not sure of how her magic had turned out.

Finwe smiled his unadulterated, warm smile.

"No Annie," he said, while gently moving a wayward lock of hair from her face. "We are most definitely sailing on the surface of the sea, and it is all thanks to you. You saved us. You saved us all."

Annie mustered up a weak smile of her own.

"Are we back on course for arriving deep within your Woodland Realm?" she asked.

Finwe confirmed that they were and suggested that he bring Elva down to check on her.

"No," she protested. "I'm Okay. I just need to rest a little while longer. Please, take my mind off the wretched sea with some tales of your wonderful Woodland Realm."

More than happy to do her bidding, Finwe settled down on the floor beside Annie's bunk to spend the remainder of their journey on the seas, regaling her of the antics of his youth.

But, less than ten Human Realm minutes later, all hell let loose once more. And this time, Annie's resources were far too depleted for her to be of any use.

Chapter Eighteen

Unbeknown to everyone on board, while the draining and re-flooding of the sea had served to dispel the lethal whirlpool, it had also stirred up life from the belly of the sea canyon and brought it writhing and angry to the surface, alongside the shallow hull of the ship.

Just as Finwe was describing his comedic hunting antics amid the various luscious greens of the Woodland Realm — before the Labradorite Amulet was stolen — the ship suffered an almighty punch to the gut which sent him sprawling across the floor. Simultaneously, Annie was jolted out of her bed to smack down alongside him.

As they lay with their faces turned towards each other, there was the briefest of expression on Finwe's face that Annie just couldn't read. A split second later, there was another punch to the ship's gut and the pair were unceremoniously slammed hard into the wooden wall that partitioned the captain's cabin from the stairs up to the deck.

"What in all héllè is that?" asked Annie.

She was desperately trying to stand, but discovered that she was as weak as a newborn kitten and her legs instantly buckling beneath her. Easily springing to his feet, Finwe lifted her and, staggering in response to the lurching of the ship, made towards the bed.

Just as he was about to place her on the scratchy blankets, a third gut-punch took his legs out from under him. This caused him to roughly dump Annie onto the mattress and pitch forward such that his face became buried in her chest. Struggling to extract his arms from underneath her and gain some purchase to lever himself up, his face remained buried for quite some moments.

When he finally surfaced, Finwe was flushed pink with embarrassment — not an easy shade to show on his bronzed skin, but he was so mortified, that it was plain as day.

"Please, please forgive me," he begged. "I had no intention of plunging amid your... your —"

"Boobs," Annie interrupted, while smiling broadly.

"Boobs?" Finwe quizzed.

"Boobs," Annie verified. "And it's quite all right Finwe. It was an innocent mishap. It really doesn't matter."

And there it was again. The mysterious expression that fleetingly occupied his face as he looked at her. A fourth gut-punch instantly broke the moment and this time, it came from the other side of the ship, sending Finwe tottering backwards, and windmilling his arms in an effort to keep his balance.

"I must go and assist the others," he said, making for the stairs. "You must stay here, Annie."

And with that he was gone. Ordinarily, Annie would have argued, hauled herself out of the bed, and struggled up the stairs behind him. However, she could feel the absolute absence of any energy or magic after her monumental ship-lifting, whirlpool-plugging feat. So, instead, she remained where she lay and tucked the rough sheets tightly across her in an effort to prevent herself from being flung across the room again.

Finwe, Elva, Lucan, and Varis are fantastic warriors, she told herself. *They've got this — whatever this is.*

And then her eyes involuntarily closed and she was unconscious once more.

<><><><><><><><>

Finwe came up on deck to find one of the Shadow Elves being seized and shattered between the protrusible jaws of an airborne Stréglöbe Ürina — a terrifying and rarely seen, deep-sea fish that would ordinarily patrol the seas at depths of more than four and a half miles. The fifty-nine-foot-long Stréglöbe Ürina was clearly, seriously vexed with regard to the Shadow Elf ship. It essentially blamed the ship for ripping it from its deepest, darkest dwelling and for unceremoniously thrusting it into the well-lit, and painfully low-pressure shallows.

Having demonstrated its utter displeasure by ramming its nemesis several times, the Stréglöbe Ürina had managed to dislodge a Shadow Elf from the rigging and into the foamy waters beneath. As the sailor helplessly flailed around in the waves, the creature zeroed in, not wanting to pass up on an easy snack for the taking.

The Stréglöbe Ürina swallowed the Shadow Elf whole.

On deck, Finwe's comrades readied themselves to dispatch the deep-ocean beast. None of those aboard could afford to have their ship ripped asunder and sunk. It wasn't just about the potential end to their mission. It was about the potential end to their lives. Once in the water, it would only be a matter of time before the Stréglöbe Ürina made swift work of them all.

Having rapidly made light work of the wretched sailor, the Stréglöbe Ürina swam a wide and menacing arc around the ship to approach the it from the other side. All those aboard did a prompt about-face, readying themselves for the next attack.

"The only weak spot on such a beast is just under the large snout, yet above the upper, ribbon-thin lip," Varis called to the others. "We have to bring it to breech the waves in order to stand a chance of ending this "hiatus" in our favour."

"Then we need to entice it with some suitably juicy bait," shouted Lucan and, before anyone, let alone Varis, could stop him, he had climbed the rigging and struck a Shadow Elf flare with which to lure the beast.

Upon seeing it, the Stréglöbe Ürina homed in on the intensely bright light of the flare, mistaking it for the bioluminescent signature of its favourite meal, the chemiluminescent, twenty-five-foot choteumesonythis squid.

There was no time to wrestle Lucan down to relative safety and send up a Shadow Elf in his place. Instead Varis unsheathed his weapons and readied himself to dispatch the creature before any one of its three hundred, nail-like teeth could harm a hair of his soulmate's head. Elva and Finwe similarly readied their arrows, holding their bows in a sustained state of maximum tension.

"Hold," Varis ordered. "Hold."

This first counterattack had to count. Varis was convinced that there wouldn't be another chance to use Lucan as bait. Using its flat, sail-shaped caudal fin, the electric violet-skinned Stréglöbe Ürina cranked up its speed enabling it to breech the waves and reach heights of around forty feet, to put Lucan well within its reach.

As the Stréglöbe Ürina's body arched out of the water and high above them, both Finwe, and Elva let loose their arrows to strike the fish at its weakest point. While their arrows hit their mark, they served only to graze it. Its skin was far thicker than they had thought. The Stréglöbe Ürina completed the highest point of its arc, then locked its eyes, and homed in on Lucan, who was now directly below it.

In desperation, Varis yelled at Lucan to grab his attention and threw his broadsword up to him, pommel first. Lucan seized Varis's sword and, in one strong, sweeping motion, he brought the point of the blade to ninety degrees with the Stréglöbe Ürina's weak spot. Using all his might to hold the sword steady, Lucan allowed the momentum and weight of the sea beast to skewer its own head. Letting go before the mass could rip his arm from its socket, Lucan watched as the lifeless Stréglöbe Ürina plunged to the deck with only the hilt of Varis's sword protruding from above its lip.

Anticipating the lethal force of the creature should it land squarely on the deck, the remaining Shadow Elves had used their seamanship and worked at lightning speed. Rather than sinking them, they shifted the sails to tilt the ship in such a way as to minimise the impact of the enormous corpse. Hitting the forty-five-degree tilted deck, the Stréglöbe Ürina slithered head first into the depths to become a welcome smorgasbord for thousands of smaller sea-life creatures.

As the others stood staring at the Stréglöbe Ürina's body slowly sinking out of view, Lucan carefully climbed down off the rigging and stood behind them.

"I am so sorry about your sword, Varis," he said.

Varis whirled round and hugged him, hard.

"I shall just have to be content with using one of the Shadow Elves' swords that I have seen in the meagre armoury on board," he replied, his voice muffled by Lucan's neck.

Everyone was exhausted and needed to recuperate, and regroup. Adopting the role of the captain's second-in-command, Elva instructed the Shadow Elf sailors to also rest a while before resuming their duties to continue the journey on their original course.

The Shadow Elves couldn't quite believe their luck, for never before had they received such compassion and kindness. In fact, they had never received any compassion and kindness, from anyone — ever. Meanwhile, the "top Shadow Elves warriors" made their way down to the captain's quarters.

There they were surprised to find Annie sleeping soundly. Disturbed by the noise of her friends entering the cabin, Annie half roused.

"Have I missed much?" she asked, with her eyes still closed and her eyebrows arched in enquiry.

"No, Annie," Finwe replied, wearing a broad grin that she couldn't see. "Nothing much at all."

The elves chuckled quietly and arranged themselves around the room to snatch some restorative sleep.

Chapter Nineteen

As the suns were beginning to dip behind the distant horizon, the Cruel Claut uneventfully docked in a little-known cove — little-known to the Woodland and Shoreland Elves at least — where the waters were shallow and riddled with rocky outcrops just below the surface. The hulls of Shoreland and Sun Elven Realm ships would have been too deep to get near to such a place. Trying to head into the Shoreland dock, deep within the Woodland Realm, in a Shadow Elf ship, would have only invited the wrath of the Woodland trebouchets. With such a small crew, they couldn't have defended themselves and would, most likely, never had made it close enought to reveal their true identities.

A posse of Shadow Elves were camped at the shoreline of the cove. To avoid getting embroiled in an unnecessary and time-wasting scuffle, and attracting questions about why there were Sun Elves, Woodland Elves, and a human, in command of a Shadow Elven ship, Annie made two trips up and down the gangplank to offload her friends in a state of invisibility.

Lucan made a mental note of where they were, with a view to sending a centuria of his army to the spot, once he'd returned to the Sun Elven Realm.

Back on the ship, the Shadow Elven sailors were under the impression that their captain would return once she had escorted their warrior passengers to an important and secret location. Not until the following morning would the enchantment placed upon them by Tathlyn, wear off.

They would come to, completely at a loss as to how they were in the Woodland Realm and would slope off, back out to sea in the hope that they wouldn't be subjected to too many questions, punishments, or worse, by the posse or their 'higher-ups'.

<><><><><><><><>

Elva and Finwe were delighted to be back in their Woodland Realm, even if it was only for a short while. They had hoped that, by the time they had reached their realm, their beloved forest would, once more, be providing rich habitats for hundreds of species of animals, birds, and plants, and would have significantly improved water quality in the rivers, and lakes. They had been looking forward to hearing lively, thriving birdsong and seeing the majestic Thritralé eagles soaring overhead.

They were bitterly disappointed.

Nothing had improved.

Nothing at all.

Annie's heart ached when she saw their expressions of dejection. She wanted to tell them the truth. To tell them her plans to ensure Carric's freedom and then steal the amulet back from Tathyln, so that the Labradorite Amulet could genuinely be restored to its rightful place.

But she just couldn't.

She knew that as soon as she spoke up, at the very least, Lucan would immediately put her under close arrest and take her straight back to the Sun Elven Realm to restore the Labradorite Amulet. The sacrifice of Carric to save the very many would be absolutely assured.

She knew that re-energising the Sun Elven and Woodland army would take too long, and that Tathlyn would give Carric an agonised death as his first act of anger at Annie for not fulfilling her part of the terrible bargain. She also knew that her immediate arrest and desperation to resist, could well result in her magic ramping up to catastrophic proportions, and result in the deaths of many elves, including her friends.

No. She just couldn't risk it.

She had to stick to her original plan. She had to remain silent and hope against hope, that the guilt eating away at her insides didn't consume her altogether.

Varis broke the silence, trying to lift the Woodland Elves' spirits.

"Perhaps it may take some time yet for all the damage to be undone and reach this distance from the centre of the Sun Elven Realm."

"Perhaps," Elva replied, her voice unusually flat and disheartened.

Lucan took charge.

"This is no good. No good at all. We cannot simply wait here, moping and wishing that the Labradorite Amulet's powers had already reached these lands. We must remain focused on our task of freeing Prince Carric from that loathsome, succum cocotte, Tathlyn."

"I am sure that, by the time we pass through here again, with Carric in our midst, things will be much improved," Varis offered hopefully. "Much more alive and... and thriving, even."

Lucan gave the order to make camp for the night with the intention of pressing on at first light. Finwe created a lively, crackling fire from what felt like a never-ending supply of dry, dead leaves, and Elva set to create a stew that would have been hearty were it not for the lack of succulent berries, and roots available to her. Nobody seemed to notice that Annie was being unusually taciturn.

She was grateful for the small mercy.

<><><><><><><><>

At first light, following an uneventful night, they headed out. It was clear that Finwe, in particular, was still feeling distressed by the barren, infertile state of his realm. It was so unlike him to be trapped in the doldrums, but they all knew better than to ply him with patronising platitudes that limply clutched at the fragile, brittle straws of hope.

Once again, Annie was able to grab a booster to her speed and endurance, by holding on to Elva. As a result, they were able to cover ground much quicker than they had when they were last there.

They had agreed to keep moving throughout the day, setting up camp again, overnight. As the suns were setting once more, they came upon the outskirts of a village. The elves strode on, but Annie suddenly came to a complete standstill.

She recognised where she was.

This was Lilyfire's village.

All the horror of what had happened with Lilyfire and the fatal accident in the nearby pool, rose up in Annie's throat like a relentless, acidic tide. She froze, and the ground, and trees closest to her instantly whitened in a spontaneous hard frost.

"I can't," she croaked, her voice breaking under the weight of her emotion. "I can't go into the village."

The elves glanced at each other and then walked back to stand with her.

"I can't go there," she repeated, finding it hard to breathe. "I can't cope with the joy of the villagers hearing about the return of the amulet and all the grief at the loss of Lilyfire. It would be too much. I think... I think I would... break."

Annie had turned everything so cold that, despite it being a hot summer day, her breath could be seen as she spoke. Standing close to her, the elves' breath was also visible.

The plan had been to stock up on what meagre provisions the villagers had available to offer, before pressing on to the Crystal Caves that would take them into the Shadow Realm. Varis gave Lucan a meaningful, hard stare and, after some initial, silent resistance, Lucan sighed, and threw his arms up in the air in surrender.

"Very well," he said, clearly unhappy about it all. "We shall manage on the provisions we currently carry, proceed around the village rather than through it, and set up camp again once we are well beyond the other side."

Relieved that they would be giving the village a clear and wide berth, Annie's hoar frost evaporated, and the air returned to its summer evening heat. The group headed west before turning south.

Only a little while later, they came upon a glade flooded with the light of the rising moons. Unlike the rest of the Woodland Realm, this small area was filled with strong, healthy plant life. Although the moons' light naturally subdued the colours, the glade was clearly bursting with life and vigour. Leaves and flowers of all shapes, and sizes occupied every available inch of the area. Ornate, winged insects fluttered in the moonbeams and buzzed lazily to create pleasing harmonies. Annie marvelled at this glimpse of what she supposed the Woodland Realm looked and sounded like before the theft of the Labradorite Amulet.

The group walked on.

Once within the glade itself, Varis, Lucan, Finwe, and Annie suddenly and spontaneously became weakened, and distracted. They instantly entered into a dazed and dreamlike state. Each of them descended to the ground to curl up among the flowers, their faces turned upward towards the flitting insects above their heads. While their eyes were open, it was clear that they were seeing and hearing nothing.

Elva, however, maintained a sure grip of all her faculties. Yes, she found the glade attractive, stunning even, but she wasn't mesmerised by it. She wasn't weakened and felt absolutely no compulsion to curl up like the others. She didn't know what to make of it. She tried insisting that each of them get up. She tried snapping them out of it by shaking them. She tried to drag each of them out of the glade, to where she felt they would return to her, but strong as she was, they had quadrupled in weight and she couldn't move them. It was like they were being held down in place by something that she couldn't see, or feel.

All efforts to rouse and rescue her friends, and her brother, failed.

She was afraid. She was very afraid.

It became clear to Elva that she wasn't going to be able to save them by herself. She needed help and probably lots of it. And she needed that help right now. Taking a moment to gain her bearings, she took one last worried look at the four prone figures among the foliage and took off at speed, in the direction of Lilyfire's village.

Chapter Twenty

All was quiet. The whole village was in deep and peaceful slumber.

At least they were, right up to the moment when Elva came steaming into the village square, shouting for help and rapping wildly on all the doors. She wasn't one to get flustered and so this fluster-igniting situation in which she currently found herself, was completely alien to her. She did not like it. She did not like it at *all*.

The desperate urgency in the elf's shouting and urgent knocking on doors, instantly ripped the villagers from their blissful sleep. With considerable effort, they tore themselves away from their cosy blankets and made their way outside by candlelight. While doing so, they instructed their younglings to remain safe inside.

Meara, from the inn, was one of the first to emerge, blinking the heavy sleep from her eyes.

"Why Elva," she said softly, when she saw who it was that had been causing all the commotion, "whatever is the matter?"

There was quite a crowd around Elva now, and Meara suggested that she stand on the large, flat-topped rock in the centre of the square, in order to address everyone at once. Forcing herself to take a full, deep breath in and a slow, long breath out, Elva tried to settle her unfamiliar nervous energy before she spoke from the top of the rock:

"It is... it is my friends and my brother. They are... asleep."

"Well, there is absolutely nothing wrong with that at this time of night," said a rosy-faced and most probably heavily inebriated elf, who was tottering out of the inn on extremely unsteady legs. "It is what we have all been doing, until you came along and scared the very shéats out of us!"

"It is more likely that you were passed out on a table in the inn, Alberic," shouted another male voice among the crowd.

Some of the older male elves laughed at this and were promptly jabbed in the ribs by their, most likely, better halves.

"This is Elva," announced Meara assertively, while joining her on the rock. "Many of you know her, or know of her. And if you do, you will also know that she is a much revered and celebrated warrior of our Woodland Realm."

Those who had laughed, shut their mouths and looked suitably chastised.

"She has obviously come here needing our help," she continued, "and we are happily going to give it. Unreservedly," she added with a particularly hard stare at the flushed faced and wobbling Alberic.

Giving a grateful nod of thanks to Meara, Elva continued addressing the crowd. She was much calmer and focused now, thanks to the few moments' grace given to her by the innkeeper.

"Finwe, Annie, Varis, and Lucan are not so much asleep as... as deeply unconscious. We were on the west side of the village and came upon a beautiful, healthy, and thriving glade. As we walked through it, the others suddenly became very weakened and curled up on the floor. I could not wake them. I could not move them. I could not help them. They are still there now."

There wasn't the slightest whiff of hilarity now. As soon as the villagers had heard about the glade, they all visibly stiffened and looked afraid. Elva noticed the seismic shift in their demeanour.

"What? What is it?" she asked, her eyes intensely scanning across all the worried faces. "You *must* help me. I cannot save them on my own. I *have* to save them. I have to."

"We cannot help you," Meara replied, holding Elva gently, yet firmly by the upper arms. "At least, most of us here cannot."

"What? Why the héllè not?" Elva yelled, angrily wrenching herself free of Meara's grasp. But Meara simply and calmly took Elva's upper arms in her grasp once more and looked her in the eye with a warm, and open expression on her face. She told her not to take her word for it, and to listen to one of their elders.

A shorter female elf, bent nearly double from the weight of wisdom gained across more moons than anyone else there could remember, unhurriedly made her way through the crowd. With the gentle assistance from several elves at the front of the crowd, she joined Meara and Elva on the rock. Her name was Zovia. In a voice that crackled with great age, Zovia unhurriedly began to explain.

"This is the work of the moertemakana," she explained, raising a gnarled finger into the air. "They come creeping out and hunt at night. The moertemakana hunt for folk to kill and consume in order to reanimate, reinvigorate, and sustain themselves. This is why the villagers here never venture beyond our village boundary after dusk. The moertemakana cunningly lure their victims with the appearance and illusion of a part of the forest that's bursting with health, and life."

"So, are you saying they are already dead? Is that why they cannot be helped?" Elva shrieked, blasting through Zovia's unhurried explanation.

She was flustered and at risk of diving headlong into blind panic. Since she could remember, Elva had assumed that Finwe would always be in her life — born in the same few minutes and, eventually, dying in the same few minutes, either by the sword or nature's decree. Seeing that Elva was beginning to spiral and unravel, Zovia held up a calm, yet halting hand.

"They may still be alive, but we will not have long to help them."

"So now you are saying that you can help them?" Elva's mind was still reeling. *What is all this nonsense?* chattered her mind. *You say you can help me, then you cannot help me, then you can help me. I cannot wait around while you lot talk in riddles!*

"Not all of us, no. But some of us can," Zovia replied. "Namely, the younglings."

Elva was now monumentally incensed.

"How the héllè can the really young save my friends," she blurted, "— save my brother?"

"The moertemakana prefer as their victims, those who are romantically in love," Zovia continued, taking no apparent notice of Elva's frustration. "It would seem that such individuals supply them with greater invigoration for less effort, on their part. The younglings are not yet in love, romantically. They are unaffected by the moertemakana, just like you, apparently."

So that is why they did not affect me, Elva thought. *I am not in love with anyone.*

She could understand why Lucan and Varis had been affected, since they loved each other. She could understand why Annie had been affected, since she was in love with Carric. But what of her brother? Who was *Finwe* in love with?

While Elva had been corralling her thoughts, Zovia had sent out the order for around thirty of the younglings to be roused from their beds and gathered in front of the stone on which she, Elva, and Meara still stood. Zovia passed a large, leather, flask-like pouch to Elva.

"Here," she said, with a mischievous twinkle in her eye. "Spitting this böccék nhây mixture at the moertemakana will deter them while the younglings drag each member of your group away from the glade and back here to safety."

Elva looked dubiously at the pouch.

"What is it?" she asked, and Zovia chuckled.

"I strongly believe that it would be so much better for you not to know," she said.

And with that, she signalled it was time for Elva and her troop of youngsters to march out of the village, and back to the lethal glade illusion.

<><><><><><><><>

When Elva and her undersized rescue party approached the glade illusion, she was shocked at what she saw before her. She could now see that there were eight creatures — the moertemakana. Two leaned menacingly close to each of her comrades. They were at least twice the height of a taller Woodland Elf and yet not much more than skin and bone. Long, straggling hair draped over their razor-sharp shoulders. Their bulging, milky eyes stared intently at their victims and their primitive mouths, with three rows of fang-like sharp teeth, gaped wide enough to have swallowed a mature restoreff deer.

Elva could see that something was being drawn from Lucan's, Varis's, Annie's, and Finwe's faces. It looked like intertwined tendrils of a brilliant violet and bottle-green smoke.

"What *is* that?" she asked, not at all expecting any answers such young ones.

"That green smoke," said one of the older youngling males, "is the essence of life. The purple smoke is the pure essence of being in love. In pairs, the moertemakana are sucking it out of their victims, through their faces."

"We had better take action now," added what looked like the youngling male's younger sister. "The moertemakana are strengthening and, before long, it will be too late. Very soon your friends will all be dead."

Staring at the moertemakana, who were looming over Finwe, Elva could see that their milky eyes were beginning to clear and the skinny limbs were starting to fill out with healthy muscle. The younglings were right. There wasn't a single moment to lose. Before Elva could give any orders, the younger sister took charge. She divided up the younglings into teams and dispatched each group to an adult elf and the human.

"Now," she said to Elva, "you are to take a generous mouthful of the böccék nhây mixture and spit it into the face of each of the moertemakana. The böccék nhây will burn them and reverse the flow of the essence of life and the essence of being in love. Each group of us younglings will then drag our elf or human to safety."

"That sounds easy enough," Elva smiled. She couldn't help but admire the young elf's organisation and leadership skills.

"Not necessarily as easy as you may think," said the older brother, and several of the others giggled. "You have yet to taste the böccék nhây mixture."

And with that, he moved off with his group towards the glade.

<><><><><><><><>

"Oh my brùkling grüla!" Elva exclaimed as she reeled away from the opened pouch and held it at arm's length. The böccék nhây mixture's fetid stink was truly horrific. A foul mix of rotten eggs, sweaty feet, and decaying fish would have been a fragrant bouquet by comparison. The younglings were all in position, keeping a little distance from their quarry, and yet obviously ready to spring into action.

There was nothing else for it.

Elva was going to have to "suck it up" — quite literally.

Still holding the pouch at arm's length, she carefully made her way over to the first pair of moertemakana. They were so intent on draining Varis that they paid her no attention. Holding her nose in a futile attempt to block out the smell, Elva bravely took a large swig. She had absolutely no problem with fiercely spitting the mixture out at the moertemakana. As soon as the mixture touched her tongue, she had a monumental gag reflex.

The very moment the böccék nhây mix sprayed and made contact with the pair of moertemakana, they instantly recoiled, emitting shrill, piercing shrieks. The moment they ceased sucking out the essence of love and life from his face, the essence reversed its flow back into Varis.

Had Elva not been spewing herself inside out among the bushes, she would have seen this. While she was girding herself for the next pair of moertemakana, Varis's team of younglings arranged themselves around him. As soon as all of his essence had flowed back into him, the younglings swiftly and efficiently worked together to pick the unconscious warrior up, and carry him all the way back to the village. Although Varis was a bulky elf, the sheer determination of younglings meant they didn't stop until he was within the safety of the village boundary.

With her eyes streaming and an intense pain in her gut from the relentless vomiting, Elva repeated her valiant sip-gag-spit-spew, cyclical process, a further four times.

She had decided to disconnect Finwe's moertemakana last of all. She seriously doubted that she could have repeated the process if she had freed him before the others. She just hoped against hope that she hadn't left him too long. There was the very real and frightening chance that the final individual to be freed might be too far gone to be saved.

The younglings were impressive with regard to their fearlessness, their focus, and their collaboration. Each group efficiently whisked away their moertemakana victim and didn't stop until they were back in the square at the centre of the village.

As soon as Finwe's moertemakana were spattered with the böccék nhây mixture, the glade illusion faltered and completely evaporated. Where the glade had been, everything returned to be as dry and impotent as the rest of the forest. All eight moertemakana, still reeling from the böccék nhây mixture, screamed as their emaciated bodies were blown away, like thin paper napkins from a picnic table on a breezy day.

Clutching at the searing pains in her stomach, Elva had one final acidic barf into the bushes before following Finwe and his team of younglings into the village. Seeing just how sweaty, pasty, and pale Elva's complexion was, Meara put an arm around her shoulders and offered her a flagon of honey beer to start combating the residual taste of the horrific böccék nhây mixture.

Knocking back the whole flagon in one go and handing it back to Meara for another, Elva was hugely, and quite possibly eternally, grateful. It didn't iradicate the terrible assault she had just taken to her tastebuds, oesophagus, and stomach, but it did, at least, start to take the unbelievably disgusting edge off.

Before her, Finwe, Annie, Varis, and Lucan had been placed in an arc. Several village elders were tending to each of them. They lay sprawled out and unconscious, on roughly-woven rush mats. The elders had stripped each of them to the waist and were wiping them down with oils infused with tréviljèa jönipetriné petals. Slowly but surely, each of them regained consciousness, but remained drowsy, groggy, and extremely confused.

Elva rushed to Finwe's side as his eyes fluttered open. He was quite bewildered as she hugged him tightly to her, and even more so when he realised that tears were freely rolling down her cheeks.

Having been redressed by the elders and left to rest, Annie awoke to find a dozen elven youngling faces looking down on her and grinning.

"Lilyfire?" she croaked and promptly burst into floods of tears. She erupted into a howl like a mortally wounded animal. "I'm sorry. I'm sorry. I'm so, so sorry!"

Woozily leaping to his feet, Finwe staggered over to her. Younglings scattered hither and thither, to avoid being squashed as he landed heavily, and with minimal control, beside Annie. Without hesitation, he put his arms around her and held her tightly to his bare chest. Annie was too distraught to argue and was simply grateful to have someone ease her emotional pain.

"It is all right, Annie," he murmured into her hair. "We all know that you did your very best. No one could have done more. You have absolutely nothing to be sorry for."

Elva was making her way over to Annie to further console and reassure her, but then abruptly stopped in her tracks. As she watched Finwe with Annie, it suddenly all became absolutely crystal clear.

Lucan loves Varis, she thought. *Varis loves Lucan. Annie loves Carric. And Finwe? Finwe... loves... Annie.*

Her heart painfully ached for her brother.

Chapter Twenty-One

Upon the suns' rise of the following morning, once the companions had recovered from either their stupor, or, in Elva's case, from turning herself inside out on the böccék nhây mixture, the villagers insisted on having an impromptu celebration banquet for the heroes of the Sun Elven and Woodland Realms.

No one cared that it was occurring at breakfast time.

Since the realms were yet to recover, the banquet was a very modest affair, and positively pauper-ish, by palace standards. In fact, it was more of a pauper's potluck buffet, but it meant so much more to the companions than any lavish palace affair. *This* banquet was heartfelt, unpretentious, free of politics, generous, and involved the whole community — even Alberic, who was still steaming drunk.

For the past few weeks, the villagers had been enjoying blue skies and warm days that were typical of the season. As their saying went, the weather had been "hot enough to poach a hlöcce on the flat rock in the square". It, therefore, surprised them to find that the morning brought with it a stiff and chilly breeze, heavy dark clouds, and drizzle. It was, of course, an expression and reflection of Annie's mood, and she was too drained from the combination of the ship-lifting, and the run-in with the moertemakana, to do a thing about it.

Undeterred by the unusually inclement weather, the villagers simply took the banquet, to be shared by all, into Meara's inn. Conditions were extremely cramped, but spirits were extremely high. Ordinarily, such high spirits would have been infectious and infused the most sullen of folk to have at least a modicum of joy. The truth was that Annie felt utter self-loathing and didn't feel she deserved to feel any positive emotion at all.

That all these generous and trusting Woodland Elves were giving her what little they had to eat, in gratitude and the belief that, before much longer, the impact of the Labradorite Amulet would reach them, made her feel utterly wretched. What she was doing for the love of one elf filled her with self-contempt, but she felt helpless to do otherwise. She had to choke her food down — what little food she managed to put in her mouth.

All this, coupled with the younglings constantly reminding her of Lilyfire, meant Annie found herself perpetually on the very brink of tears or screaming, or both. Pretending that she was full of joy and hope was too exhausting. She had strategically placed herself in a far corner with her elven friends either side of her to act as a kind of "joy buffer".

For Annie, leaving the village couldn't happen soon enough and she was hugely indebted to Lucan when he announced that it was time for them to move on.

As they left the village, surrounded by the younglings for the first mile or so, Elva, Finwe, Varis, and even Lucan formed a sort of elven cocoon around Annie, and engaged with the younglings so that she didn't have to.

It kept drizzling until the younglings were left far behind at the outskirts of their village and the Crystal Caves stood before them.

<><><><><><><><>

Looking at the entrance to the Crystal Caves, Annie appreciated just how raw and unskilled her magic had been when she was last here. Black sand radiated out from the ragged, gaping mouth to the caves and covered everything for a half a mile or maybe even more. Scattered among the sand were shards of crystals that had been shattered by the blast that Annie had generated when they last came this way. Tiny slivers of every colour of the rainbow twinkled from every surface.

It's funny how something that looks so innocently pretty could be so very lethal, she thought. Before she had unleashed her magic, all this black sand and these crystals had been inside caves.

"A word of warning," Varis said as they trudged through the shin-deep sand and into the first cave. "Following the seismic explosion, care of our Annie here, the crystals and overall structure of these caves will probably be even more unstable than when we first encountered them."

"Excellent," bit Annie, sarcastically.

"It is most definitely not excellent," sniped Lucan.

Annie rolled her eyes. As time went on, she felt sure that Lucan would never be able to loosen his virtual straightjacket.

"I know it isn't," Annie sighed.

"I think," Varis loudly whispered to Lucan, "that she is expressing some sort of human humour."

"You mean that by saying excellent, she in fact meant quite the opposite?" Lucan replied.

"Now you're getting it," Annie said, patting his upper arm while in her other hand, creating a palm light to illuminate their way. She had none of the apprehension that she'd experienced the first time she had been down here. She had survived these caves before and, with regard to her magical powers, she had become far more proficient, and had significantly expanded her repertoire. This time she wouldn't need to coax the crystals to light their way — assuming that there were any crystals left since their last visit. No, this time, she would effortlessly light the whole way herself.

Her palm light revealed the light-absorbing, black sand floor densely punctuated by the remains of exploded stalactites that had rained down from the ceiling. Surprisingly, the ceiling was festooned with the beginnings of fresh stalactites of every colour imaginable, and some colours never before seen by human eyes. Although she was very well aware that this place was, at the very least, inhospitable, Annie couldn't help but marvel at its beauty and astonishing rate of recovery. Varis broke her moment of awe and wonder, with a warning.

"Remember also, that we must tread lightly. We do not want to attract the attention of Ravbition Worms again."

The others shivered, recalling their last encounter. Remembering Finwe's nifty dispatch of the Ravbition Worms, Elva readied her Naur mál powder, that was ordinarily used to make fire in fire-reticent places. She passed some to her brother for him to dip his arrowheads into. With Annie and her palm light leading the way, everyone walked as softly and as silently as they could.

Unlike the others, Annie felt confident that they wouldn't experience any plummeting crystals. Last time, Shadow Elves had caused the crystals to lose their power and rain down on them. Since Tathlyn wanted the Labradorite Amulet, she was confident that he wouldn't be instructing his elves to hinder or cease their progress. Of course the others knew no such thing and kept furtively glancing upward.

Before long, they had re-entered the main cavern with its plum-purple sandy floor. The rapid self-repair within the caves meant that, once more, thousands of jagged crystals of all shapes, sizes, colours, and infused with light, covered the walls and ceilings of the cathedral-sized cave. The lights created a kaleidoscope of patterns that cast across everything they touched, including the elves and Annie. Annie put out her palm light.

Their previous attempt to make camp in this crystal cathedral had been abruptly cut short by, not only the plummeting crystals, but also the arrival of Ravbition Worms.

After a brief discussion, it was agreed that, rather than make a second attempt of making camp here, they would push on and make camp once they were out the other side of the caves. They would rather take their chances against potential posses of Shadow Elves and the biting cold, than be sliced, and spliced by stalactites, or ripped asunder by the thirty-two-foot, lime-green, faceless worms with their gaping mouths housing row upon row of serrated teeth.

Once on the other side of the largest cavern, everything was pitch-black. No one noticed that there was more than one tunnel leading away from the huge cavern. No one, that is, except Annie's golden fleck, which darted and zigzagged in an attempt to gain her attention. Sadly, Annie paid it no heed, assuming the jittering was all about the anticipated discomfort of being in a dark, enclosed space. After just a few steps into the tunnel they thought was *the only* tunnel, Annie lit her palm light once more and, slowing her breathing to quell any hint of claustrophobia, she forged ahead.

The others followed.

Everyone was so focused on getting out of these narrow tunnels to make camp above ground, that no one noticed the change in the floor from the deep, gritty sand to a wetter, stickier, blancmange pudding sort of texture. Just ahead was something emitting an ultra-violet glow from the ceiling. On closer inspection, it turned out to be several glowing, fleshy tubes that lazily and rhythmically, curled, and unfurled.

"What are they?" Annie asked, quite mesmerised by their hypnotic movement. Elva could see them over Annie's head and was similarly fascinated.

"I do not know," Elva confessed. "But, in their own way, they are quite beautiful."

As Varis now saw the glowing tubes, his reaction was radically different to that of Annie and Elva.

"Stop," Varis hissed loudly. "Those are Ravbition Worm wormlets."

"Really?" Annie asked, her hand following the sway of the wormlets. "But, like Elva says, they are so surprisingly beautiful. What are they doing here?"

"I do not know," Varis replied, his whisper imploring Annie to leave them well alone. "At such an early stage in their infancy, they should be feeding from their mother, by latching on to the roof of her mouth cavity."

With a herculean effort, Annie's fleck performed every shape and shift it could muster to shake her out of her mesmerised state, and firmly grab her attention.

Thankfully, it worked.

"Oh my god," she mouthed.

Her hand recoiled and she turned to face the others. Varis's face showed her that he was thinking the exact same thing.

"Slowly and steadily go back the way we came," he hissed. "We are in their mother's mouth."

But it was too late. The mother had felt the presence of this unwitting snack and had, for the last few moments, been creating a ripple in her muscles from the tip of her tail, some thirty feet away, that would culminate in a projection of highly acidic bile to immobilise her prey before macerating it with her rows of serrated teeth.

Feeling the gathering tsunami of rippling muscle heading their way, Varis changed his hissed order to the shout of,

"Run!"

With Annie at the back of their line now, those at the front couldn't see a thing and were ricocheting off the sides of the Ravbition Worm mother's mouth, and then latterly, the sides of the tunnel. This was slowing them down and Annie was getting a whiff of the acidic bile as it progressed up the mother's body towards her. To speed up their progress down the one-elf-wide tunnel towards the crystal cathedral, she threw her palm light over the others' heads so that it was once more at the front and lighting the way.

A moment later the acidic bile was launched from the mother's mouth and spattered where Annie's feet had been, less than half a moment before. It caused the sandy floor to bubble, fizz, and hiss.

Frustrated that its prey was still getting away, the mother shut its gaping mouth and pursued its potential meal by propelling itself forward through muscular contractions up the length of its body. The muscular contractions quickly got into an impressively coordinated rhythm that enabled it to move at a surprisingly fast pace.

Soon Lucan, now at the front of the line, could see the light from the crystals through the archway to the huge cavern. Annie's fleck, now having her undivided attention, suddenly and violently jabbed to the left of her eye. Heeding its instruction, she yelled,

"Turn left!"

"There is no left," Lucan shouted over his shoulder.

"Do it anyway," yelled Varis.

And just then, Annie's palm light revealed to Lucan a partially hidden tunnel entrance to the left. Needing no further prompting, the palm light and Lucan, followed by Finwe, Varis, Elva, and Annie all darted into it. This tunnel was narrower than the previous one and afforded them more time to create greater distance between them, and the mother Ravbition Worm. The huge worm was only slowed down by the necessity to rearrange the cells in her body and to reconfigure them to create a much longer, slimmer Ravbition Worm, enabling her to continue the pursuit of her irksome prey.

From the back of their line, Annie continued to relay directions that were given to her by her golden fleck. Had there been far more time and far less urgency, it would have been an interesting facet of her magical development that would have been interesting to explore. Annie made a mental note to pursue this at another time, and upped her speed to avoid yet another projectile-spewing of the acidic bile.

After yet another narrowing of the tunnels forced the mother to stop again and once more rearrange her cells, the palm light, elves, and human all burst out of their confined space and into the open night sky. Never had they been more glad to see the stars, even if it did mean that they were now in the Shadow Realm.

Not wanting to risk the Ravbition Worm getting out from the system of tunnels, Annie smartly turned about-face and laid her hands on the rock just inside the tunnel's narrowed entrance. As she was gaining mastery of her powers, she quickly placed all her intention into the rock. The lava of magic inside her belly instantly boiled on command and she directed it out through her hands.

At first, the only thing that seemed to be happening was the sounds and vibrations of the Ravbition Worm getting closer, and closer. Annie forced herself to pay this no attention and remained one hundred percent focused on the task in hand. The mother came closer still and the others readied their various forms of weaponry. They needn't have bothered for, just then, there were rumbling and cracking sounds from within the tunnel that crescendoed from the sound of a mouse to the roar of a whole pride of angry lions. As the crescendoing peaked, the sides and roof of the tunnel caved in, sealing off the entrance. When the sounds of the falling rock had subsided, Annie placed her head against the blocked entrance. Straining her ear, she could hear the sounds of a hugely frustrated Ravbition Worm, retreating into the distance.

She turned back to her friends and found a mixed response to her spontaneous, and extreme hard landscaping. Elva and Finwe congratulated her on her quick thinking and decisive action. Varis was less enthusiastic and Lucan was out-and-out annoyed.

"You do realise that you have blocked the only protected route back home to our realms, do you not?"

"Protected?" Annie exclaimed. "So you're saying navigating through potentially lethal crystals and killer Rabbit Worms, or whatever the héllè you call them, was the *protected* route?"

"They are called *Ravbition* Worms, and yes," Lucan persisted. "Now we will have to make our return journey by traversing over land and across the terrain of the Kàdàvérsité Region."

"And is that bad?" Annie asked while starting to feel a little contrite.

"Yes," said Lucan and Varis, both forcefully and together. There hung several, uncomfortable moments of an awkward silence before Varis spoke again.

"And what is done is done. We must head on with our mission and navigate the Kàdàvérsité Region when we come to it, with Carric in our midst."

At the sound of the name Carric, Finwe dropped to his knee with his head down, "busying" himself with something that really didn't matter. Without Finwe knowing that she knew what he was doing, Elva moved to stand before him so as to assist with the masking his feelings.

Chapter Twenty-Two

It turned out that Lucan hadn't been the least bit exaggerating when he'd said the night air in the Shadow Realm dessert would be bitterly cold. If anything, his description had been conservative. Although Annie had gained plenty of experience sleeping out rough, this wind's chill factor brought the term 'bitterly cold' to a whole new level. Hunkering down in front of one of the larger sand-smoothed rocks that sat in the sand close to where the cave's entrance used to be, only served to make things marginally better.

Digging into their satchels, each one of the group brought out a ration of raw narmo meat. Since Elva, wisely, didn't want to waste any of her naur mál powder to start a fire in this barren place merely for the extravagant purpose of cooking, everyone had to eat their narmo in its raw state. Even in her time as a homeless teen, Annie had never had to resort to such a 'meal', but she appreciated Elva's stance on the matter, closed her eyes, and tucked into the slimy chunk of meat. Surely nothing could be as bad as the raw fish they'd had in Glasgow. To her surprise, after combating the initial gag reflex, it actually wasn't so bad — definitely nowhere near good — but, not so bad.

In addition to this, and really a more pressing reason to not light a fire, was the need to not draw the attention of any Shadow Elves posses that might be within thirty miles of where they were. Their current location was completely different to the woods where they had lit small fires before. Here, in such an area of flat, uninterrupted terrain and dense darkness, where even the light of the moons was dimmed, a fire would attract all manner of unsolicited and undesirable attention.

Just when I thought it couldn't get any colder, Annie thought as her teeth started to chatter, *it gets colder. Fabulous!*

To preserve themselves from the inevitable and potentially lethal further drop in temperature, Lucan instructed everyone to huddle up together. And so it was that Annie found herself tightly snuggled between Varis and Elva, with Lucan, and Finwe taking the outer positions. They had draped every cape over themselves, to even cover their heads, and Lucan, and Finwe had worked to scoop up sand over them all, making them all into one sandy hillock. Varis had assured everyone that being semi-buried under the sand would give them extra insulation from the cold.

Once they had settled down, and much to the bemusement of the others, Annie valiantly tried to stifle a fit of the giggles, and failed. She kept thinking of how similar they were to "pigs in blankets" at a traditional English Christmas dinner, and the arctic penguins from the nature programmes she had seen. She simply couldn't get the mental visions of jumper-wearing Antarctic penguins sitting down to dinner, out of her mind. When she tried to explain, and Elva couldn't quite believe that there were birds that couldn't fly, Lucan put a stop to the frivolity by reminding them that they all needed to rest up, as the hardest part of their mission was yet to come.

This instantly sobered Annie up. With everything that had gone on in the caves, the tunnels, and with the wormlets, and the Ravbition Worm mother, she had virtually erased any thought of the skulduggery and deception that was her own, personal mission.

<><><><><><><><><>

Just as the suns began their slow ascent to peep above the horizon, the companions were gently nudged awake by intense snuffling and bearlike grunting from directly above them. Flipping the capes from her head and opening one bleary eye, Annie came face to face with — a nostril. It was a huge, cavernous, hairy nostril that, had it breathed in any harder, could have sniffed Annie's head right up inside it. Suddenly, all five friends were wide awake. As she was wedged in the centre, Annie couldn't move at all until the others did. As a result, she spent more moments than she cared to, looking up into the nostril and praying that it didn't need to sneeze.

Once everyone was on their feet, they saw that a small herd of huge, lumbering beasts, roughly the size of the Human Realm rhinoceros, were feeding on and around where they had been sleeping.

"What the héllè are those?" Annie asked, slowly backing away, with her eyes unwaveringly fixed on them. As she had come to expect, Varis — their elven version of a portable encyclopaedia — had the answer.

"Those," he said casually, as though this was nothing at all to get riled up about. "Are probos sand-eaters. They are not to be feared. They literally eat sand and nothing else."

Annie was still feeling somewhat flustered.

"There is literally sand everywhere, as far as the eye can see, in all directions," she said, squeaking a little. "Why do they want to eat *our* sand? The particular mound of sand that was on top of us."

"Ah well," he explained, like some enthusiastic and thoroughly absorbed professor teaching his favourite topic in a physics lecture of less than half-interested students, "you will notice the sand of this desert is a rich, deep purple. However, this is not the sand that the probos like to eat. They are very much more partial to the green sand that is several incrons below the surface."

"So mine and Finwe's digging last night must have brought their favourite meal to the surface," Lucan supposed.

"Indeed it did," said Varis with a relish that suggested he had a large soft spot for these creatures. "It is not the sand itself that is green, but rather, the microbial tardigroans that live among it. It is what makes this sand far more nutritious for them." Varis was really getting into his encyclopaedic groove now. "They have rough, leathery, mottled skin underneath their shaggy, green coat. Of course their coat is green because of their diet. Their hair is long and double layered so as to keep them cool in the scorching sun, and warm in the freezing night."

"Thanks for the nature talk, Varis," puffed Annie as she wrestled to retrieve her green, sand-covered jacket from the soft, wide mouth of one of the small, possibly infant, probos. While it was smaller than her, its soft, wide, and toothless mouth had a surprisingly firm, and stubborn grip.

I can't have you digesting the Labradorite Amulet, she thought, shaking her jacket to release more green sand for the little fella to munch on, which it did with enthusiasm.

"Their particularly large pupils are well adapted for seeing in the dark, which is when they tend to eat. A third eyelid acts as a protective visor, protecting their large pupils from the light of the suns and the sunlight that reflects off the sand."

"Are they dangerous?" asked Annie, not wanting to turn her back to any of the herd, just in case they turned out to have the unpredictable moodiness of the Human Realm hippos. She didn't see Lucan rolling his eyes at the encouragement for Varis to continue with his impromptu wildlife lesson.

"Oh no," he answered, offering handfuls of green sand to what looked like the eldest member of the herd and stroking the hair on the bridge of her nose. "They are extremely gentle and community minded, with the matriarch leading from the rear of the herd. And before you ask, no, they are not hunted as their hide is too tough for any elven weapons."

Lucan had reached the end of his patience. Ordinarily, he loved Varis's tendency to become lost in the fascination for the world around him, but this moment wasn't a good time. Their mission had to take priority.

"We really do need to move on," he said throwing his satchel across his chest and setting out across the soft, yielding sand. But Varis didn't move and, instead, called after him.

"We could go by foot, or we could ride these probos." Lucan stopped in his tracks and turned back to Varis.

"Why would we choose to ride these lumbering beasts when we can be fleet of foot?"

"Because," Varis answered with barely disguised triumph on his face. "While these beasts may not be as fleet of foot as an elf over short distances, they have far more stamina across the soft sands and unforgiving heat of this desert."

Lucan tried to look irritated by Varis, but couldn't sustain it. Within moments, his frown had turned into a broad smile. Annie couldn't help thinking that it would be better if Lucan smiled more.

A smile really does suit him, she thought.

Then another thought struck her. *I struggled enough with a trained and patient horse. How am I going to cope with a wild, shaggy beast, gentle temperament or not?*

It was as if Eva had divined Annie's apprehension.

"Well, I am in favour of the faster mode of transport across this energy-sapping sand," she said. "It will conserve our energies, and Annie can share a probos with me."

Finwe looked irritated with Elva, but said nothing. Annie offered a silent thank you to whatever gods the elves may have prayed to, and followed Elva to select a suitable and willing probos for them both to ride.

Within a few minutes, the herd set out across the purple desert at an impressively brisk pace for such non-aerodynamic beasts, with the elves and Annie astride four of them. Annie was surprised at how much she felt like she was sitting in a comfortable, well-worn armchair.

None of them noticed the large raptor-type bird that lazily circled high above them.

It had no eyes.

Chapter Twenty-Three

From his circling vantage point of more than ten thousand feet in the air, Tathlyn closely observed, with interest, the four elves and one human. He watched through the unseeing eye sockets of his Surrönto eagle.

Tathlyn had seized the eagle and, despite all its efforts to resist, had wrenched it from the confines of its cage. Tathlyn needed a bird's-eye view — literally.

Taking his sharp paring knife from the pocket in the folds of his cloak, he had skilfully whipped out each of the bird's eyes and plopped them into a smoking mortar that contained a brewing potion he had created earlier. The eagle was screaming with fear and pain, and was thrashing its wings in a vain attempt to get free of Tathlyn's firm grasp.

Ignoring the poor bird's commotion, Tathlyn almost casually scooped up each potion-infused eyeball and popped them in his mouth. As he bit down and swallowed each orb, the eagle instantly became eerily silent, and still. Tathlyn's head unnaturally jerked back and, when he brought his face back down to be eye-to-eye-socket with the bird, he could see his own face.

But not just his own face. Looking up, he could also clearly see a tiny woodlouse crawling on the wall the equivalent height of ten stories above him. Everything was magnified, all colours were dazzlingly bright, and he could see many more shades of colour than he had ever done with his own Shadow Elf eyes.

One of Tathlyn's minions quietly and gingerly approached him, and, barely daring to lay a fingertip upon him, guided him to sit upon his throne. Another minion, with equally extreme caution, took the huge bird, climbed up to the window, and let it loose into the sky. Immediately, the apex predator unfurled its nine foot wing span and propelled itself high above the tortured treetops, and much farther out over to the Shadow Realm's purple desert.

Having digested its eyes infused with dark magic, Tathlyn saw on its behalf and guided the eagle upward and outward, in search of Annie.

<><><><><><><><>

Tathlyn eagerly leaned forward in his seat as he spotted a herd of probos sand-eaters, not typically casually grazing, but moving with intent across the sand. Although the eagle was at the altitude of several thousand feet and some twenty-five miles from the herd, Tathlyn could clearly see every detail of the elves and the human that were riding some of the probos. By riding the hairy, sand-eating beasts, they were making impressively good progress.

Tathlyn was about to regurgitate the eagle's eyes, thus releasing the bird to fly free, when he noticed the expression on the male Woodland Elf's face, and also to whom his expression was directed. The Shadow Elf king could see that this strong, bronzed Woodland Elf was in love.

And whom is he in love with? he thought. *The female Woodland Elf in front of him? No, wait. He is in love with... Annie.*

Tathlyn recognised the depth and intensity of this elf's stare because he knew he had worn the very same expression himself when the human, Meredith, had resided in his realm.

For Tathlyn this wouldn't do.

It wouldn't do at all.

It looked like Annie was oblivious, but he couldn't afford for this elf to come between Annie and Carric. He needed Annie to remain besotted with Carric, in order to ensure that she brought the Labradorite Amulet to him. He had to inject some extra emotional motivation into this blasted human, just to make sure.

Tathlyn had the mortar brought to him and, dipping his fingers into the darkly enchanted liquid within, he coated his tongue with more of the eagle's essence.

Effortlessly, the eagle folded back its wings and dove towards the ground at a speed exceeding one hundred-and-sixty-eight miles per hour. Within seconds, the bird was flying around the companions' heads, squawking loudly. The probos were initially a little spooked, but the wise old matriarch gruffed and huffed, and soon had them settled back into a steady, light-footed jog.

"What does this Surrönto eagle think it is doing?" Lucan called to Varis.

Such behaviour was generally unheard of. The probos instinctively closed ranks around the youngsters and increased their speed in tight formation.

"Perhaps it is trying to whisk away one of the pups," suggested Varis. "But making off with such a quarry would be fruitless, since the eagle's beak and talons could never pierce the skin. Surely instinctive knowledge passed down through generations would mean he knows that."

Annie knew exactly why the eagle was flying so low around them, but she wasn't going to tell anyone else. Evidently, the others only heard squawking. Annie, however, heard the squawking that quickly transform into the voice of Tathlyn.

"What do you want?" she asked with her mind.

"Nothing very much," the Tathlyn-bird mused. "I just wanted to make sure you were still motivated to honour our deal."

Annie was incensed.

"How dare you use the word honour. You have no right to have it in your vocabulary or utter it from your mean, thin, twisted lips... beak... I mean mouth," her inner voice hissed. The bird laughed cruelly.

"I am really not sure that you have a right to such a word either," he retorted. Annie's golden fleck recoiled at the unsavoury truth in what Tathlyn had said. "Just remember," he continued, "that your friends are only alive because they are inadvertently helping to deliver the Labradorite Amulet and you to me."

Something sparked in Annie's mind.

"*The amulet and me?*" she quizzed. "*What do you mean by, "and me"? Do you mean I am also part of your dastardly plans? As well as the amulet?*"

But Tathlyn made no answer. He ignored her questions and simply carried on as if she had said nothing at all.

"I have someone here that you may like to speak with," he said, as casually as a host might introduce two unacquainted guests at a polite society soiree.

There was a pause. The next voice she heard was Carric. Tathlyn had instructed a minion to coat Carric's tongue with some of the liquid from the mortar.

"Annie?" Carric's voice was thin and reedy. "Annie, can you... can you hear me?"

Annie's reflexes upon hearing her love's pained voice meant that she surprised Elva by giving her a sudden, jerking squeeze around her waist. In addition to this, the air temperature around the two of them dropped by a few degrees, causing the exhales of the probos and their riders to form billowing puffs of water vapour.

"*Carric, Carric is it really you?*" she asked, not quite daring to believe that she was really communicating with him directly, rather than hearing him speak through a mere illusion.

"Yes, yes, my love. It is... me." Carric sounded weak and exhausted. "Turn back. Do not put yourself... or the realms at risk... just for me —"

"No. No!" Annie insisted. "I'm not leaving you in the clutches of that schteelcün!"

"But... you must, my... love," Carric urged. "I do not... know how much longer... I can survive the... torture. Death would be... a blessed... relief."

"What? No!" she screamed within her head. "We're not far away now. Hang on. Please hang on for me. I love you."

"Annie, I... love you," he said earnestly. But then his whole demeanour changed. He had become afraid and desperate. "Annie, I... what? No... please no! Not the molten lava spear again! No... no... please... no... argh!"

And with that, Carric was gone.

Annie squeezed Elva even harder and buried her head into Elva's back.

"What is it, Annie? What is wrong?" Elva asked while using one hand to slacken off Annie's vicelike grip a little.

Annie kept her head buried.

"I guess I'm just getting impatient and anxious about rescuing Carric."

Elva understood but, at the same time, felt so sorry and sad for her brother. Finwe deserved to be happy. Finwe was wonderful. She'd never liked Carric as an elf and her brother was worth at least a hundred of him. She also thought that Annie deserved better than the Sun Elven Prince. She had always had an uneasy feeling about how Carric was with Annie. She hadn't trusted him, one icron.

As abruptly as it had started, the eagle ceased its incessant squawking and, with a sweep of its magnificent, sliver-tipped wings, it swept back up high into the sky, and away in the direction of the Crystal Caves.

<><><><><><><><>

Tathlyn tightly gripped his stomach and generated strong, rhythmic convulsions from deep within. Moments later, the macerated eyeballs of the eagle were on the cold stone floor. With his energies depleted from mustering so much of the dark magic, Tathlyn slumped in his throne and was assisted over to his bed to rest, and recuperate.

At the moment that Tathyln had vomited, the Surrönto eagle had been released from the Shadow Elves king's clutches. While the eyeless bird was vulnerable, and acquiring food would be challenging, it was nonetheless overjoyed to be free. Soaring higher and higher to catch the warm thermals, the bird was soon a mere speck in the sky.

Chapter Twenty-Four

By the time the two suns were starting their descent into the horizon, the probos sand-eaters had successfully delivered their passengers to the edge of the Shadow Realm forest. The almost impenetrable tapestry of tall, brittle trees interwoven with thick, lifeless vines that were covered in barbed thorns, was no place for the probos.

Before the sand-eaters headed back out into the desert, they each fondly nuzzled each of the group of friends. Even Lucan, who, despite projecting a starchy façade, clearly enjoyed the contact and connection, gave the probos he had ridden an extra rub of its leathery nose with the back of his hand.

As with the rescue of Annie from Tathlyn's tower before, Lucan and Varis set about using their hefty swords to cut down thick, dead vines, and forge something of a pathway through the densely packed, dark, brittle-barked trees with their frail, contorted, sharp-ended branches. Just as Annie remembered, the ground was a pale putty-cum-phlegm colour. It felt soft and yielding under foot. The rise and fall of the wind rattling through the dry leaves, as they clung to twigs and branches, brought with it the scurrying of small creatures, and the gunshot snaps of branches under the feet of much larger animals. Annie was too focused to notice even the occasional terrified death screams of distant, cornered prey.

The suns had disappeared now and all that remained of them was the flicker of burnt umber and sienna kissing the edge of the horizon. Farther away, some thirty miles ahead of them, the light-consuming black tower, Tathlyn's strong keep, was silhouetted against the emerging star-studded night sky.

"Our progress through these dense thickets is too slow and draining for us to be able to wage a successful assault on Tathlyn's tower tonight," Lucan announced. "We must not alert the Shadow Elves to our presence with a campfire, so we shall have to bed down as we did last night, but with dried leaves mounded upon us instead of sand."

Having heard Carric being tortured made this news unbearable for Annie.

"But we've got to get Carric right now," she blurted out. "He's in that tower being brutally tortured. He's battered, bruised, and bleeding. His resolve and strength are almost nonexistent. I don't know if he can survive another night, another moment even."

Her tone was pleading now and the others simply stood, and looked at her, each with different thoughts and feelings coursing through them.

Finwe was not proud about the extent of his jealousy towards his friend Carric. It was eating into him, but, nevertheless, he couldn't deny that it was there. Elva was torn between the compassion she felt for Annie and that which she had for her brother. Varis was experiencing fatherly concern for Annie. But, once again, Lucan was crudely prodded by suspicion.

"You seem extremely knowledgeable and clear on the specific details around what Prince Carric has been, and is currently, experiencing," he said coldly, and with more than a pinch of accusation. "Why and how is that?"

Before replying, Annie looked to each of the other three to garner their tacit support. Finally she looked at her accuser and hoped that her fleck wasn't squirming too much to give her away.

"I don't know *exactly* what Carric is going through," she replied. Gaining confidence, which she perhaps didn't deserve, she decided that attack was often the best form of defence. She stubbornly jutted out her chin before continuing. "I'm just *guessing* what's happening to him. After all, I have been held in Tathlyn's tower myself, so I have a fair idea and... and it's driving me crazy."

To Annie's surprise and Elva's distress, Finwe stepped in, putting a hand on Annie's shoulder and looked hard, and square, at Lucan.

"I think that, rather than turning suspicions and vitriol on to Annie, you should save it for Tathlyn and his elves. She clearly loves Carric."

Elva could feel how painfully difficult it was for Finwe to say those last words and, while she couldn't do anything about it, she wished she could ease his emotional pain somehow. Closing his eyes, he took a swift breath in, opened his eyes, and continued.

"And when you love someone that much, you can feel their pain, though you be many leagues apart, and you would jump through Hüelgar's fire to save them, if that is what it took." Finwe then took a further, menacing step into Lucan's personal space and finished with, "Or have you forgotten *your* love for Varis?"

There was a extremely tense and pregnant pause, where everyone held their breath. The tight band of heartache continued to grip Elva's chest as her outpouring of silent compassion flowed towards Finwe.

Damn you, Carric, she thought. *Damn you to brùkling héllè.*

Varis was about to speak up in an effort to dissipate the tension, when Lucan spoke instead:

"You are right, Finwe," he said. Only then did Varis, Elva, and Annie breathed out an audible sigh of relief. "I should not have distrusted Annie's words for anything more than the tortured imaginings of someone who is in love."

He looked to Varis, his features softening. Returning his look, Varis gave him a nod to say, "I love you too. Now make it right with Annie." Now it was Lucan's turn to sigh as he moved to face Annie.

"I apologise, Annie. I should not have doubted you."

Annie couldn't restrain her fleck from squirming.

Oh yes you should, she thought ruefully. *You should all be doing much more than doubting me.*

<><><><><><><><>

Although they had no fire to attract the enemy, it was decided that they should still take shifts to keep watch throughout the night. No fire meant no stew into which Annie could work her magic to improve their night vision. They would have to rely on their wits.

Elva and Finwe took the first shift, while Lucan, Annie, and Varis hunkered down under a heap of cloaks and dried leaves. The twins sat leaning against each other, back to back. Elva wanted to let Finwe know that she could see how he felt about Annie, that she understood, and that she was there for him, no matter what. She just had no idea as to how one should go about starting up a conversation like that.

It turned out she didn't need to.

While Elva was repeatedly, mentally sidled up to starting the conversation, only to about-face and sidle away again, Finwe simply cut to the chase.

"I know your heart aches desperately for my heart's sorry situation. I know you are there for me, no matter what," he said out of the blue, while still keeping his eyes scanning for possible attackers.

Elva gave herself a knowing smile. How could she have forgotten about all those times when one of them simply knew what the other was thinking or feeling without having to see each other, or utter a single word. She reached a hand round behind her. She found Finwe's open hand, clasped it, and firmly squeezed it.

Nothing more needed to be said.

Chapter Twenty-Five

After a surprisingly uneventful night, Lucan and Varis woke the others at the merest hint of first light. When Varis commented on how the lack of nearby Shadow Elf patrols had served to unnerve him, it was Lucan who presented an uncharacteristically positive mindset, saying,

"Come now, Varis. Let us not look a gift närg in the snoot."

Not wanting to give the game away that she may know exactly why there had been no patrols, Annie busied herself with flattening the pile of leaves to erase any evidence that they had been there, and kept her head down.

After another unsatisfactory breakfast of yet more raw narmo meat, they set out once more. Annie admitted to the others that the more times one had to consume the slithery, tough flesh, did nothing to render it more palatable. This assertion was met with resounding agreement from them all, that came to an abrupt halt when Lucan caught sight of a posse of Shadow Elves, a quarter of a mile to their right. Without absolute clarity that was so typical of him, he indicated with a hand signal, that they were all to shut up — immediately.

They were too far apart to lay hands on Annie and be "disappeared". Instead, they all stood perfectly still, their hands resting on their weapons, and all hoping that they would blend in with the vegetation around them. The posse of Shadow Elves sauntered closer, clearly not taking their patrol duties particularly seriously.

Tathlyn would have your heads for such a laid-back attitude, Lucan thought. *And I cannot say that I would blame him.*

They were only a dozen or so strides away when the lead elf made a sharp turn to the left and the others followed suit. They were now moving in parallel to where Annie and her friends stood, and still, none of her group moved a muscle.

As the last Shadow Elf passed Annie, he looked directly at her across the space that lay between them. Annie fought to swallow a gasp as the elf's face morphed into a slyly grinning Tathlyn for a just split second, before he turned his head away, and continued marching past.

"We cannot have your friends growing too suspicious about the lack of my elven patrols," he said in her head. "And you have yet to find out what I have in store for them."

"*What? What do you mean by that?*" she demanded inside her head, but Tathyln's presence was only fleeting and he had spirited himself away before she had got her questions out — not that he would have answered them anyway.

Annie hoped to grüla that no one had noticed that one of the Shadow Elves had seen and directly stared at her. When Lucan gave the signal that they could move once more, she furtively looked at the others and was relieved to find that no one seemed to have noticed a thing.

<><><><><><><><>

The companions' subsequent progress was unimpeded by other Shadow Elf patrols and, while Finwe and Varis felt encouraged by this, Lucan and Elva started to feel distinct, and growing, pangs of unease. In less than two and a half hours, they had reached the outer curtain wall that circled Tathlyn's tower, some sixty elven strides from its base. This wall was as thick as Varis was tall, with gnarled, limpet-like hard shells covering every inch.

The suns were at the peak of their arc and yet, their rays struggled to breech the shrouding, forever-near-dusk and cloud of dense, blue-tinted dullness. This was good, as at this time of day, the eyesight of the Shadow Elves would be slightly surpassed by that of the Sun and Woodland Elves.

They were so tantalisingly close now. Internally, Annie was being roughly torn this way and that by intensely conflicting emotions. Excitement was countered by guilt. Hope was countered by fear. She was forced to consciously keep her belly of magical lava in check, and it was hard work.

Just focus on each 'now', she told herself. *Deal with each moment of now, one... at... a... time.*

She was so engrossed in her self-control that she very nearly leapt out of her skin when Elva placed a supportive hand on her shoulder and whispered in her ear,

"You have got this, Annie. You can easily calm your magical energy," she asserted. "It is quite natural to have conflicting emotions."

If only you knew the truth of it, Annie thought, feeling even worse due to Elva's show of kindness.

At her other side, Lucan's sharp whisper cut through her introspection. Some time earlier, his unusual optimism had been exchanged for his more characteristic scepticism.

"Is it far, *far* too quiet," he complained, his eyebrows knitting tightly together. "Where are the Shadow Elves? Why are they not patrolling? This area inside the wall should be crawling with diligent lookouts, and yet I can see no one."

Varis, Finwe, and Elva were of the same mind. Tathlyn's threatening words from earlier rang loudly in Annie's ears:

"And you have yet to find out what I have in store for them."

She had the awful foreboding feeling that she was about to find out exactly what he meant by it.

It was decided, by Lucan that, like it or not, they could not stay put indefinitely. They had to make a move, and the light now would be better than the lack of light later. Elva and Finwe provided cover as Lucan, Annie, and Varis climbed across the impressively thick wall, and took cover behind a large supporting buttress. They in turn provided cover so that within moments, all five of them were within the first boundary.

Still, there was no movement or sign of any Shadow Elves.

But, moments later, countless fire-tipped arrows rained upon them and landed less than an inch away from them in an arc. Instinctively, Annie knew that these arrows hadn't hit their mark because her comrades were all so close to her. The Shadow Elves dared not risk harming a single atom of her.

I can use this, she thought.

"Stay really close to me," she ordered. "Your best chance of surviving is if you stay close to me, and stay behind me."

The situation didn't really allow for further discussion, so the elves did as she said. Crouching uncomfortably low for their long limbs, the four of them used Annie, with her borrowed cloak spread wide from open arms, as their human shield. Slowly, for crouching so low didn't allow for any faster progress, they all moved across the open space together.

Just as they were halfway between the curtain wall and the base of the tower, there was a deep rumbling sound from some undisclosed source to their left. Noticeably, the wildlife noises around them had ceased any of their normal chatter. They had ceased chattering at all. Then the deep rumbling became a roar, louder than anything Annie had heard before. So deep and loud was the sound, that it reverberated through their breast bones. Each looked at the other in alarm and fear.

"Hold in tight formation," shouted Lucan over the noise. "Hold tighter than you have ever held on before!"

Seconds later, an unforgiving wall of water hit them, lifting them as a unit and carrying them a hundred feet or more farther around to their right. The water smelled beyond disgusting and, had they not been utterly focused on their mission, and surviving in general, would have had them violently vomiting. It was no wonder, since the water had been unleashed from a long-stagnant lake, high up at the rear of the tower, and had traversed through the multitudes of Shadow Elf open latrines before reaching them.

Using their combined efforts, they resisted being swept away farther to grüla knows where. They eventually came to rest, fifteen feet above the ground, in front of the tower's striking, primary entrance. The utterly foul water had accomplished the desired effect of depleting their energies. Seconds later, what they hoped was the last of the filthy waters swept past them, leaving them wet through, shaken, and literally stinking of shéat.

Before they had time to take stock of their situation, large rocks, fresh animal dung, and not-so-fresh cadavers of both beasts and captured Woodland and Sun Elven Realm folk, were repeatedly thrown down upon them through the machicolations above the large main gate.

It was becoming crystal clear to Annie, that Tathlyn had decided he was going to have his cruel fun with them, like a cat with a half-dead mouse, before finishing them off to leave only her. However, she was doggedly determined to spoil his fun in any way she could.

Without discussion or debate, she mustered and marshalled her magic, much to her fleck's delight, and, through raising her dominant left hand, created a large dome of protection around herself, and her friends.

Rocks, turds, and dead bodies alike, were repelled.

"Let us make for the side entrance where we escaped from last time," Varis shouted over the din of the hundreds of Shadow Elves now lining the very top of the tower and spiralling down the steps that hugged the outer face of the structure.

Remaining in a close-knitted formation beneath Annie's protective dome, the group inched their way around the tower's narrow ledge that sloped down towards the door they had discovered on their previous visit. They were but ten strides away, when the door in question burst open and a swarm of rabid Shadow Elves burst forth. They quickly assembled around Annie's dome and proceeded to clamber upon each other's shoulders until their bodies blocked out the weak light of the suns. Annie valiantly struggled to maintain the dome's form. The sheer mass of Shadow Elves' bodies was beginning to getting too much for her.

But her primal drive to keep her friends safe served to strengthen her resolve.

Directing her focus inward, she fervently engaged her golden fleck to stir the pot of her magic, whipping it up into a powerful frenzy. At the moment when she felt her magic would effervesce far beyond the realms of her control, she clapped her right hand to her left, above her head, as hard as she could.

Instantaneously, her dome of protection morphed into a mighty weapon of destruction, obliterating all the Shadow Elves that were in contact with the dome and ripping asunder those within a fifteen-foot radius.

At the precise moment her dome burst outward, a second wave of stinking excrement-infused water swept around the curve of the tower, taking with it Shadow

Elves' body parts, Lucan, Varis, Elva, Finwe, and Annie. The horrifically putrid waters carried them round to the far side of the tower and out into the narrow river that raced along the bottom of a tight gorge.

Violently coughing and spluttering in the foul waters, the five comrades instinctively created their daisy-chain formation, with Lucan at the front and Varis at the back. Using his superior upper-body strength, Lucan grabbed sturdy, overhanging branches and managed to halt them all from being washed farther down river, and deeper into the Shadow Realm.

In turn, each member of the group clawed, squirmed, and heaved their way out of the foamy waters and onto dry land.

Everyone, that is, except Varis.

He was floating on his back, unconscious. Seeing Varis's plight, Finwe, without any hesitation, jumped back into the foaming water to retrieve him. Turning Varis over revealed the short, black shaft of a barbed, Shadow Elves arrow, protruding from under his left shoulder blade.

Chapter Twenty-Six

Without a second thought, Lucan joined Finwe in the river to lift Varis from the water and up the slick, muddy bank. Finwe then took off to find somewhere they could tend to Varis and dry off. Lucan made to rip the arrow from Varis's body, but Elva laid a strong, halting hand over his, to stop him in his tracks.

"No, Lucan," she asserted. "You will almost certainly seal his fate for the worse if you remove the barbed arrow in this way. The wound will be far bigger than it is now and, without the arrow blocking the wound, there will be nothing to stop the heavy bleeding that would come with such a wound. Without a doubt, he would die." Lucan looked at her with large, pleading eyes. "We will save him," she assured him. "But we must do this in the right way."

Having made his way back, Finwe's hand now clasped Lucan's shoulder to both demonstrate his compassion and stress that Elva was right in her assertions. He confirmed that in the riverbank, a little way ahead, he had found the abandoned lodge of a river räbbevotèr.

"We can take refuge there, help Varis, and work out our next move," he said as he took Varis by his legs and, with a nod, indicated that Lucan should take Varis's shoulders.

Annie and Elva shouldered everyone's satchels, and the group carefully made their way down the river's slippery edge.

"How are we going to get into the lodge of a, what was it — a river rabbit voter?" Annie ask Elva. She was remembering childhood afternoons in the library, reading *The Wind in the Willows* under the table in the languages section, so that the librarian wouldn't realise how long she'd been there and ask any awkward questions that she'd rather not have had to answer. "I'm nowhere near as big as you elves, and even I wouldn't be able to get more than my arm into some riverbank animal's home."

"Ah, I think that you will be pleasantly surprised," Elva smiled.

"I hope so," Annie replied. "For Varis's sake."

She was intent on getting the amulet to Tathlyn, but she was not prepared to give him the pleasure of dispatching her friends in the process.

And there still may be a chance for us to get both Carric and the amulet, she thought, absentmindedly tapping her zipped pocket.

<><><><><><><><>

Contrary to Elva's prediction, Annie was less pleasantly surprised and far more utterly gobsmacked, as she beheld the abandoned lodge of the river räbbevotèr.

"Just how big is this creature exactly, and might we become its dinner if it comes back while we're here?" she asked, her brain still struggling to digest what what had been revealed to her.

Virtually hidden in among the droopy foliage on the riverbank — that was, Annie guessed, about ten feet deep, from the thorny bushes down to the river's surface — was a perfectly circular opening reenforced with supple, woven branches. Rather than just being able to fit her arm through, Lucan and Finwe, carrying Varis between them, were able to enter without either of the them having to bow their heads.

"River räbbevotèr are about as tall as Finwe and heavier than all of us put together," Elva explained.

"Great. Now please tell me something that's *not* going to have me freaking out," said Annie, as she parted the thorny trailing tendrils of the bushes above, and followed them in.

"Well," Elva replied. "They only eat the mudplate muscles that are found at the bottoms of rivers here in the Shadow Realm. The mudplate muscles migrate with the seasons, and so the river räbbevotèr migrate with them. The river räbbevotèr that built this lodge will not return for some moons yet, and when he and his family do, the entrance will be concealed by the high level of the river water that accompanies that season."

Annie let out a sigh of relief.

"Now that's much more settling," she breathed.

Just inside the entrance it was pitch dark, so Annie created a palm light to hover a little way in front of them.

The floor before them rose steeply for what Annie guessed was around a hundred feet. It then levelled off and there was the sound of brittle twigs, and branches snapping beneath their feet. It was warm and dry, and would have had a comforting earthy smell were it not for the obnoxious odour from their wet hair and clothes. Elva started a fire using her naur mál powder.

In the meantime, Finwe and Lucan had stripped Varis down, and were rubbing dry his unresponsive, naked body with moss they had taken from what Annie guessed had been the river räbbevotèr's bed.

I'm sure Mr. Räbbevotèr's not going to be too thrilled about that, she thought.

They then carried Varis over to Elva's fire and covered him over with his heavy cape that had remained dry within his satchel. Gathering up more moss, Finwe distributed it between them.

"Now we must do the same for ourselves," he explained while removing his belted waistcoat and shirt.

Turning his back, he suggested that Elva and Annie might want to undress, and dry off with the moss in the darkness where the light of the fire didn't reach. Once they were all snuggly wrapped in their cloaks, Lucan and Finwe arranged everyone's clothing around the chamber to be dried by the fire, while Elva and Annie tended to Varis.

In her peripheral vision, Annie saw Lucan shaking out her jacket before draping it over the end of a branch.

"You need to be careful with that," she blurted and instinctively made a grab for it. But it was too late. Lucan had already felt that there was something in one of the pockets and had started to unzip it.

"Whatever is inside here will dry much quicker if it is not zipped away," he assured her. But his face suddenly fixed like granite as he fingers were violently repelled from the pocket's contents, like a sharp and painful electric shock. "What is this?" he asked as he accusingly held up her jacket in front of her.

Annie burst into spontaneous, nervous laughter and her fleck shrank to an ashamed, ousted pin-prick. But it needn't have worried, for in the next moment, Annie brought forth a beautifully crafted lie. Such a lie was a skill she had begun cultivating at around the age of five and had perfected at about thirteen. This lie was beautiful because it had many elements of truth woven within it.

"Okay, Okay," she said, holding up her hands in mock surrender. "You've got me. I brought the dud amulet with me from the Necropolis." She reached into her jacket pocket and brought out the enchanted amulet. "It just didn't feel fair or right to leave it there at a gravestone when its twin was being brought to the elven realms. It had been left alone for so very long and I was able to do something about it."

She left her explanation there, very much aware of how a lie can reveal itself with unnecessary over-explaining and detail.

"I can readily relate to that," said Elva, resuming her rummaging around in her satchel for what she would need to heal Varis. "I would find it a terrible heartache to be kept in a different realm from my brother for all that time. And then be found only to be separated once more."

"Why, thank you sister," grinned Finwe, bowing flamboyantly and instantly lightening the mood within the lodge.

Annie took this moment of lightheartedness to quietly return the enchanted Labradorite Amulet to her pocket and zip it up. Hoping he wouldn't start asking as to why the dud amulet had repelled him, she handed her jacket back to Lucan for him to hang on the drying branch. He gave her the slightest of nods.

But Lucan was not that easily deterred from his original train of thought.

"So, how was it that Elva was able to hold the dud amulet back in the Human Realm, but I cannot go near it here in our elven realms?" he asked.

Annie was marginally relieved that Lucan's tone was more quizzical than accusatory, but she would still have to supply him, and the others, with a plausible answer. Once more, her fleck shrank and her mental cogs whirred.

I think it was my portal, came a small voice from somewhere deep at the back of her mind.

"It was my portal," Annie said, with a forced confidence that made her jump a little. "My portal." She prayed to whichever gods might be listening, that she could create another, believable lie. *What a thing to hope for,* she chided herself. *Not now,* she insisted. *Let's discuss this later.*

"In my portal," she continued with a calmer confidence, "when everything atomised and reassembled, I think it did the same thing to the dud." She was getting into her mentally acrobatic stride now. "Ever since we've been back in the elven realms, although it hasn't got the same powers, the dud has felt more and more like the enchanted Labradorite Amulet."

Again, she stopped herself from overcooking her explanation and just allowed her words to hang in the air while Lucan thought. Eventually, through tight lips, he responded.

"I apologise," he said, giving a curt nod. "And now, I need your full attention on assisting Elva to save Varis."

Annie, hoping she hadn't given the game away by looking relieved, returned the nod and crouched down by Elva. She was now crumbling some form of root and a generous pinch of the naur mál powder into a small pot that she had placed into the edge of the fire. Annie looked at her quizzically.

"We have to get this arrow out of Varis if he is to recover," she explained. "When we pull the barbed point out, he will have a much bigger wound and he is almost sure to rapidly bleed to death. I am hoping that the naur mál powder mixture, together with some of your magical intention, will serve to neutralise the poisoned tip and cauterise the wound from the inside out. If it works, it should give him instant relief."

"And if the naur mál mixture and my magical intention don't work?" Annie asked. Elva paled and shook her head a little.

"Then the naur mál mixture may well set all his internal organs on fire and kill him. But, sadly, not instantly enough to save him from an excruciating death."

Then it was Annie's turn to go pale.

Well, if I didn't want the answer, I should never have asked the question, she thought as she exhaled heavily. A warm and encouraging grip of her shoulder came from an unexpected quarter.

It was Lucan.

"Varis would tell me that he had every faith in you, and so I am deciding to be confident, and trust that you will succeed."

You trust in me, eh? she thought. *If only you knew how misplaced your trust in me actually is.*

They'll all know soon enough, came the jabbing dig at herself.

Not now, she protested. *I have to focus on Varis. I can't have him die here, or die at all for that matter.* And in that moment, she realised that once she had saved Varis, she would need to, somehow, head to Tathlyn alone. *There will be no more bloody game of cat and mouse.*

Lucan positioned himself to hold Varis's unconscious body down. Finwe readied himself to yank the arrow from Varis's back. Elva held the hot pot, ready to pour its potentially healing, or potentially lethal, contents. And Annie, engaged her core of magic ready to...

"Don't tell me," she said, before Elva could speak and not lifting her head to look at any of them. "I'll be using my intention."

The corner of Elva's mouth twitched a brief smile before counting down so everyone could coordinate doing their part.

Lucan had to use all his might to resist against Finwe's strong and steady pull. Just as it looked like the arrow was never going to come out, it exited from Varis with a sickening squelching schlop. The force with which Finwe had needed to pull, now sent him sprawling backwards.

The resulting wound was a large, ragged, and bloody hole.

Without wasting a single moment, Elva quickly poured the naur mál mixture into the gaping wound. As soon as the mixture made contact with the blood it made it boil and burst into flames. Annie firmly pushed Elva to one side to get as close as she could to Varis. Drawing her magic up through her throat to her face, Annie felt lasers of her intentioned magic pierce through from her fully dilated golden fleck, to where the wound was deepest in Varis. In her mind's eye, she could see that the back of Varis's left lung had been sliced into, and a lethal poison was making headway in spreading through the capillaries in the alveoli.

She imagined her magic soaking up this poison like a sponge. Then, she envisioned her magic, combined with the naur mál mixture, causing his cells and membranes to rapidly repair, one cellular layer at a time. After what felt an absolute age, the final, topmost layer of skin cells were cauterised and Annie sat back, feeling spent, yet satisfied.

The others were looking at her, mouths agape.

"What?" she panted. "What is it? Did it work?"

"Your face," whispered Elva, amazed. "You had your face right in the flames, but it seemed like you felt nothing and the flames did not even touch you, never mind singe or burn you."

"I did?" asked Annie, finding it hard to believe herself.

"And yes," came a muffled voice from below them, "it appears to have worked."

It was Varis. He had regained consciousness and was making an effort to get up. They all huddled and hugged around Varis in sheer relief, and joy.

When their chattering about how they had found the river räbbevotèr's lodge and how they had worked together to save him, died down, Varis asked,

"But why have we not been set upon by Shadow Elves? Why did all but one arrow miss us?"

They agreed that it was suspiciously odd.

"What do you think, Annie?" Finwe asked.

But there was no answer. They all looked up from where Varis still lay. Finwe looked over to the branches with their drying clothes and saw that Annie's weren't there.

When they had all huddled and hugged around Varis in ecstatic celebration, Annie had surreptitiously wriggled her way from the middle to be on the outside of the group.

Silently, she had crept over to the branches, grabbed her warm, damp, still stinking clothes, and her satchel. Without pausing or daring to see if her actions had been noticed, she had softly exited down the slope to the riverside, and up onto the bank.

She was now striding towards Tathlyn's tower with granite-like purpose.

Alone.

Chapter Twenty-Seven

"What the brùkling héllè does she think she is doing?" Finwe demanded as he leapt up and hastily made for the exit. But Lucan firmly blocked his way. With his hand on Finwe's chest, he spoke with crystal-clear authority.

"We must work as a team, together. Dashing off individually will weaken us, and our chances of success would be dramatically reduced, most likely to nil."

Finwe glowered at him and was sorely tempted to force his way past, but Elva interceded.

"None of us want to see Annie in danger, but, as you know, such occasions call for a ruling from our heads and absolutely not from our hearts." Finwe shot her an angry look, but she chose to ignore it a continued unabashed. "Lucan is right. We stand a far better chance of saving Annie and Carric if we work as the cohesive unit that we usually are."

After a couple of failed attempts to sidestep him, Finwe puffed out a hugely frustrated sigh and conceded to Lucan's and Elva's point.

"But why the hüelgar would she go and do this?" he demanded, his voice cracking with his heady mix of emotions. "By going out there alone she has dramatically reduced her chance of survival."

Varis weighed in on the debate as he slowly and carefully rose to stand, loosening up his left shoulder, and testing out its strength as he straightened up. He found that the site of the injury smarted somewhat, but was, overall, up to any task the Shadow Elves may, quite literally, throw at it.

"Perhaps she did not want anyone else injured or worse in the attempt to rescue Carric. Perhaps she feels it is her burden and hers alone."

Finwe went icily silent and roughly shrugged off Elva's consolatory hand that she had tentatively placed on his shoulder. Lucan and Varis exchanged a knowing look, and pretended they hadn't noticed anything.

Once they were dressed, the four elves made their way out of the river räbbevotèr's lodge and up onto the bank. Ordinarily, they would have smeared themselves in mud for camouflage. However, since their clothes were already smeared in far worse than mud, courtesy of the stagnant lake, the open latrines, and the flotsam, and jetsam tossed down through the machicolations, such a measure was rendered totally unnecessary.

The ground cover had been beaten into a rudimentary pathway and packed down hard from the weight of thousands, possibly tens of thousands, of Shadow Elves over time. Being smaller and lighter than any adult elf, Annie's footsteps had left no imprint for Finwe to track. Exasperated, he wondered if there would be no end to his agonised frustration.

Elva nimbly climbed a taller tree to scan the area, but Annie was nowhere to be seen. Surely Annie couldn't have reached the tower already — could she? From ground level, Finwe stared hard at the stretch of land between them and the tower. For a moment, in the distance, he thought he could see Annie. It was a paler version of her, as is she were a washed out water colour painting.

It cannot be her, he thought woefully. *If it was Annie, then Elva would have seen her too.* He decided it was simply his desperate wishful thinking and said nothing of it.

"And where are all the Shadow Elves?" Varis queried, again. Their marked absence had been niggling him on and off, from the moment they had left the probos at the edge of the desert. "We are basically huge sitting kwarns here, out in the open."

The others agreed that this situation ran contrary to any experience of the Shadow Elves that they had gone through before.

"But why is that?" Varis continued. "It feels so completely out of character, so completely wrong."

"I agree that my initial optimism was seriously misplaced and that this feels like some sort of trap," Lucan replied. "But trap or no trap, we have our mission. We are here to rescue Carric —"

"And probably Annie too, now," Finwe finished.

"Yes, although she is not strictly part of our mission, most likely Annie too," he agreed. "And I, for one, am going to honour my commitment. I am the commander of the guard of the Sun Elven Realm. It is my job, it is my duty, it is my calling."

Elva placed her hand on his shoulder and gave it a firm squeeze.

"We are all going to honour our commitment, just like you said. Together. As a team."

<><><><><><><><><>

Annie had made good progress, but hadn't reached the tower — not quite yet. To make sure that she could not be seen by her friends once they realised she had gone missing, she had worked hard to make herself invisible even to them. On the Bridge of Sighs in Glasgow, while she was invisible to the police, her elven friends could still see her.

It hadn't been so easy to increase the opaqueness of her invisibility, and she could only hope that it was working. It was made all the more difficult by her golden fleck that was voicing its objection to what she was about to do by rotating its movements of darting, zigzagging, and straining. It was distracting, uncomfortable, and sometimes downright painful.

Twice, she had reappeared accidentally and had been compelled to wrestle with herself to achieve her greater invisibility once more. On the second occasion, she had reappeared beside a small troop of Shadow Elves. They had leapt out of their skins, and one would have taken her head from her shoulders had his comrade not had the wherewithal to parry the swing of his double-bladed sword. Her eyes had bulged in terror and she had readied two palm bombs with which to defend herself. But, she soon realised that self defence wasn't at all necessary. These Shadow Elves were clearly under strict orders to allow her safe passage through to the tower, without any hindrance. Once she thought she was out of view of her elves, she decided to conserve some of her much needed energy, by remaining visible.

Surely Tathlyn knows that I'm just a few steps away now, she thought, her mouth going terribly dry with fear, and the heavy clouds in the sky above, simultaneously increasing in density. If this carried on, she would create an almighty deluge without a moment's notice. She sought some solace. *At least the shiedait retpoilè isn't getting my friends served up on a plater.*

The watery suns were only half visible above the horizon and their rays created blood-red edging to each cloud as well as the dark tower itself. Annie thought that if ever there was a visual representation of ominous, impending evil, this was it.

As she reached the curtain wall, she discovered that a pontoon-like bridge had been erected to provide her with easy access up to the main gated entrance. As she passed under the machicolations above the main gate, she had to step over many boulders and bloody body parts that had not been washed away by the torrent of filthy water. She looked straight ahead, forcing herself not to pay any attention to what she inadvertently kicked, stepped over, or trod upon.

<><><><><><><><>

Once inside the initial gate, Annie found herself in a surprisingly large, inner courtyard that was open to the blackening skies many hundreds of feet above. About four hundred, or maybe more, Shadow Elves stood to attention, all looking blankly straight ahead. She had no doubt about where to go. She was to head down the centre of the courtyard and up some stone steps to a tall archway. The Shadow Elves had created a kind of corridor with their bodies, down which she was to traverse.

This is it, she thought, terrified that she might freeze or turn heel and run. Instead, she forced herself to take the all-important first step among them.

The deathly silence was eerie and oppressive. She was surrounded by at least four hundred of them, and yet she couldn't even hear them breathe. As she moved on past them, the Shadow Elves silently turned and filled in their makeshift corridor behind her.

She had, most definitely, gone past the point of no return. And then she realised that the point of no return had probably been passed quite some time earlier — quite possibly when she had placed the dud amulet in the grand window in the Sun Elven Realm palace.

With sure steps, she slowly climbed the worn stone stairs and unhurriedly walked through the archway, looking straight ahead, and hardly daring to breathe.

Chapter Twenty-Eight

Tathlyn was fizzing with delight and anticipation, and could barely contain his excitement. He was like a macabre giddy child, and it was an unsightly, and disturbing sight, even to his faithful minions.

Finally, the enchanted Labradorite Amulet was going to be his.

He could almost taste it on the tip of his black tongue.

Oh, the devastating damage I shall wreak upon the Woodland and Sun Elven Realms, and the irritatingly, lèplà-livkakt, neutral Shoreland Realm, he thought. Those pustid shiedaits. As if neutrality would protect them from my vision.

If Tathlyn's vision was realised, before long, the elders of the Woodland Realm and the pompous, arrogant, and loathsome King Peren, would be grovelling at his feet, and begging him to spare the lives of their elves.

Well, the Woodland elders at least would, his thought train continued. *Peren will, undoubtedly, beg for himself to be spared, the néate, succum cocotte.*

There were a growing number of Shadow Elves, within both the upper and lower ranks, who thought that King Peren and King Tathlyn had many traits in common. Not that any of them would dare to voice such thoughts, or indeed dare, within the tower's compound, to even *think* them for fear of cruel and probably lethal consequences being exacted upon them.

The Labradorite Amulet is not yet in our hand, his internal voice reminded him, in an attempt to steady him. *Let us not be too presumptive in our celebration of such a delicious triumph.*

Tathlyn snorted like spoilt child being told that they couldn't have the sweets or toy that they so desperately desired. The various birds and other creatures that swung from primitive cages around his hall, all fell silent, and shrank back against their bars for fear of becoming Tathlyn's outlet of his petulant frustration.

They needn't have worried for, a moment later, Annie passed from the darkness of the corridor and into the dim, and foreboding light of Tathlyn's chamber.

<><><><><><><><>

Meanwhile, Lucan, Varis, Elva, and Finwe were within spitting distance of the tower's curtain wall. The complete and continued lack of any Shadow Elves as they had made their way from the river räbbevotèr's lodge, had only served to increase their concern, and heighten their alertness.

"This is just all serving to convince me further, that this is some sort of trap," Lucan whispered as they leant their backs on the wall and faced away from the looming tower. "It feels like we are being lured in, and yet we cannot resist the pull upon us because our Annie and prince are in there. I feel like a limpöd caught in the lure light of the phischlè."

"I am very much inclined to agree with your analysis, Lucan," said Varis.

Elva, Varis, and Finwe exchanged slight, furtive smiles. This was the first time that Lucan had coined the phrase, 'our Annie', not to mention placing a human before an elven prince, and they had all noticed it.

"So, I guess that we are going in through the front door, then," Finwe said. He was itching to get going.

"I think that we may as well," Varis chipped in, still rolling his shoulder to ensure it didn't seize up when he, inevitably, needed to wield his sword.

It was agreed that Finwe and Lucan would leap the curtain wall first, with cover from Elva's bow and arrows. Finwe would then use his archery to cover for Elva and Varis as they sprang over. They moved in tight formation across the expanse between the wall and the tower itself.

Still everything was quiet.

Far, far too quiet.

The only noise they heard was their own breathing and the soft squelching of their boots in the stinking dregs left behind by the spontaneous tides of fouler-than-foul water. Still remaining on their highest alert, they knew better than to take anything for granted.

A couple of sections of the pontoon-like bridge had been left to stretch towards the curtain wall. Using this large structure as cover, they climbed up underneath it. By swinging hand over hand from one horizontal slat to another, they made their way to the main gate entrance.

This was clearly a test for how well Varis's shoulder had healed, and he was very pleased when it caused him no grief whatsoever. In fact, it felt stronger and more supple than it had in a long while. Varis knew he had Annie's magical skills to thank for that.

Once at the tower, they really had no choice but to lay themselves vulnerable to possible attack. They each pulled their bodies up over their heads so that their feet were planted on the bridge itself. Without waiting to ensure they had complete control over their balance, they each sprang to stand tall, and pressed their backs flat against the slick, black bricks of the tower, either side of the expansive main-gated entrance.

The gates were wide open.

Still there was the disconcerting, eerie silence.

Lucan fished out a mirror from his satchel and used to see if there were any Shadow Elves lying in wait beyond the entrance.

There was no one.

Stepping over the boulders and bloody body parts that hadn't been washed away by the water, the four elves moved light of foot, within the confines of the tower itself. There was absolutely no opportunity for a change of heart now. They were all tightly bound to their commitment to face whatever awaited them within.

Unlike when Annie had arrived, the large inner courtyard was completely deserted. Only the light of the moons rising high on their nighttime trajectory gave away the fact that the courtyard was open to the skies. Directly opposite them were the stone steps that led to the tall archway.

Rather than leaving themselves exposed more than necessary, they made their way — two one way and two the other — around the sides of the courtyard, keeping tight to its edge until each pair stood either side of the steps.

Without warning, out from under the archway, came a single-minded swarm of Shadow Elves.

Chapter Twenty-Nine

Annie completely ignored the menacing figure of Tathlyn. Instead, her eyes searched wildly for Carric. At first she couldn't see him anywhere. But then there came a weak and reedy, cracked voice of someone whose spirit had been brutally broken.

"Annie... Annie?"

At first she simply couldn't comprehend what her eyes were seeing. As her thoughts, like some mental form of Tetris, struggled to make sense of what she was looking at, the filthy, animal skin held high up on the wall became the limp and bloody body of Carric.

"Oh... my... god," Annie whispered faintly as she dashed towards him.

She could only reach his filthy, bloodstained feet, but she held them and kissed them as if she were holding his entirety to her. Looking up at him, she saw that his near-naked body was hung like some curing venison on a meat hook. His hands and feet were bound tightly with strong, thin wire that looked like it was cutting into his sallow skin. His hair was filthy and lank, rather than lustrous, and thick. It fell across is sunken eyes and protruding, razor-sharp cheek bones. He had an unkempt beard and he was thin. How he could have become so painfully thin in such a short time, she didn't know. She didn't really want to know. His body was stained from top to toe with blood. He had many wounds — some old, some fresh, some clearly inflicted by tools of torture, and some from a source unknown.

Fat, silent tears rolled down Annie's cheeks.

Tears of joy.

Tears of sorrow.

Tears of love.

But, primarily, tears of absolute rage.

"How could you, you loathsome, brùkling clätck?" she growled, as she whipped round to face Tathlyn.

A Shadow Elf bravely, but definitely unwisely, put himself between her and his sovereign. Annie's lip curled into a wrathful sneer as she encouraged her magic to cook, bubble, and make a sharp exit through her left hand, which she had held up to the ill-fated Shadow Elf. The sheer brutal force of her ejected power lifted him and gut-punched him into the far wall. The Shadow Elf, now unconscious, and quite probably dead, slowly slid limply to the ground and, to the unsuspecting eye, resembled a pile of dirty old rags.

Seeing just a mere taster of what Annie was now capable of doing, Tathlyn decided he would be wise to take no unnecessary chances. Unable to muster powers naturally from within his body, he seized his nearest minion round the back of the neck with one hand and plunged what looked like an ivory-handled curved and serrated knife, in his other hand, into the elf's chest. The sound of the elf's splintering ribs was sickening. So shocked was the minion by the speed of Tathlyn's actions, that he had no to time to register or make a sound. As Tathlyn slowly and purposefully turned the knife, and muttered some ancient words of dark magic, a pearlised dome of protection formed around him. While he still had hold of this husk of a freshly slaughtered Shadow Elf, Annie wouldn't be able to get to him and mete out her wrath.

"You *knew* I was coming," she continued. "You knew I was bringing the damned amulet. There was no need to hurt him. To pretty much *kill* him!"

From within his protective dome, Tathlyn felt particularly at ease enough to show his true nature.

"But it was simply so very fun to do," he said, his wicked twinkling, steely grey eyes enjoying the furious contortions of Annie's face.

Annie was readying herself to dispatch more Shadow Elves and, hopefully, Tathlyn himself, when Carric spoke again from behind her.

"Annie? Annie... my love. You came... for me. For me."

Her heart promptly melted and her boiling powers instantly simmered down.

"Of course I came for you. I love you. You love me. We complete each other."

"Do you... have it?" he croaked. "Do you have... Do you have... the amulet?"

"Hmm?" she said, her mind working quickly on how best to get him down. "Yes, yes. I have it."

Tracing the barbaric, rusty chains that held him so high, she saw that they passed through a large pulley before being tied off around a robust, wooden capstan that was fixed to the floor.

"Untie him and carefully, very carefully, lower him to the floor," she demanded. "Do it now!"

Tathlyn gave the slightest nod to a guard by the doorway.

"Do as she says," he ordered.

Seeing that her initially explosive anger had subsided, at least for the time being, he let go of the unfortunate elf in his grasp and, seemingly without a single care in the world, stepped over the desiccated corpse as the protective dome vanished.

Once lowered to the ground, Annie was far better able to inspect Carric's condition. Her entire focus was on him rather than Tathlyn. It was clear that he was suffering greatly from dehydration, possible hypothermia, animal bites, probably from ratlike creatures, and several severe beatings.

She saw a pot of water nearby and, by soaking the corner of her cape, dabbed and wiped away much of the dried blood, and dirt from his face. He winced, but all the while, his beautiful, yet sunken, eyes were fixed on her, unblinking, unerring.

She kissed his split lips as lightly and as gently as she could. Her kiss was as soft as a feather. He made an effort to return her kiss, but clearly found it too painful. As she looked down at him, their flowing tears mixed together on his cheek.

Tathlyn tutted. He had seen more than enough.

"That is quite enough of that," he snapped. "You can carry on where you have left off once I have the Labradorite Amulet."

Then a thought struck her.

Only I can touch the Labradorite Amulet. He can't touch it. It will repel him. She felt the slightest flutter of elation. Perhaps she wouldn't have to betray everyone after all. Perhaps she could come away with both Carric and the amulet. The flutter dared to grow into a little hope.

She smiled when Tathlyn spoke again.

"Hand it over to me, now," he demanded, then looked a little confused and very irritated. "What is it? What are you smiling about?"

"You're a fool Tathlyn," she said, her smile broadening in self-congratulatory satisfaction. "Only *I* can touch the Labradorite Amulet. Me. The human with the hands of Meredith the Thief. You can't touch it."

Tathlyn's body stiffened and his face twitched.

She could see that hearing the name, Meredith, stung him. But then, it was Tathlyn's turn to arrange his face into a broad smile of self-congratulatory satisfaction. Now Annie's expression faltered. She was worried. Had she missed something? Her golden fleck shivered in confirmation that she most likely had.

But what? she thought. *What have I missed?*

"Actually, I think you will discover that I can touch it," he said, all smug and self-righteous. "I too can be the hand of Meredith the Thief."

Annie felt bile rise up into her throat.

"Oh brùkling héllè! Please don't tell me that we're somehow *related*," she said, utterly horrified by the thought that his might be the case.

Tathlyn looked as completely appalled by the notion as she was.

"Good pisht, no!" he exclaimed. "I would rather have my gömrickts shredded by a vanböurg than be in any way related to you."

Although she didn't know what his gömrickts were, or why he wouldn't want them shredded by a vanböurg, whatever that was, Annie understood him perfectly, and knew she felt the same way.

At least that's something we can vigorously and wholeheartedly agree on, she thought.

"So how can you possibly be the hand of Meredith?" she asked, clocking another fleeting shudder from Tathlyn at the utterance of the name, Meredith.

Did she have that much of an influence on you? she thought. *What did she really mean to you? Obviously* the emotion and memories are strong. *Did she hurt you? Did you hate her?* Her fleck kept twirling as if to encourage her to think of more possibilities. *No... wait. I was right before. You. Loved. Her.*

Bingo! she replied to herself. Her curious nature instantly wanted to know more, but she knew that now was neither the time nor the place to mine this intriguing seam.

Tathlyn tussled with his muscles to force his face into a neutral expression, and then made an exaggerated show of nonchalantly reaching for a tall, corked vial from the table beside his throne. It was held in an ornately carved, wooden frame and looked like it had been there for a very long while. He held it in front of him, between his long, silvery forefinger and thumb, so that Annie could clearly see.

"I can be the hand of... her... with this," he announced, his eyes sparkling maliciously. "I have had this prepared for over twelve hundred moons."

He tipped the vial this way and that, encouraging the three distinctly differently coloured liquids within to mix — the sapphire blue, the Syracuse orange, and the salsa red, together becoming a sort of glittering opal. But the liquids weren't the only things within the vial. There were also several strands of something. Was it wire? String? Fibres?

No, Annie thought. *No, it's... it's hair.*

"Meredith's hair," Annie whispered, her eyes like saucers.

"Yes indeed," he drawled. "It is *her* lustrous, wavy, pale hair." There was a sordid twinkle in hie eyes. "I *procured* it while she slept beside me."

Her fleck instantly curled up and shuddered in disgust. Had it been able to make a sound, that sound would have been "Ewww". Agreeing, Annie thought,

What a total creep of creeps.

Tathlyn knocked back a large slug of the vial's contents. His face screwed up tightly and Annie rather enjoyed the fact that the hair infused liquid was clearly, utterly revolting. Forcing himself to swallow, his eyes sparked open to reveal they had changed from their steely grey to a deep ocean blue. He then held out his long-fingered, long-nailed hand.

"The Labradorite Amulet, if you please."

"Not so fast," Annie replied, taking a sizeable step back towards Carric, who had managed to get his shaking legs beneath him and was now, just about standing. "You let Carric go and *then* I'll hand the blasted thing to you."

Tathlyn made a big show of contemplating whether or not to humour her, and then came to a decision.

"Very well," he said and indicated to the two minions left in the chamber, to assist Carric over to the exit.

Looking at the two remaining minions, Annie knew how to ensure Tathlyn's adherence to their deal.

"And be aware that, by tasking your Shadow Elves to help Carric, you are moving them out of your reach to create another dome of protection," she warned. "Any more pratting about, and I will exact my increasingly powerful and *natural* magic upon you — and it will *end you.*"

Tathlyn looked suitably chastened and assured her that the Labradorite Amulet was far too important to warrant him "pratting about".

"I am not entirely sure what that phrase specifically means," he continued. "But I believe that I get the general gist."

When Carric was at the exit's doorway, Tathlyn held out his hand once more.

"Now, hand it over," he insisted, with a thinly veiled threat in his tone.

Am I really going to do this? she asked herself.

Yes, she asserted. *I need Carric to be safe, and then we can set about stealing the amulet back, and saving everyone.*

Very well, came her internal reply. It stung her to note that it was full of reproach. Before she lost her nerve altogether, Annie unzipped the pocket of her jacket. She plunged her hand within, and brought forth the enchanted Labradorite Amulet.

Even within the dull lighting of the tower's interior, the delightful, iridescent, cyan blue hues of the labradorite stone shone. For a moment or two, all those present were mesmerised by its dazzling, bewitching beauty. It took considerable effort for everyone to extract themselves from its captivation.

Both Tathlyn and Annie took a step forward towards each other. Her hand, with the amulet nestled in her palm, was only inches away from his.

"Wait," he said, making her jump and recoil.

"Wait for what?" she asked. "Do you want it or not?"

"Of course I want it," he snapped, peevishly. "Just not... quite... yet."

"What the héllè?" she retorted, surprised to find that she was capable of being even more vexed with this Shadow Elf king than she already had been. She glowered at Tathlyn intensely and her internal volcano bubbled, and swirled ominously.

"Just do as he says, Annie," Carric pleaded from somewhere behind her. "I could not withstand the consequences if he... if he changed his mind and kept me any longer."

She couldn't bear the thought of Carric having to endure a single moment more of Tathlyn's torture, so she dutifully waited, her fleck impatiently turning figure of eights. There was a sudden change in Tathlyn's demeanour. What was it? Was it — was it unadulterated triumph?

"Hand it to me now," he suddenly ordered. "Slowly."

What is he playing at? she asked herself, while also doing his bidding. *There must be something extra in it for him. He's obviously playing some cruel game. But what's the game?*

She stretched her hand towards his, but he maintained a distance between them.

"Slower... slower... that's it."

He had his eyes fixed on the amulet, but Annie didn't notice that he was simultaneously paying attention with his peripheral vision, to what was happening near the door.

At the moment that the amulet was touched by both her hand and his, there was a wretched and collective howl of,

"No!"

As Tathlyn took possession of the amulet, Annie's eyes snapped towards the doorway, from whence the howl had come.

There stood Finwe, Elva, Varis, and Lucan.

Chapter Thirty

The very moment that Tathlyn had full possession of the Labradorite Amulet, his whole body spasmed and his head unnaturally arched backwards. He started to recite an incantation in ancient Elvish and the amulet's labradorite stone shone brightly, burning white hot. Beams of intense light broke out from between his fingers that clasped it. Although struggling to keep hold of the violently vibrating stone, Tathlyn repeated his incantation several times until the light casting outward was reabsorbed into the stone. In that instant, Tathlyn's body relaxed and sagged, and his head fell forward onto his chest.

He slowly raised his head and, threading a thick silver chain through the back of the amulet, he hung it around his neck. He spoke with swelling, egotistical smugness, his voice crescendoing as his wicked enthusiasm grew.

"And now my skills and power in magic are elevated such that the magic is within me. There is no longer any need to sacrifice my energies, my beloved creatures, or my Shadow Elves in order to exact my magic on my enemies. Now, I am unstoppable. Now, I am invincible. And I shall be ruthlessly unrelenting in my assured domination to be Emperor of All Realms, everywhere!"

<><><><><><><><>

Annie's companions had their hands haevily bound. They were surrounded by excitable Shadow Elves riding the crest of their leader's oratory wave. Elva, Varis, Lucan, and Finwe had just witnessed the staggeringly deceitful handing over of the enchanted Labradorite Amulet to their arch enemy, King Tathlyn. All four of them violently struggled against their binds and the elves around them, in an effort to get to Tathlyn, but it was totally futile.

"You brùkling treasonous retpoilè!" Lucan spat towards Annie.

She had never seen Lucan so angry. His usually buttery complexion was now crimson, his eyes bulged wildly, and he was staring directly at her. "I would have expected all of this from Tathlyn. But from you? From *you*? *Never!*"

His expression of unbridled wrath was echoed by Varis and Elva. But, the expression on Finwe's face? Well, that was the hardest of all to take. His face showed sorrow and hurt — deeply cutting, scarring sorrow and hurt. Annie squeezed her eyes tight shut, but this only served to show their faces in her mind, in even brighter technicolour. Her guilt and self-loathing shrank her fleck to a speck, and turned her magical lava to a hard and heavy block of ice. She knew that nothing she could say would change their view of her, but in a small, weak voice, she spoke anyway.

"I had to ensure Carric was saved. I *love* him."

This only gave rise to a deep, snarling growl from Lucan and Varis, and several explosive expletives from Elva. And was that a cry of pain from Finwe? And there was another sound.

What was it?

A harsh, barking laugh?

From Tathlyn?

No — not from Tathlyn. He was simply grinning and thoroughly enjoying the scene unfurling before him.

Who then?

Who was laughing?

Carric?

No.

Yes.

Carric.

<><><><><><><><>

All eyes were on Carric. When he was absolutely certain he had got everyone's attention, he gradually transformed his thin, listless, cowering, shrinking stance into his far more familiar upright, square, and strong one. All but Tathlyn, were confused. Their minds were unable to acknowledge, assimilate, or comprehend what they had just witnessed.

Carric then casually and confidently stepped forward to a large, copper-coloured, metal bowl and jug that was full of water. Using large, pristine white cloths, the two minions set about cleaning Carric's body. He just stood facing his stunned audience with his arms out wide and his chest bare. He looked... he looked... amused.

Before long, he was cleansed of all the dirt and blood. The blood had never been his own. Rather, it had been acquired from captured Woodland Elves who had been hung upside-down and had their jugulars cut to drain their blood into earthenware jugs beneath. The white cloths, now stained, were discarded on the stone floor. Carric stood before them, hands on hips. He was still a little thinner and no where near his usual high standard of personal grooming, but otherwise, he was completely unharmed.

Elva was the first to find her voice.

"You brùkling, schteelcün shéats! I am going to rip off your cléttiès, feed them to the kystrallas, and take small comfort in knowing that your gaping, weeping wound will become infected, and afford you an agonisingly slow, shameful, and humiliating death."

"And we three shall be beside her as she does it, to throw acidic salt into your gaping, festering wound!" Lucan spat with gallons of venom that he wouldn't have ordinarily stooped to.

The throng of Shadow Elves detaining them pressed the points of their serrated daggers to Elva's and Lucan's throats. It was clear that while they outnumbered the Sun and Woodland Elves, they wisely respected the supreme skill of those they had captured. Sheer numbers wouldn't necessarily overpower these highly trained, masterfully skilled, and exceedingly angry warriors.

Annie was yet to think, say, feel, or do anything. She had been instantly rendered menatlly, emotionally and magically impotent. She had been struck dumb by the revelation that Carric was actually in league with Tathlyn. This handsome, endearing elf had inveigled his way into winning her much-guarded trust. He had wormed his way into her heavily shielded heart. He had taken her trust and taken her heart, and then gleefully trampled upon them both. He had ground them into dust and, apparently, taken great delight in the whole charade.

Large tears of agony and self-loathing welled up in her eyes and tipped over her lower lids to roll silently down her cheeks. She struggled to assemble her thoughts into some sort of tangible order. It was like she was in a labyrinth, blindly running and continuously careening into walls. The same walls. Over and over and over again.

She desperately didn't want to believe it, but here it was, right in front of her, as plain as day. She had thrown everything away in order to save him. She had deceived her elven friends — friends being something she had never really made in the Human Realm. And she had potentially condemned thousands, possibly millions of elves to death by starvation or by a Shadow Elf sword.

She was filling up with the beginnings of wretched grief, despair, and all-consuming self-hatred for becoming the very things that she so deeply despised. For ignoring, and subsequently falling foul of, the beliefs she'd held all her life. Valuing consistent honesty, fairness, trustworthiness, and all that sat under the umbrella of integrity. She had betrayed everyone. She had betrayed herself.

Then, other torturing thoughts came flooding into Annie's mind and neatly slotted together to create a fuller, more detailed, picture of what Tathlyn had been cunningly masterminding all along. She now knew that she was never the intended target of the Shadow Elves that had swarmed over the ship on their first journey across the seas. Carric was their mission, and Carric had known it too. Tathlyn had needed to hold Carric as the ultimate leverage over Annie, for her to sustain the motivation to retrieve the Labradorite Amulet and bring it to him. And for that to work, he needed Carric to find his way into Annie's affections and take root there — for her to love him.

Carric must have informed Tathlyn that Annie had arrived through her portal. He must have noticed the resemblance she had to Meredith. Most likely, together, they had formed the cruel plan for the prince to win her over. Or maybe that was all Carric's idea. It didn't matter which was the case. The terrible consequences were the same.

Had Carric taken her to see The View, knowing full well that there would be a Shadow Elf there to pounce upon her? Was it all a ruse to show Carric to be her saviour, her hero? Was it all created for him to start becoming all the things that were missing in her life up to that point? It certainly seemed like it.

She blamed Carric for ruthlessly and unscrupulously fooling her. She blamed him for abusing her trust, which she had never truly given before. She blamed him for grooming her by playing on her insecurities and using her need to find acceptance, and love. But most of all, she completely blamed herself for lowering her ordinarily impenetrable guard. For lowering the guard that she had begun to build since before she'd turned five. For letting someone in. For letting the guard around her heart fall away. For daring to fall in love. For stupidly daring to believe that she was loved — that she could ever be loved.

I mean come on, she thought, sneering at herself in disgust. *As if someone would love me.*

She then cringed at how she had told Carric that he completed her. She'd never before bought into the notion of the "other half" and how one person can make another one whole. She'd always mimed vomiting whenever she'd heard someone say it. She'd believed that each person is whole, is complete, and a romantic partner is just that — a partner. And yet, despite this, she'd unwittingly allowed Carric to undo all that and bring her to believe that without him, she was somehow 'less than'.

She was swiftly yanked from her spiralling thoughts by Carric and the two remaining minions strolling over to stand beside Tathlyn. Staring straight at her, Carric pointedly situated himself on Tathlyn's right-hand side.

"What the shéat is this? Is it some sort of kitsch symbolism?" Annie hissed, making a half-arsed attempt to scrape together her self-protecting, pithy sarcasm. The faces around her showed that while they had no idea what she had specifically meant, they knew it was some sort of sarcastic, scathing dig.

"Why?" came Varis's question, quiet and simple. "Why do this, Carric? You are a prince. You had the ultimate privileged life, devoid of any hardship."

For a fleeting moment, Carric looked a little subdued and abashed, but then, he bounced back with renewed venom, and bile in his voice.

"A privileged live devoid of hardship? You mean a life of irrelevance as the powerless laughingstock of the Sun Elven, Woodland, and Shoreland Realms." He was practically pouting now, wallowing in his own excessively self-pitying narrative. "A prince garnering no respect from his underlings, with no real power, and with a father who sees him with nothing but disappointment in his eyes. A father who openly calls him a stupid pellopé to all and sundry!"

Lucan had heard more than enough of Carric's self-righteous and snivelling carping. For all his time in the Sun Elven Army at the palace, Lucan had borne constant witness to the self-obsessed and selfish prince as he grew up. He had passed no comment, purely as part of his duty to his king and his realm. Now, as a consequence of Carric's own actions, there was no need to hold back any longer. He strained against the four Shadow Elves who were holding him in place.

"All of which you had within your gift to change. But instead, you chose to blame anyone and everything outside of yourself. You have persistently pouted, preened, belittled, and bullied your way through life. You could have chosen to do good with the power you *had* been given. But oh no. Instead, you threw your considerable royal weight around and treated others like they were the lowest of shéats. You know absolutely *nothing* of hardship, you loathsome, brùkling skänè!"

"Lucan speaks the truth," Varis chimed in, in agreement. He too had witnessed the prince growing up. "You constantly demanded and craved respect, and tried to punish those who didn't give it. But respect cannot ever be demanded. It must be *earned* and, once earned, one must work selflessly to retain it."

Carric was purple with rage and indignation, and was about to attempt to defend himself, but it was Tathlyn who unexpectedly chipped in.

"You are both completely right, of course," he said languidly, like one engaged in casual conversation discussing a petulant, self-centred child. Carric's pallor morphed to an embarrassed hue of red, but he made no attempt to speak up against Tathlyn. "But, I am sure you will appreciate how all these... these *qualities* and behaviours made Prince Carric the perfect candidate with whom I could make an exceptionally enticing deal."

"And what have you promised the stupid pellopé, who I had called friend?" Finwe asked. Carric didn't even bother to try and look like he could make a reasoned argument against the slaying of his character that he was being submitted to.

"I am unsure as to who is the most stupid pellöt," Finwe continued, his eyebrows knitted together in anger. "Carric in general, or me, for always trying to see the good in him where there probably was none. I strongly suspect the answer is that we *both* are. We are both brùkling stupid pellöts."

"He has promised me everything that I desire and deserve," Carric tried to assert, standing up to his tallest, puffing out his chest, and jutting out his chiselled chin. All present, except Annie, shared the one thought — that his actions merely revealed a lack of real conviction in what he was saying, and that he was trying to prove his case to himself as much as to anyone else.

With eyes glazed and seeing nothing in particular, Annie was deep within her head, rerunning all the interactions she'd had with Carric and finding them all turning bitter, and sour.

"I will be king of the Sun Elven and Woodland Realms combined," he continued, his voice booming and full of self importance. "I will be loved and feared by my millions of subjugated subjects. I will — "

"You will answer to *me*," Tathlyn reminded him firmly, but not too unkindly. Rather like a father would remind his toddler that the family rule is not to have an ice cream just before dinner. "You will be king in name only, since I shall be the Emperor of All The Realms."

Carric looked down embarrassed, like a child who feels they've said or done something silly in front of the older kids.

"Yes," he mumbled into his unkempt beard. "But I will no longer be the spare, and my schteelcün father will be dead."

"And I am guessing your brother Adran will also be dead, if you are to be on the throne," Varis pointed out. "What has he ever done to you other than be generously and selflessly kind, encouraging, thoughtful, and forgiving?"

Carric looked sharply at Varis, as if the question was completely stupid because the answer to it was so glaringly obvious.

"What has he done?" Carric scoffed. "Why, he was born before me," he said, simply.

<><><><><><><><>

Annie finally roused from her tortured reverie, with a kernel of realisation.

"So, this was the plan you had in store for my friends," she said in a thin whisper.

"You can *never* call us friends again," Lucan seethed. Annie winced and physically cringed, but she knew he was right.

"I thought you simply wanted to kill them. But your plan was so much worse that. You wanted them to know, firsthand, that I had betrayed them all. To know that Carric betrayed them all and made the biggest fool, and accomplice, out of me."

"And then kill them, of course," Tathlyn added, with what — was that glee? "But not before they have returned through their realms with the news that I am coming, stronger and more powerful than ever, and that you were instrumental in making it all possible."

Tathlyn and Carric thoroughly enjoyed watching distress, anguish, and heartbreak move through her body. They also noted the ferocious bluster of anger sweeping across the faces of Lucan and Varis, that was pointedly aimed at them.

"And what is that I see, Finwe?" Carric mused, cruelly. "Not anger, not fury. No. You are not even looking at us. No, I believe that is sorrow, pain, and anguish, and your mind and heart are lost in looking at — "

"Hush your brùkling wretched, poisonous mouth, you loathsome, shéatting skänè!" Elva interrupted, in an effort to protect her brother and deflect their attention away from him, and onto her.

It worked.

"And there she is," Carric said, his face leering and his hand spread in a gesture of mocking welcoming friendship. "The most macho warrior she-elf of the Woodland Realm. You have more cléttiès than the rest of this snivelling lot put together."

"And like I said, you repugnant, worthless spare," she retorted, while making it difficult for the surrounding Shadow Elves to contain her. "I shall be serving your cléttiès up to the kystrallas any time now."

He laughed harshly, although the reference to him being "the worthless spare," again, still clearly rankled.

"I knew that you never liked or trusted me, and it turns out your were absolutely right. How utterly vexing that must be for you... you fusty, barren clätck."

"Enough of this posturing and pillicok waving," Tathlyn ordered sternly. He was plainly bored of the verbal skirmish, and Carric, again, looked suitably chastened.

"That told you," Elva grinned and she fired off a loud, scathing, and triumphant laugh.

Chapter Thirty-One

Tathlyn was becoming really rather comfortable in presenting his plans to his literally captive audience. He was revelling in the bile, anger, and frustration that it inspired among them. With the enchanted Labradorite Amulet in his possession, he delighted in the thought of the terror these elves' messages about everyone's impending slaughter and oppression, would have on his future realms.

He now strolled nonchalantly, back and forth, his long, bony fingers clasped behind him. He addressed them all as if they were eager, disciples hanging on his every word, rather than the literally captive audience that they were.

"Of course, my magnificent campaign will not be limited to the Sun Elven and Woodland Realms — and héllè, why not — the Landshore Realm as well. I shall commandeer the skills of our Annie here to give us access to the Human Realm also. She will gradually transport tens of thousands, if not hundreds of thousands, of my Shadow Elves through her portal, and we shall conquer the Human Realm by stealth. By the time they realise what is happening, it shall be all but over for them. I shall be Emperor of All Realms Everywhere, and not simply the elven ones."

"Well good luck with that," Finwe declared. "Firstly, you completely underestimate those in the Human Realm. Since the time of Meredith the Thief, things have dramatically changed. Secondly, I strongly suspect that Annie would rather *die* than do your bidding again. And thirdly, if you have the means to force her to transport your elves, you cannot use Annie if you do not have her."

Tathlyn laughed loud and long.

"My dear, lovesick pouchéllè," he patronised Finwe. "I already have her. While I allowed her to enter my tower unhindered, do you seriously think that I would allow her to leave?"

A broad smile spread across Finwe's face. It unsettled Tathlyn.

"Where is she then?" Finwe asked, simply.

Tathlyn and everyone else in the chamber looked to where Annie had been standing dumbstruck, overwhelmed, and crestfallen.

She wasn't there.

Tathlyn's control on the situation wavered a fraction. His eyes frantically searched the chamber, as did those of everyone else.

No one could see her.

She had disappeared.

<><><><><><><><><>

While Tathlyn had been absorbed in waxing lyrical about his plans for all-realms domination, Annie had gathered together enough of her wits to realise that she may be able to foil his plans before they had got any real traction. There was a chance that she could retrieve the Labradorite Amulet and save everyone, everywhere.

Her internal magic cauldron had melted from its heavy, static, iceberg-like quality to the much more familiar and useable viscous lava-like consistency. Together with her golden fleck, she encouraged her magic to heat up to the point where it bubbled and circled, ready to be unleashed into action.

She realised that direct hits from her palm bombs, where she currently stood, would guarantee fatal injuries to her friends — even if "friends" was no longer what they viewed themselves to be with her. To ensure this didn't happen, she had, with the additional energy required to render her unseen by elves, made herself invisible, and had climbed up the rough, protruding stones of the back wall, to be above Tathlyn, and Carric. Here she could direct her palm bombs to maximise the damage to their targets, while simultaneously minimising damage to Lucan, Varis, Elva, and Finwe.

She took particular delight in seeing the uncertainty and fear flashing across Carric's face as he searched for her. The tiniest kernel of doubt about what she had ever seen in him, started to take root at the very back of her mind. But there was currently no space for it to grow. In this moment, her whole mind, her whole being, was preoccupied with her single mission of the moment:

The mission to stop Tathlyn and Carric in their tracks.

"Here I am," she announced loudly from her somewhat precarious vantage point. "And I shall end you both, you brükling despicable pair of clätckes."

And, I'll admit that I feel very nearly as despicable as they are, she thought.

Yes, she agreed with herself. But, in this moment, all that matters is that, right here and right now, I start making amends for my blind stupidity. There's a chance that I can still put this right.

But your friends will still hate you, she countered.

And this is not about me and getting them to stop hating me, she curtly asserted. This is about doing the right thing, even though it is crazily hard. It's all about saving millions, more like billions, of lives, and leaning back into my integrity.

And then, with pinpoint accuracy, she let loose half a dozen fierce palm bombs directly at Tathlyn and Carric. Their force and potency would have been sufficient to cause twenty elves to be scattered into mostly unidentifiable, bloody body parts.

Much to her disbelief and distress, the palm bombs were repelled from their target and instead, obliterated the Shadow Elf servants that had been with Tathlyn when she had first come in. Everyone, bar Tathlyn, was confused and unnerved. They had seen the palm bombs' trajectory and couldn't fathom what had happened. The Shadow Elves surrounding Lucan, Varis, Finwe, and Elva, quickly shuffled themselves, and their charges, back towards the relative safety of the doorway's arch.

Tathlyn simply and confidently smiled. Carric, realising that he was still in one piece, blew out a huge sigh of relief and also fashioned his face into a smile, to be like Tathyln. Annie's forehead screwed up into deep furrows of confusion and frustration. Even when she had first discovered that she could create palm bombs, they had never failed her. Yet now, when she had mastered her self-generated weaponry, they had been batted away like tiny, irritating flies.

"Yes," Tathlyn smirked. "Surprising and probably somewhat annoying, isn't it? Have you already forgotten that, thanks to you, I can now conjure and deploy more powerful magic from within me? I cannot deny that I am rather impressed and pleased with myself."

Growling in her response to being thwarted, Annie unleashed another pair of palm bombs and, again, they were easily swatted away. This time, they ricocheted and instantly dismembered the two Shadow Elves standing at the front of those holding her companions. Once again, the surviving guards retreated to move even farther away, actually into the corridor behind the doorway.

Tathlyn had successfully and spontaneously created a protective bubble around himself and Carric, without the need to sacrifice one of his creatures or minions. Changing tack, Annie attempted to pierce the bubble by unleashing her magic through just one hand, and focusing it at a single point. It was possible to see the skin of the bubble as the point of Annie's attack caused it to glow white-hot, and created a radiating red, and burnt orange glow. Despite this intensely concentrated effort, the protective bubble remained in tact and the level of Tathlyn's smugness multiplied exponentially.

Annie ceased her attack and, looking at the faint scorch marks on the bubble's skin, she acknowledged that it was hopeless. She knew that there was only one thing she could now try in order to put an end to Tathlyn's power-crazed and maniacal plans.

She would bring the whole damned tower down on top of him. It would most likely mean that she too would be killed in the process, but anything that saved all the realms was worth it. She doubted that she deserved to live anyway. The deaths of her once close friends, however, was not something she was prepared to cause, so, before focussing on the tower itself, she directed several of her palm bombs to strike directly above the doorway's arch.

The arch was blown asunder, as were many of the Shadow Elves who had stood in front of her elves, in the corridor. Large bricks and Shadow Elves' body parts completely blocked the entrance into Tathlyn's chamber at the base of the tower. She just prayed that Elva, Finwe, Lucan, and Varis had managed to get far enough down into the corridor so as not to also be crushed to death.

If this goes how I think it will, she thought, allowing a little sadness and regret into her heart. *I shall probably never know.*

She made herself invisible once again and moved so that Tathlyn wouldn't know where to strike. But there was no retaliation from him.

Why is that? she wondered. And then, glancing at Tahlyn and Carric, the answer came to her. *Of course! If you want to strike at me, you'll have to remove your protective dome. You've not yet mastered your newly acquired powers, and... and I'm scaring you.*

Her confidence boosted by Tathlyn's fear of her, she turned to place an intense beam of all her attention on the tower itself, starting with the very top. She figured that starting at the top could produce an unstoppable and relentless waterfall effect of bricks, mortar, and timber pouring inward, that would pulverise everything beneath it. She worried that starting at the bottom might cause the tower to fall outward or concertina down without touching what was inside the tower itself.

At first nothing happened.

But then, just as Tathlyn was starting to roll his shoulders and crick his neck in preparation for taking down the dome, and attacking her, the arched, timber roof of the tower imploded.

The sound of the enormous beams splintering and snapping, was deafening. As they careered towards the ground, they spun and toppled end over end, ricocheting off the curved walls, and off each other. The trick of perspective made it look like they were growing larger as they fell. The slate roof tiles smashed and rained down like razor-sharp confetti.

Annie didn't wait to see what damage the implosion of the roof had caused. She was hell-bent on complete destruction, complete annihilation. She maintained her full attention on the task in hand.

From way up at the very top now roofless tower, there came a faint tinkling sound that became louder and louder as individual bricks broke free of the overall structure, and fell to the ground. Initially it was the equivalent to a light shower of rain, but within moments, it had transformed into a lethal deluge. Soon the entire floor was knee-deep in bricks and rubble.

High above, fierce storm clouds shrouded the night sky. It began to rain, heavily.

Many of the cages dotted around the chamber, had been bent out of shape or ripped open by the falling debris. The feathered and fury creatures within needed no invitation to extricate themselves and head for freedom.

Although trapped in among the bricks herself, Annie carried on unperturbed, as thousands more bricks rained down. Somehow, her concentrated beam of intention repelled any bricks that would have directly hit her. However, it was entirely probable that the sheer weight of the tower upon her, would easily crush her to death.

She didn't care. She didn't stop. She would never stop.

Nearly half the tower had come tumbling in, but still, frustratingly, Tathlyn's dome stayed intact. The bricks were rapidly piling up all around it, and Annie could see that Tathlyn was having to work very hard to maintain the dome's integrity. The layers of bricks were starting to crush her chest and yet she still kept the bricks coming. She just prayed that she could keep the onslaught going until Tathlyn's dome could no longer cope, and it, Tathlyn, and Carric were similarly crushed beneath the tower's ruins.

Then the worst thing Annie could have imagined, happened.

As Annie was struggling to breathe, being consumed by the ruins, she saw the dome of protection burst and, — horrors of horrors — Tathlyn and Carric escape. With Carric tightly gripping onto Tathlyn's shoulder, the pair disappeared in a burst of plum-purple smoke. Finally, Annie was completely smothered by the bricks and rubble. The very last thing Annie saw was the trapdoor.

That damned trapdoor, she scolded herself as she was starting to lose consciousness. *Why didn't I think about the blasted trapdoor? The very same door through which I escaped when Carric tricked the others to join him and save me!.. To save me... Carric saved me... Carric...*

The rain abruptly stopped and the clouds instantly cleared to reveal a beautiful star smattered and encrusted sky.

<><><><><><><><>

Moments later there was a deep and rhythmic rumble from somewhere beneath the ruins. At first it was a mere whisper, but soon, it steeply crescendoed into a guttural, primal roar of volcanic proportion. As the noise reached its peak, bricks, timber, rubble, and dust violently exploded with a blast radius that sent debris up to, and beyond the tower's curtain wall.

From the epicentre, Annie ascended, limp, and unconscious. Riding on the wave of the sound, she was carried up, and onto, the side of the mountain of building materials that had come to rest against what little remained of the tower's foundations.

As Annie had disappeared from view, suffocating, unconscious, and merely a hair's breadth from death, her golden fleck had taken firm control. Twisting and spiralling at an ever increasing speed until it was simply a blur, the fleck had whipped up her magic, and let it rip loose.

We are not done here, it declared, as Annie's body lightly touched down from having been buried alive. *We are not done here at all.*

Annie's chest was still.

Her heart was still.

In her lifeless, open eye, her golden fleck crouched, waiting, not daring to move.

It's all up to you now, Annie. Come on. Unable to stand it any longer, her fleck lost all patience and emitted a screeching scream inside Annie's mind.

Come on!

The piercing scream effectively kick-started Annie, back into the land of the living. She coughed out mushroom clouds of brick dust from deep within her lungs. Her eyes fluttered, trying to clear her vision, and she very gingerly rolled onto her side.

And there she is, her fleck announced with a heady mixture of triumph and relief. *That's it. Get your breath, get your bearings, and get your arse going. We can't stay here. There'll be Shadow Elves swarming all over us in minutes.*

Annie was in no state or mind to argue and simply did as she was told. Her legs were shaking beneath her and her arms felt incredibly numb, and weak. However, with a monumental effort, she still managed to scrabble up to the apex of the rubble mountain. From the top she saw elves running hither and thither with flaming torches. Shadow Elves, with their silvery skin glinting in the light of the flames.

Then she saw someone else.

There were four elves without torches, just outside the curtain wall, and heading towards the woods, their hands now unbound. She recognised their silhouettes immediately. Still coughing up dust, she called to them with a voice that sounded like grinding gears. She waved, forgetting for a second that she would now be sharing the top spot for the elven realms' "most hated" list, with Tathlyn and Carric.

Lucan, Varis, Elva, and Finwe stopped dead in their tracks and spun round. Three of them looked dumbstruck, but Lucan wasted no time in seizing Elva's short yet powerful crossbow from her satchel. He stood sideways adopting a strong and deadly stance. His arm was outstretched and Elva's loaded crossbow was pointing straight at Annie. As he unleashed the arrow, something firmly knocked his arm, sending the arrow spiralling off past her and far to her left.

That something was Finwe.

At the top of his lungs, Finwe shouted just one word:

"Run!"

Chapter Thirty-Two

Annie wished she'd never fallen through her portal and discovered the elven realms.

She wished she'd never met Carric.

She wished she'd never allowed herself to become vulnerable and trusted him.

She wished she'd never fallen in love with him.

She wished she'd never believed that he loved her.

She wished she'd never put Carric before the needs of everyone and everything else.

She wished she'd never betrayed her newly found, firm friends.

She wished she'd kept her integrity.

She wished, she wished, she wished.

She wished she was dead.

Annie had been running, scrambling, and staggering for quite how long, she didn't know. It must have been for at least three hours since the suns' glow was weakly reaching up over the horizon of mountaintops and piercing the night.

She was utterly exhausted, but her golden fleck and magic had kept her going — one miserable, wretched foot after the other.

These wishes had persistently played over and over, and over in her head as she went along. But now she was utterly spent. Not even her magic could keep her going. Her desperately weary legs buckled under her, and she slumped heavily down onto the dewy ground.

She had absolutely no idea where she was and she absolutely didn't care.

No Shadow Elves had pursued her to this place.

Why is that? she wondered, but she didn't bother to task any brain cells to think about it because, again, she simply didn't care.

She just knew that she had run in the opposite direction to her ex-friends and the Shadow Elves. She had purposely put as much distance as she could between herself and the purple dessert, the Crystal Caves, the Woodland Realm, the sea, the Sun Elven Realm, and the Human Realm — away from anything she knew, and anyone that might know her.

Her self-loathing continued to relentlessly multiply, as she thought of how she had betrayed the trust of all those in the Woodland and Sun Elven Realms. How she had lied and tricked her friends. How disappointed in her, Lilyfire would have been — had Annie managed to save her — yet another, devastating failing to add to her list. And, at the last, when she was prepared, and willing, to die while thwarting Tathlyn, she had even failed to stop him and Carric from escaping.

There was not one single thing that could redeem her.

"I don't even deserve to be redeemed," she screamed into the darkening skies. "Not ever!"

She didn't believe that she deserved anything — anything good at least. Anything bad? Well, yes. That she deserved in spades.

She was utterly furious with her golden fleck.

You should have left me to be crushed and die under the ruins of the tower, she wailed. *You had no right to save me. No right at all.*

But you have so much more yet to do, her fleck replied pragmatically.

Annie screamed out loud, in frustration.

Haven't I already done enough? Isn't it enough that I have condemned three elven realms to death, destruction, and domination? And for what? An elf who tricked me into thinking he loved me, thinking that I could be loved, and tore down my defences so that I dared to love him.

She burst into loud, pitiful, sobbing tears, not even attempting to hide her face. She could hardly breathe as her sobs caught in her throat. She had absolutely nothing and no one, just like before she fell into the elven realms. No, wait. It was far worse. She'd had something, something precious. She'd had friendship, purpose, and, even though it had turned out to be a complete falsehood, for a little while, she'd believed she'd had love.

And now?

Now, it had all been forcefully ripped away and she had only herself to blame.

She was broken.

Utterly, despairingly broken.

<><><><><><><><>

Realising that no amount of encouragement, coaxing, or peptalk was going to shift Annie's state of mental and emotional torture, her fleck shrank to the size of a pinprick, and quietly waited. What it was waiting for, it wasn't entirely sure.

Through her tears, she saw that she was on high ground. There were mountains behind her and in front of her, the earth steeply fell away to show the ruins of the Tathlyn's tower way below and far away. She could see the purple desert beyond the Shadow Realm forest and what must be the Kàdàvérsité Region that Lucan had been so furious that they would have to traverse on their way back to the Woodland Realm. In that area, Annie could see the moons' light reflecting off what looked like bone-white, flat-topped rocks that were roughly interlocking. And, on the very edge of her view was the thinnest sliver of the Woodland Realm.

Wait. The earth steeply falls away, she thought. She carefully traced the immediate geography with her eyes. Not far from where she was sitting, the land cut in to create a wide scar to the base of the nearest mountain. Hauling her weary body to its feet, she unsteadily walked, and stumbled, in a semi-zombie state, towards the scar.

A dark idea was forming.

As she teetered at the top of the scar itself, she discovered that it was a deep ravine. The bottom of the ravine was way, way below. Along the very bottom was the thin blue-and-white line of a raging river.

The forming idea crystallised.

Her fleck was unable to take control while Annie was conscious. It violently shook. It was terribly afraid.

Standing to her full height and setting her shoulders square, Annie breathed slowly in and out... in... and... out. The wind suddenly died down to nothing. Her bubbling, fluid magic within her, once again turned to impotent ice. She breathed more slowly and even slower still. The pauses between breaths became longer and longer, until she almost forgot to breathe at all.

An eerie calmness swept over and enveloped her.

Annie lightly closed her eyes.

And then, without any hesitation, she stepped off the edge of the ravine, and into thin air.

A Word from Hil

I really hope that you have enjoyed reading the second book in the Annie Harper Trilogy as much as have enjoyed writing it. If you could see your way to leaving an honest review, I'd be ever so grateful — honest reviews are all welcome and useful.

If your appetite is whetted for more of what I'm penning, take a gander below.

Prequel Novello of the series:

To get a free copy of **Betrayal**, please go to hilggibb.com

The Golden Fleck Series:

The Dying Realms — Annie Harper Trilogy, Book 1
 The Worst Deceit — Annie Harper Trilogy, Book 2
 The Final Hope — Annie HarperTrilogy, Book 3
 Devotion — Lisa's Story Part 2 (free to subscribers)
 Outsider — Meredith Harwood Story

Books for younger readers:

The Tale of Two Sydneys
Archie Brittle Saves the play

NB:
As I am an advocate for people with dyslexia, I decided to make the print version of my novels in the OpenDyslexic font so that they are more readily accessible.